Crushed

Also by Laura and Tom McNeal

Crooked
Zipped

Crushed

Laura & Tom McNeal

Alfred A. Knopf
New York

THIS IS A BORZOI BOOK PUBLISHED BY ALFRED A. KNOPF

Text copyright © 2006 by Laura McNeal and Tom McNeal

www.randomhouse.com/teens

Library of Congress Cataloging-in-Publication Data
McNeal, Laura.
Crushed / by Laura and Tom McNeal. — 1st ed.
    p. cm.
SUMMARY: Seventeen-year-old Audrey's life is turned upside down when she falls in love with a mysterious newcomer and a vicious gossip sheet exposes the secrets of both students and teachers at her school.
ISBN 0-375-83105-3 (trade) — ISBN 0-375-93105-8 (lib. bdg.)
ISBN-13: 978-0-375-83105-8 (trade) — ISBN-13: 978-0-375-93105-5 (lib. bdg.)
[1. Gossip—Fiction. 2. Interpersonal relations—Fiction. 3. Family problems—Fiction. 4. Secrets—Fiction. 5. High schools—Fiction. 6. Schools—Fiction.] I. McNeal, Tom. II. Title.
PZ7.M47879365Cru 2006
[Fic]—dc22
2005004320

Printed in the United States of America
January 2006
10 9 8 7 6 5 4 3 2 1
First Edition

For Sam and Hank,
and in memory of Christine

Besides, there was
truth in his looks.

—from *Pride and Prejudice* by Jane Austen

Part
One

The north wind doth blow
And we shall have snow
And what will the robin do then, poor thing?
—Traditional rhyme

Chapter 1
Something Happening

The door opened, and a tall boy Audrey Reed had never seen before entered the room. It was early November, clear and mild—the season's first snow wouldn't fall for another two weeks. Through the windows of the second-story classroom, the midmorning sun lit up Audrey's fingers and the edges of her book, and when the boy stepped into this light, it gave his face an artificial radiance.

He had dark hair, a little on the long side and wavy, and he wore a heavy black sweater and faded khaki pants, the whole look loose and slouchy but in a put-together kind of way. He was so different in appearance and yet so at ease with himself that Audrey wondered if he was a foreign exchange student from some place like France or Italy, or wherever it might be that people grew up feeling okay about themselves. He wasn't embarrassed by his tallness or his newness, the very things Audrey herself had been embarrassed by when she'd enrolled as an incoming junior at Jemison High two months earlier.

Mrs. Leacock twisted the ring on her left hand, stared at the documents the new boy handed her, and let a look of weary exasperation cross her face. She was one of those adults Audrey could least imagine becoming, a middle-aged woman with hairsprayed curls in a style that belonged exclusively to old women.

Whether she was reading announcements or passing out tests, the creases in her face made her look like she was scowling. She began going through her file drawer for a series of papers that she handed the boy, one after another, while speaking to him in a low, businesslike tone. The boy stood easily, without any of the impatience to find a seat to sink into that Audrey herself would have felt. He merely stood there and nodded at Mrs. Leacock, and smiled, and lazily scratched the back of his neck.

Audrey glanced up at the wall clock, then opened her green composition book. In its back pages, where she put notes to herself, she wrote: *11:13 a.m., Nov. 2. Something happening. Something definitely happening.*

She put her pen down. Up front, Mrs. Leacock twisted her ring and gave the room a long scan before fixing her gaze on the empty desk behind Audrey, and suddenly the boy was looking her way, too.

Audrey lowered her eyes, and a few seconds later felt his approach and saw his shoes pass by—soft leather loafers a man would wear—and took in the faint, sugary smell that swept along behind him. She wasn't sure what the smell was, but it reminded her of Christmas. She heard the boy slip into the metal desk behind her and shuffle some papers. A few seconds later, Mrs. Leacock walked up the aisle to give him a worn copy of their physics textbook.

"Chapter seven," Mrs. Leacock said in a low, tired voice. "I don't suppose you've heard of Heisenberg?"

The boy let out an easy chuckle and said, "Oh, you'd be surprised the folks we manage to hear about down there in South Carolina." He spoke in a low, gentle, bemused drawl that Audrey suddenly craved hearing again.

4

Mrs. Leacock seemed to feel differently. "It would behoove you not to guess what might surprise me, Mr. Hill," she said stonily, and without waiting for a reply returned to her desk. As she went, the boy drawled under his breath, "It would also behoove me not to think you're a peabrain, lady, but there it is."

Audrey found herself grinning, not because Mrs. Leacock was peabrained—she wasn't—but because she was rude to students and indifferent to anything not strictly related to her lectures. Audrey liked the idea of someone having the spunk to say that tall, rigid, imposing Mrs. Leacock was peabrained.

In a stage-whisper drawl and to no one in particular, the new boy then said, "So who the hell is Heisenberg?" and Audrey—she couldn't help herself—let slip a small laugh.

At the Tate School, where Audrey had spent the previous four years, a new student was cheerfully introduced to the entire classroom, and then (the Tate School was hopelessly and, to Audrey's mind, endearingly fogyish) the new student was assigned an "Honorary Helpmeet" to initiate him or her into the Tate School's intricate ways. But that was Tate, and this was Jemison.

Still, it didn't mean you couldn't be polite.

Audrey composed herself as best she could, turned in her seat, and prepared to introduce herself. She wasn't, however, prepared for what she saw. He'd looked handsome when he was at the front of the room, but seeing his face up close, she felt a little dizzy.

In a low, shaky voice, she said, "Hi. I'm Audrey Reed."

In a whispery drawl, he seemed to say his name was Wiggim Hill.

"Wiggim?" Audrey whispered. It was the oddest name she'd ever heard.

"Wickham," he said, and made a turned-down smile that seemed almost to imply the name was a mystery to him, too.

Audrey didn't know what to say next, but she knew she had to say something. She whispered, "Are you here for good?"

This time he broke into a loose smile and fixed his eyes on hers. "As opposed to evil?"

She laughed. She shouldn't have, but she couldn't help it.

Chapter 2
Tatesters

Ten minutes later, Audrey was sitting with C.C. Mudd and Lea Woolcott, her best and only friends, as they ate their lunches where they always ate their lunches—on an isolated knoll far from the lunch quad. They were wearing their sweaters without coats, and Audrey could feel the faint heat of the sun on her back and the crown of her head. Audrey ate currants from a cardboard carton and looked up at the blue sky while Lea and C.C. talked about a teacher who'd made some mistake in class, one that Lea had wanted to correct but had decided not to.

"Good thinking," C.C. said. "Everybody already suspects we're freaks. If we start correcting the teacher, it'll only confirm it."

C.C. had thick, dark hair, black eyelashes, brown eyes, and what she called the body of an inflated gymnast. She had been short and narrow at eleven, short and voluptuous by thirteen. Audrey thought she was pretty, but C.C., of course, disagreed.

Lea was the quietest of the three. She wore glasses but still seemed to squint, so that you didn't notice, until you'd known her for some time, that her irises were faceted, and blue like quartz. Her face was fine-boned and recessively attractive, and she had a soft way of talking. Her hair was white-blond and utterly without interest to her—she wore it in a ponytail unless C.C. or Audrey insisted on fixing it for her.

The three had been best friends since starting sixth grade at the Agatha Ingram Tate School, a tiny private school in Cazenovia, New York. C.C. had been the bold, flashy, wise-cracking one; Lea had been the pale, bookish one with two parents; and Audrey had been the one who wanted to be a bold, wisecracking girl with two parents.

The Agatha Ingram Tate School went through tenth grade—as far as its only teacher, Edie March, felt she could go in math and science. It was a one-room school with eight students, an upright piano, a parquet floor, and a fireplace. You couldn't possibly get lost there. Whereas on Audrey's first day at Jemison, she couldn't find anything and was late to every class. The one time she'd asked for directions, a girl wearing a skimpy T-shirt with *Hubba-hubba* inscribed across her breasts said, "Like I would know." No one knew who Audrey was, no one said hello, and when she'd searched for a place to eat at the lunch quad, three girls looked up at her, then looked at one another, and one of them said something that made the other two break into harsh, stinging laughter. Audrey had turned and staked out the remote, deserted knoll, where Lea and C.C. had found her.

Their first morning had been as bad as Audrey's, and as they ate their lunch together that first day, they were quiet for a long while. Then Lea had squinted at the massive cafeteria building and said, "We're like pet rabbits released into the wild. This is supposed to be our natural habitat, but it's not."

Since then, they had made the knoll their habitat. They met there at lunch to discuss whatever freakishness they had detected in others or had been accused of themselves, and to bolster one another for the rest of the semi-terrifying day. Today, Lea and C.C. had rearranged themselves so they were sitting back to back, like bookends, grilling each other for a trig quiz. Audrey had closed her eyes and was thinking idle Wickham Hill thoughts when she sensed that someone was looking at her. *Wickham Hill*, she hoped (preposterous as she knew that was), but when she flicked open her eyes, she found she'd been both right and wrong.

There *was* someone staring at her, all right, but it wasn't Wickham Hill. It was a tall boy in black pants and a pinkish shirt, possibly that semi-creepy, semi-handsome boy she'd caught staring at her once or twice in World Cultures. Now, caught staring again, he readjusted his gaze and pretended not to have been staring, which was kind of embarrassing for them both. He turned and walked hurriedly away.

Audrey closed her eyes again and when, within her imagination, the face of Wickham Hill presented itself with perfect clarity, she kept them closed.

"Yo, Tatesters!"

C.C.'s brother, Brian, approaching from below.

Brian Mudd was a sophomore, small for his age, but with big hands and feet. He'd been in the public school system for three years now and liked it. For him, the Tate School hadn't been a serene island. He liked computers, and Edie March had liked fountain pens. Every time Edie had asked a question he didn't know the answer to—which, as he put it, "was like a gazillion times a day"—he felt himself getting

9

squished. "That wasn't a schoolroom, dudes. It was a trash compactor."

Today Brian was cradling something against his neck, something brown, spiky, and reptilian.

Lea seemed alarmed. "What is it?" she said. C.C. looked at the reptile, then at her brother, and said, "Where did you get that? And don't you dare bring it home."

Brian nuzzled the creature and gave it a nibbling kiss. "Found it sitting by a bush," he said. The lizard had a flat triangular head with gold eyes, and spikes ran down the ridge of its spine. It seemed designed for gladiatorial work.

"Bearded dragon?" Audrey asked.

"Well done, Miz Reed!" Brian said, mimicking Edie March; then he loosened the enormous lizard from his neck and held it out in his big hands for general presentation. "So how stellar is this?" he said.

"Not very," C.C. said, "and don't you dare let loose of that thing."

Which of course Brian immediately did. The reptile blinked, looked around, and then began slogging very slowly downhill, through the dirt. "Lookit 'im scoot!" Brian said.

Audrey didn't share Lea's and C.C.'s aversion to reptiles. She got up and followed Brian and the lizard until, perhaps twenty yards along, Brian reached down and scooped the bearded dragon back up. The reptile seemed pleased, and nestled restfully against Brian's neck.

"Wanna hold it?" Brian asked. "He's totally gentle."

Audrey handed her box of currants to Brian and took the animal—it was a strange combination of roughness and plumpness—and it seemed to relax against her neck, too.

Brian was nodding his head and smiling. "Blissing out. Animal's blissing out."

"That's its name? Animal?"

"If you say so," Brian said.

Like C.C., Brian had thick, dark hair. He wore it mostly uncut, which meant he occasionally had to push it aside with his fingers in order to see. When they had all met at the Tate School, he'd been a skinny little kid with teeth too large for his mouth. Now that he had grown into his teeth, he wasn't bad-looking, but he was still Brian, and normal conversation with him was impossible.

"Is it male or female?" Audrey ventured.

Brian gave a who-knows shrug. "Before you came up with Animal, I was thinking of going with a gender-neutral name. Pat or Terry, or maybe Kiki." Brian's grin suddenly broadened. "Did you know that male lizards have two penises? Technically, one penis split in two. It's called a 'hemipenis.' But it takes some real effort to expose it."

Audrey paused, her hands on the lizard. "Then let's not," she said.

Brian smiled and shrugged. He took one of Audrey's currants and popped it into his mouth. "What are these things, anyway?" he said. Brian was six inches shorter than Audrey and had to look up, which made Audrey feel enormous. She wished they could sit.

"They're like raisins," Audrey said, "only more exotic."

"Ah," Brian said, and then he did something he occasionally did. He smiled and let his eyes settle gently on Audrey. "Raisins with snob appeal."

Audrey laughed, but it was a laugh cut suddenly short.

From behind them, C.C. was reading aloud, in a reciting voice, *"11:13 a.m., November 2. Something happening. Something definitely happening."*

Audrey turned abruptly. "What're you doing, C.C.?"

C.C. flipped the page of Audrey's green composition book and read: *"Here's the fortune I got last night at Ming Garden with Dad. 'For you the time is auspicious for romance.'"*

"Give me that, C.C.!" Audrey said. She shoved the bearded dragon back into Brian's hands and hurried up the knoll. "That's spying!" she said, and after grabbing her composition book, she said to C.C., in a softer voice, "You're terrible."

C.C. grinned her pleasant grin, and in an exaggerated Asian accent said, "For you, time velly auspicious for romance!"

"That's not funny, C.C.," Audrey said.

Brian, standing aside and smoothing a finger over the dragon's flat head, said, "Yeah, well, you know what they say. The taller they are, the farther they fall."

C.C. gave her brother a deadpan glance and said, "Nobody says that, Brian."

Brian gave the lizard a little kiss and said, "Evidentially untrue. I just did."

"Bye, Brian," C.C. said, and her brother, shrugging, shambled off with the bearded dragon happily cradled against his neck.

"So, Audrey, honey," C.C. said after Brian was gone. "What does that mean—*'Something happening. Something definitely happening'*?"

Audrey felt her skin pinkening. What was she going to say?

That at 11:13 this morning she'd had oddly ardent feelings about a boy she'd just laid eyes on and hadn't even talked to? No, it was too embarrassing, so she said, "I've been trying to figure out the days when my period's starting, and I wrote that down when I thought I felt it."

C.C. gave Audrey a dubious grin. "Really, or maybe?"

The bell rang. A smile broke across Audrey's face. "Maybe really," she said, and waved good-bye.

Chapter 3
To Do

Heisenberg's uncertainty principle, as Audrey understood it, had to do with a subatomic particle moving through space, and the fact that you could know its velocity or its position, but not both. The more accurately you defined where it was, the less you knew about how fast it was going, and the more you knew about how fast it was going, the less you knew about where it was.

As Audrey moved within the stream of students in the hallway of the south wing, she saw them briefly as subatomic particles. She could see what they were doing, but not what they intended to do. If she could measure their velocity, could she still know their positions? She knew that physics wasn't psychology, but she couldn't help feeling that there was an uncertainty principle at work in her own life, where there was so much to measure and so little to know.

"Cheer up, dudette. It may never happen."

It was Brian's voice, carrying with it the pleasant smell of citrus. Audrey, jolted from her thoughts, said, "*What* may never happen?"

Brian shrugged and popped a wedge of tangerine into his mouth. He was leaning against his locker. "Whatever it was you were toddling along all worried about. You looked like the doctor just gave you ten minutes to live."

"Oh, sorry," Audrey said, and made a little laugh.

"What for?" Brian said.

"I don't know," Audrey said. It was true. She didn't. She couldn't help it if she got lost in her thoughts.

"Close your eyes," Brian said.

"What?"

"Close your eyes and open your mouth."

She did, and he slipped a section of tangerine between her lips. When she started to open her eyes, he said, "Keep them closed and chew slowly, and it'll be like nothing you've ever done before in the hallowed hallways of Jemison High."

She did, and it was.

Brian shrugged. "Yeah, well, I told you."

Something occurred to Audrey. "Where's the bearded dragon?"

"Busted. Turns out none of the reptile nation are welcome on campus. My guy's in Murchison's office, in the reptile slammer." Mr. Murchison was the assistant principal.

"But you'll get him back?"

"Oh, yeah. Right after the closing bell." Brian stretched out one of his wide, lazy grins. "You just can't keep a boy from his dragon."

Audrey glanced at her watch and said, "Gotta go."

Brian said, "No, you don't, but you will."

She laughed and set off.

"Hey," he called after her, "if you're heading for Patrice's class, stay away from the temps. Theo's over there."

Patrice was Patrice Newman, who taught World Cultures; the temps were the temporary classrooms; and Theo was Theo Driggs, a steel trap of a boy who, along with his hulking friends, hung out in the unsupervised recesses of the campus and waited for prey.

Audrey's personal introduction to Theo Driggs had occurred soon after enrollment. Mr. Daly, her trig teacher, had asked her to take a notice down to the journalism classroom on the basement floor of the vocational education wing, and as she'd turned at the bottom of the stairs, a group of boys in big shirts, leather jackets, and low-slung jeans stood against a wall. Most of the boys were mountainously big, but a compact, muscular boy of medium height stood at the center of the group. He had oily blond hair, fleshy lips, and a soft, moist-looking neck. When he saw Audrey turn their way, he closed his eyes, exaggeratedly sniffed the air, and said, "Denizens, I smell a snob." With his eyes closed, he reminded Audrey of a basking lizard.

Now all of the boys were making sniffing sounds. One of them said, "Oh, yeah, I smell it, too."

"It smells like caviar."

"Know what else smells like caviar?"

Audrey kept her stiff limbs moving and stared woodenly ahead. "Aren't you in the wrong section of town?" Theo said. "Ain't no AP classes this part of town."

As she drew closer, the huddle of boys tightened, leaving only a narrow channel between them and the wall for her to pass through.

"Attention, shoppers!" one of the boys said. "We have a snob lost in the basement!"

Hard laughter, and Audrey, leaden, numb, passed close to the group, close enough that she smelled the boys' leathery, sweaty smell. Their voices nipped at her ears. *Eyes straight ahead*, she thought.

"Where's Her Majesty going?"

"Talk to us, Miz Caviar."

"You too good to talk to us?"

Theo Driggs leaned forward, brought his thick lips and softly flattened triangular nose within inches of Audrey's, and said, in a whispery voice, "I've got my eye on you. You're on my to-do list."

They'd receded slightly, and Audrey had moved woodenly through the group.

"God!" C.C. had said with real vehemence when Audrey later told her and Brian about the incident. "He said you were on his *to-do list?*"

Audrey nodded.

"Theo Driggs," Brian said, his voice full of mild wonderment. "Now there's a dude there's no handy explanation for."

"Where were the teachers?" C.C. said. "How do a dozen guys stand around harassing girls without any teachers finding out about it?"

Audrey shrugged.

"What we need is a Mafia contact," Brian said, almost talking to himself. "We would say, 'Rocco, we got a punk in need of a popping.'" Brian made a gun of his hand, closed one eye, and, pointing his index finger off toward the distance, let his thumb hammer down three times, saying, "*Pop pop pop.*"

C.C. had stared blankly at her brother, then turned to Audrey. "This is what happens to a sensitive youth left too long in the public schools."

The incident with Theo had occurred six weeks earlier. Since then, Audrey had seen Theo from time to time—in the halls, out in the quad, once even at Bing's Restaurant on a

Saturday morning—and each time he saw her, a smirk formed on his plump lips and he let his eyes fasten onto her. *Like a tick*, Audrey thought. It made her blood crawl. Which was why, today, Audrey went back through the quad and all the way around to the humanities wing to avoid letting Theo fasten his eyes on her again.

Chapter 4
Barter

Lea and C.C. shot grins Audrey's way when she burst into World Cultures just before the bell rang, and as soon as Patrice Newman turned her back, C.C. slid Audrey a note that read: *One more day almost over and we're still unbloodied.*

Audrey wrote back, *Day ain't over yet,* and added a smiley face.

Then, fingering her long hair, Audrey turned to glance at the craggy boy across the room, the one she'd thought had been staring at her at lunch. He sat now as he always sat, bent over his desk as if trying to make his large self small, but it was the same guy all right. Heavy eyebrows, scruffy unshaved jaw, brown eyes that never seemed to settle on anything. Different, and not necessarily good-different. No one else wore pink bowling shirts that said HARRY'S FRIES on the back. To C.C. Audrey wrote, *Who's the guy in pink and black, due west?*

C.C. wrote back, *ID unknown but Audrey, honey, why dost thou ask?*

Audrey was thinking how to respond when Patrice Newman, who had requested that the students call her simply Patrice, announced, "Okay, kiddos, we're going to have some fun today."

World Cultures had always been a mixed blessing. Patrice wore her graying hair long and dressed in clothing made of hemp. Sometimes class consisted of nothing harder than listening to music samples and guessing which country they came from. On the downside, the class was chock-full of cheerleading, dancing types who used the "creative" structure of the class to prey on the fashionless. C.C., Lea, and Audrey referred to these girls as the *snobbae popularae*, and assigned them individual flavors ranging from Battery Acid to Lemon Tartlet.

Today Patrice was breaking the class into groups of four to play a card game meant to imitate the process of barter among migrant sub-Saharan herdsmen.

C.C., Audrey, and Lea collected at one table, but the fourth chair remained vacant. This was fine by them, but Patrice noticed and said, "We've got an empty over here, kiddos." She spotted Sands Mandeville loitering by the window and said, "Sands, that empty chair's got your name on it."

Sands turned and took the situation in. "Can't, Patrice. If I go over there, then Zondra's group, which is where I belong, is down to two, so we've only made matters worse."

Patrice seemed hardly to hear, in part because of the din building in the room. "Okay, listen up, kids," she said, and when the noise didn't diminish, she began to shout over it. "Okay, you'll find a sealed envelope in front of you!" she began, and someone yelled, "Not me. I already opened mine!" which drew raucous laughter.

Hopeless. That's what Audrey thought this class was, and she began to write the word over and over on the cover of her green composition book, just above her name and address.

When everybody else began opening their envelopes, Audrey opened hers, too. Inside, she found three index cards.

One read, "2 baskets flax." The others read, "1 olive press" and "5 flagons olive oil."

From two tables away, she heard Zondra Freese yell, "I'll trade you a camel and two asses for your flagon of red wine," which most of the students found unmatched for hilarity.

Audrey flipped back to the cover of her notebook and kept writing. *Hopeless*.

About ten minutes later, Patrice Newman slipped out of the room, and shortly thereafter Zondra Freese cracked open the door, peered both ways, and then turned back to the class. "Gone," she said, and the noise in the classroom, already loud, grew louder.

Lea and C.C. got out their French homework. Audrey brought out her literature anthology, and soon became so absorbed in it she didn't notice that the room had gradually grown quiet. When she looked up, Sands Mandeville and Zondra Freese were standing over her.

"So who *are* you guys?" Zondra said. She hooked one French-manicured fingernail around the necklace she wore and slid the pendant from side to side.

"What do you mean, who are we?" Lea asked.

Sands cut in. "She means, like where did you come from?"

From behind them, someone, a boy, said, "Nerdstone Terrace," which drew clamorous laughs.

Audrey felt the class watching. They were waiting to see what Battery Acid and Lemon Tartlet had in store for the new girls.

"So what school did you go to before you came here?" Zondra said, still sliding the pendant.

Lea had lowered her eyes, and to keep C.C. from saying

something regrettable, Audrey said, "The Agatha Ingram Tate School."

Sands Mandeville smiled. "I've never heard of"—she prissified her voice—"the Agatha Ingram Tate School."

A girl's voice behind their table said, "It's a tiny little private school for freaks and lesbos."

"Really?" said Sands. "So which are you?

When the laughter from that remark abated, Zondra said, "Why either-or? Maybe they're both."

More hard laughter moved through the room.

Audrey felt her skin turning hot. Lea squinted at her book.

"We're neither," Audrey said, but her words came out brittle and small.

Zondra and Sands ignored her. Sands said, "So who's the hubby, that's what I want to know. Who's the hubby and who's the hussy?"

More hard laughter.

"You're so rude!" Audrey heard herself say. She knew at once that this was a mistake.

Sands said, "Golly, Zondra. We're so rude!"

Zondra said, "I'm thinking Miss Audrey's the man-dude. Telling us what's what in her he-manly way. Trying to protect the wee little wifeys."

More general laughter. Audrey felt sweat slide from her pores and glaze her body. C.C., usually impossible to intimidate, clenched her teeth and worked her jaw, and Lea just squinted at her book, sitting perfectly still. Audrey thought Lea was actually studying until a tear fell on the book. Saying "Please excuse me," Lea rushed from the room just as Patrice Newman reentered it.

"What happened to her?" the teacher said, looking back.

Nobody spoke until Sands said, "I don't know, Patrice. She didn't look well, and then she said she felt nauseous and then—" She gave a vague wave of her hand toward the door.

Patrice Newman shrugged, then glanced at the clock. "Okay, kiddos, three minutes, then we look at your inventory and decide whether you've gained or lost stature in the eyes of your tribe."

Zondra said, "Sands has increased in stature big-time. She now has three asses."

This seemed to make everyone laugh, even Patrice, but Audrey noticed that the boy in the bowling shirt wasn't laughing. His look was cold, and he was staring at Zondra.

Chapter 5
Ally

After class, Lea was waiting for Audrey and C.C. down the hallway, and as they were walking away together, the bowling-shirt guy caught up to them. "Hey," he said, and the girls turned.

He carried a motorcycle helmet under his arm, and he was much taller than C.C. or Lea, taller even than Audrey. For once he let his brown eyes connect with Audrey's. The coarse stubble of his chin made Audrey flinch a little, as if he had actually touched her face with his.

"I just wanted you to know," he said in a tight, gravelly voice that made Audrey want to clear her own throat. "Not everyone thinks Sands and Zondra are funny."

The boy's words were kind, Audrey supposed, but he spoke with such awkwardness and intensity that they seemed to be coming from some mysterious well of emotion that made him seem out of balance, and scary. He was staring so hard at Audrey that she wished he would be shy again. She looked down and hugged her green composition book to her chest. She was trying to think what to say, but nothing at all came to mind.

The boy tried to smile. "That's all I wanted to say," he said, and turned and walked off with his book bag over his shoulder and his helmet under his arm.

When he was beyond earshot, C.C. said, "Who was that? Dr. Death?"

Audrey watched the boy—he'd just stopped and seemed to be writing something on the palm of his hand—and tried to think of something charitable to say. "Somebody trying to be nice, I guess." But the truth was, he'd seemed more odd than nice. And what was the deal with the helmet? Did he own a motorcycle?

"He had eyes for you, Aud," C.C. said, grinning, "and the time is velly auspicious for romance."

Audrey laughed. "I'm thinking he's not my type, whoever he is."

She glanced at Lea, who at the Tate School had been known as "the Database."

"His name's Clyde Mumsford," Lea said quietly, "but I've heard people call him The Mummy."

C.C. said, "Well, The Mummy just spoke."

Audrey, Lea, and C.C. shared a laugh—which helped a little—and walked on together, their own small, movable, on-campus island.

Chapter 6
Address in Hand

Clyde Mumsford owned an old Vespa, and at the moment all he wanted to do was jump on it and ride away from Jemison High and never look back.

The day had gone from bad to worse. He'd just sat there seething while Sands and Zondra had taken over the class and started playing one of their ugly little tunes on the new girls, and he'd wanted to leap up and yell, "Stop! Just please for once in your lives act like human beings!"—which of course would've come out like croaks from the crypt, and then they all would've turned on *him*. So he'd just sat seething. And then, after class, he'd caught up with Audrey Reed and her friends to try to tell them he was on their side, but he'd done it in such a dweeby way that they stood there staring at him as if he were the kind of retardate fool that now, as he headed for the cycle parking lot, he knew for a fact himself to be.

Up ahead, two of the Theo Driggs group turned a corner and came into view, so Clyde took an alternate route and was glad, finally, to get to the cycle area, glad to get to his Vespa; glad to turn the key, pull on his helmet, and put it in gear. Once you were on the scooter and moving through traffic, you couldn't think. You could only drive and feel the scooter beneath you and the wind in your clothes and the cars in motion and the blurring, rushing colors of shops and offices, shrubs and lawns, signs and fences, a euphoric feeling of being both of the world and beyond its reach. But then you would get where you were going and pull off your helmet and let the world back in, and the thinking would start again.

Clyde locked his scooter in the underground garage of his apartment building. For a second, he turned up the palm of his left hand, stared at what he'd written there—*1501 Van Buren*—and then closed his fingers over the writing, making a loose fist. He took a deep breath before stepping into the elevator, which smelled heavily of Lysol and, behind that, something he was pretty sure was urine. Some days he could get to the third floor without having to take another breath, but today wasn't one of them.

Inside Clyde's apartment, the smell was pleasantly neutral. His mother was sitting up in a bed in the middle of the living room. It was a hospital bed, metal-framed, adjustable, and too big to get into his parents' bedroom. A metal intravenous drip stand had been rolled close to the bed, with tubes leading from a plastic bag to a catheter inserted in his mother's side. On the other side of the bed was a table stacked with novels, cooking magazines, *The Field Guide to North American Birds*, and a pair of binoculars for identifying the birds who nested near the duck pond.

She looked as if she'd been napping, because when she said, "Hello, Clydefellow," her voice seemed to float.

"Hi, Mom."

He kissed her on the forehead and patted her nose, something he'd started doing, he was told, when he was two. He was now sixteen, but his mother still liked the kiss and the nose pat, and expected it at certain ritualized moments of the day, including his return from school.

Clyde's mother had been sick for the last five years, since her diagnosis of stage four ovarian cancer. When Clyde had heard the term *stage four*, he'd asked his father what it meant, and his father had stared into the distance without answering. "Is there a fifth stage?" Clyde had asked, and his father had had to look away from Clyde when he shook his head no.

But his mother was still alive. She wasn't well, she wasn't cured, she wasn't even in remission, but she was alive. In the past five years she'd been through three operations, two full courses of chemotherapy, and another course of radiation treatments. For one full year she couldn't eat and had to take everything she needed intravenously. In boxes under the bed, there were six or seven different wigs she'd used to cover the baldness caused by the chemotherapy. His mother sometimes got discouraged, but if she ever once complained—and she must have, she absolutely must have—it wasn't when Clyde was around to hear it.

His mother's hair was presently growing back from the last chemo—it looked okay, really, almost like she'd had it chicly buzz-cut—and her skin was still a smooth olive brown, but her eyes had sunk deep into their darkened sockets. He'd thought once that she looked like a prisoner of war, and then realized that was exactly what she was—a prisoner of her own private war.

"So how was school?" she said now.

"A seven," he said, a complete lie. It'd been a two, maximum, until he acted like a wimp in Patrice's class and then like a sub-idiot in front of Audrey Reed and her friends, which had dropped the day's score to something fractional, but he knew it was better not to mention any of this to his mother (once he'd told her how some kids had called him The Mummy and she'd obsessed about it for days and had actually wanted to call the principal). Today, for insurance, he added, "Maybe an eight."

She nodded. "How about the tests?"

"Good." At least that much was true.

His mother shifted under her covers. "Could you do my feet?"

Her feet were cold. Her feet were always cold.

Clyde refolded and tightened the blanket that his father had wrapped around her stocking feet before going to work about half an hour earlier. Everything in the room was neatened up, the way his father always left it.

Clyde's father was an accountant at Bor-Lan Plastics and had never been an around-the-house type, but once Clyde's mother was diagnosed, he'd quickly adapted his life in order to extend hers. They'd needed money, so they'd sold their house in Jemison and rented this apartment on the south side. His company tried to accommodate his new situation. They'd let him change his hours to coincide with the swing shift (the factory was open twenty-four hours a day, and his office overlooked the factory floor) so he could be home during the day, and they'd let him assume responsibility for security screening of employment applications, which he could do at home on the computer, in order to make extra money. He'd become good at dealing with doctors, insurance companies, intravenous medications, and food prepared as Clyde's mother needed it. He'd even become good at mopping the apartment's linoleum floors and vacuuming the rugs.

The Parkview Apartments were a mistake from the '70s, a plain three-story rectangle of brick plunked down at the rim of a plain rectangular park. The walls were thin and the doors were hollow, but the rent was low and his mother had loved the view of the park.

Today, down on the sunny lawn, a group of guys were playing touch football, five against five, the kind of game Clyde had loved before his mother had gotten sick. The ball was snapped and one of the ends, a tall boy, started a slant pattern, then went long. He broke completely free, but the quarterback underthrew him.

When Clyde had been talking to Audrey Reed that afternoon, he'd seen the word *hopeless* on the cover of her green notebook. He'd also seen a street name and number, and after walking away from Audrey and her friends, he'd pulled out a pen and written this address on the palm of his hand before he could forget it.

Now, facing the window with his back to his mother, staring down at the park as if waiting for the next play in the pickup football game, Clyde casually brought his left hand in front of him. When he unrolled the fingers, the address was again revealed on the palm of his hand.

1501 Van Buren.

He started slightly when his mother said, "Homework?" But as he was turning around (careful to keep the palm of his left hand turned inward), he gave her an easy smile and said, "Pope Catholic?"

This was his standard line, and his mother replied with her own: "Unless there've been recent developments."

She then put on her earphones—the TV was wired so she could listen to it with earphones and not disturb anyone else—and Clyde glanced at the screen. She was watching some kind of cooking show, and how did you make any sense out of that? With her sickness, she couldn't cook, couldn't digest anything that couldn't be poured, and here she was, watching cooking shows and marking recipes in cooking magazines.

Clyde's desk was on the other side of the living room. He opened his book, but his mind kept returning to Audrey Reed. The first time he'd really noticed her was one day early in the school year when he'd gotten up in World Cultures to check something in the big dictionary at the other side of the room and found Audrey Reed's long, bare legs extended out into the aisle, and her all at once realizing she was blocking his way and smiling up at him and pulling her legs in and saying in a friendly, whispery voice that she was sorry.

He'd begun watching her after that, especially when she was lost in her reading and sliding a finger through her long sandy hair to separate a small cluster of strands that she would make into a little brush that she moved nervously across her lips.

And then, today, when he'd spotted her and her friends up on their little knoll and she sat facing the sun with her eyes closed so that, in that light and in that attitude, she looked not so much like a girl at Jemison High as some goddess he might invent for his own personal Greek myth.

1501 Van Buren, he thought.

He slipped into the kitchen and looked up *Reed* in the phone book. There were two columns of Reeds, none on Van Buren. Clyde brought a glass of water back to his desk, glanced at his mother—she was lost in her cooking show—and then booted up the computer and logged on to the program his father used for screening potential employees at Bor-Lan. The program searched every place a person's name might be recorded: newspapers, magazines, legal documents, television interviews. It found addresses, phone numbers, liens, and crimes. Clyde wasn't supposed to use it, but he found it interesting to slip unnoticed among the file cabinets of the world, peering in at everything that had been recorded about one individual or another.

He typed in *Reed* and *1501 Van Buren*, and watched as the name *Jackson Luther Reed* came up on the screen. Jackson Reed seemed to owe a lot of money to Citibank, and there seemed to be two large loans on the house on Van Buren—but one thing was certain: he had a daughter named Audrey Anne.

Audrey Anne. At 1501 Van Buren.

If he hurried through his homework, then made something simple for dinner—spaghetti, say, for himself, and some kind of creamed soup and smoothie for his mother—then he could tell her he needed to go to the library, which was true, but on the way back he could detour to 1501 Van Buren.

Just do a little drive-by.

What could it hurt?

Chapter 7
House

Audrey's car was an old white Lincoln Continental that her father called the *Queen Mary* and Audrey called the *Titanic*. He considered it her armor in any possible collision, and she had considered it the death boat of her social life before she realized that being small-chested, tall, and academically earnest would have sunk her anyway. As she cruised into the driveway at 1501 Van Buren that afternoon, she was surprised to see that her father was home. Usually he worked late.

Like her car, Audrey's house was white and overlarge. The huge white columned porch, the gleaming cupola, the Adamesque door, and the Palladian windows were enthusiastically described in *Around Jemison*, the historical society's guidebook, which praised "the exotic sunken garden of the gracious McNair mansion" and noted that "since 1918, a light has gleamed in the upstairs window, left on in memory of the owner's only son, who died in World War I."

Audrey's mother had grown up walking by the McNair house, staring up at that light, and sneaking in to play in the exotic sunken garden. After the house was sold and the light went off, she'd made excuses to drive, walk, or cycle by, trying to get up the courage to ask the new owners to turn the light on again in memory of Grady McNair. When she finally did, though, "they looked at her like she was crazy," Audrey's father later related, "and told her not to set foot on their property again."

Audrey's mother had died of something called acute myeloid leukemia when Audrey was three. The McNair house came on the market soon after, and Audrey's father, almost vindictively, bought it. He could not quite afford it, but he told himself that was just temporary—he was doing well in his firm and would do even better as time passed. He put a lamp in the upstairs window and left it on, more in memory of his deceased wife than of Grady McNair.

In Audrey's four-year-old mind, the belief formed that if she turned off the light, her mother would go out, too. And that wasn't her only fear. The whole house was terrifying: the darkly papered walls, the carved posts and paneling, the smells of coal and mildew, and—her father immediately regretted telling her the legend—the memory of the dead soldier. When the wind inflated a curtain, four-year-old Audrey thought she was seeing the soul of the soldier, or of her mother.

After they moved in, a sixty-year-old German woman named Olga Hoffmann—"Oggy," to Audrey—had joined the household, first as nanny and then, later, as cook, driver, and mother-substitute. Room by room, Oggy painted and papered the walls so that, in time, the house became lighter and cleaner. The framed pictures of Audrey's mother smiling in the Queen of Jemison Days float and lighting the candles on Audrey's first birthday cake were joined by photographs of black-eyed, white-haired Oggy serving Audrey oatmeal, stabilizing Audrey's first ride on a Schwinn, and supervising one of Audrey's early swimming lessons.

Audrey's memories of her mother were visual, and remote: the white crown of roses on her mother's head in the bridal and Jemison Days photographs; the white pearls at her throat; her eternally young face. Audrey's memories of Oggy were deeply physical: the Werther's butter toffees she carried in her purse, her German vocal groups harmonizing on the stereo, the watery jasmine of Echt Kölnisch Wasser, a cologne that came in gold-and-turquoise-labeled bottles that Oggy always gave to Audrey when they were empty. There were many images of Oggy waiting—waiting for Audrey to come down for breakfast in the morning; waiting with German cheese-cake when she came home from school; waiting in the car, reading *Frau im Leben* magazine, until Audrey's piano lesson was over. And finally, as Audrey reached adolescence, she'd found Oggy surprisingly frank about sexual development. ("I think today we go buy our Audrey a *Büstenhalter,*" she'd announced matter-of-factly one day after studying Audrey's barely budding breasts. "Maybe also supplies for your *Periode.*")

This afternoon, Audrey opened the front door and said, "Hallo?" She wished, impossibly, that Oggy would call, "Hallo!" in return. To Oggy, she could have described how handsome Wickham Hill was, how horrid Sands and Zondra had been, and how intense Clyde the Mummy was, preferably while slicing yet another thin piece of *Käsekuchen.* But this past August, Oggy's sister in Germany had broken her hip, and Oggy had taken a leave of absence to care for her in Berlin.

Without Oggy's counterbalancing weight, the world of Audrey and her father seemed to tip slightly, with everything sliding this way and that. Audrey didn't know how to cook, clean, or iron. (In truth, she hadn't realized that clean clothes were initially wrinkled, or that Oggy had ironed her sweatpants.) The house began to remind Audrey of the way it had looked when they moved in: dust on the stairs, spots on the windowpanes, dead flies on the windowsills, rust-colored stains in the washbasins and tubs. Oggy had been gone nine weeks now, and her sister was still bedridden.

Audrey stood in the hall and waited a second longer to see if Oggy had magically returned. Then she said, "Hallo?" again.

There was no answer, but Audrey followed the smell of frying meat into the kitchen, where she found her father standing over the stove, still wearing his business clothes. When she tiptoed up behind him and gave him a light poke in the ribs, he gave a start and turned with a stricken look that dissolved upon seeing Audrey.

"Stealthy little Polliwog," he said.

"Jumpy ol' Dad."

Audrey could always tell how much her father loved seeing her by the way his face would lose its haggardness for a second or two. "Jumpy, *hungry* ol' Dad," he said. "How about you? Hungry?"

"Was, until I saw the frying fatty meat," Audrey said with a grin.

"Cheeky, cheeky," her father said. "I'll have you know I went to Oggy's favorite butcher shop for these morsels." He converted to a bad Teutonic impression of Oggy. "Dis *Wurst* is de best!"

Audrey laughed because it had been a while since her father had even tried to be funny.

While her father cracked eggs into a mixing bowl, Audrey split English muffins and set the table with apple butter (his favorite) and orange marmalade (hers). His suit had a strange shine to it, as if it were worn, or inexpensive.

"That jacket's showing its age," Audrey said.

He smiled over his shoulder. "I know. I need to buy a few new suits. Problem's making the time."

"What about Enzio?" Enzio was the tailor who brought suits to the firm for him and other executives to try on.

Her father seemed not to hear her, and as he slid eggs and sausage onto the china plate, it was clear he was distracted.

"Dad?" Audrey said.

He didn't answer. He was just standing with the skillet in his hand, staring toward the wall.

"Dad?"

This time he heard her, and turned. "Oh, sorry, Polliwog," he said. "But you know what? I just thought of something that might be important to a project."

So, after gulping down a couple of bites of food and giving Audrey a kiss on the forehead, her father headed out the door and back to work. She listened to the sound of his car recede into stillness.

Suddenly the house felt deeply silent. Audrey ate another bite or two, then scraped her plate into the trash, cleaned up the kitchen, and walked down the hall to Oggy's room.

Oggy's bedspread was white chenille, and Audrey tried not to wrinkle it as she lay down. She studied the painting Oggy looked at when she went to sleep and when she woke up: a woman harvesting wheat. Beside her on the nightstand was a round silver-framed picture of Audrey at about five years old, wearing a Halloween princess costume. Audrey slid open the drawer of the nightstand and selected a white handkerchief with little pink flowers silk-screened in the corner. It smelled faintly of the Echt Kölnisch Wasser, and Audrey laid it over her face and closed her eyes. She pretended that she was five years old and Oggy was in the kitchen frying *Reibeplätzchen*. This worked the way it always worked—within five minutes, Audrey was asleep.

Half an hour later, she woke up, refolded the handkerchief, and looked at the woman harvesting wheat. She smoothed out the chenille spread. Then she headed upstairs, turning off lights behind her so that, by the time she started her homework, the only illumination within the old McNair mansion shone from the empty memorial room and Audrey's bedroom window.

Chapter 8
The Distance Between Them

A bad feeling had risen in Clyde when he'd brought up Jemison on MapQuest and found Van Buren on the east side of town. Half an hour later, as he turned his scooter into Audrey's neighborhood, the bad feeling grew worse. Right and left, huge trees spread over wide lawns that fronted two-, three-, and even four-story houses. At the end of long brick and stone driveways stood Audis and Land Rovers, Mercedes and Escalades.

Most of the house numbers were illuminated, and though 1501 was not, it was easy to find. Clyde's eyes were drawn at once to the house's only lights. One shone behind a drawn upstairs curtain, but the other lighted window was open. A person could be seen sitting at a desk.

Audrey Reed. He was pretty sure it was Audrey Reed.

Clyde circled the long curving irregular block and passed by again, a little slower. This time she was looking up and her face seemed spotlighted. The pull of Audrey Reed's lighted window was almost gravitational.

Clyde parked the scooter about a hundred yards down the block and sneaked back to Audrey's house on foot. Clyde had never been in a residential area so quiet. There were no voices, no radios, no TVs—everything seemed sealed completely shut. He crouched behind the low, serpentine rock wall that ran along the street frontage of 1501, but when he looked over the wall, something was changed.

The light in Audrey's room was out—itself alarming—but there was something else. Without her lighted room as a focal point, Clyde became aware of the cupola; the wide, curving, columned porch; the length of the lawn; the height, width, and depth of the house—the almost ungraspable *bigness* of it all—and, without quite knowing why, found himself backing away, as he might from a terrible accident. Beyond the lawn, he turned and ran for his scooter.

What he'd seen and what he was feeling had gathered together to form a fact, and by the time Clyde reached the Parkview Apartments, he carried that fact like a deadweight.

She was rich, and he was not.

Even when he and his parents had lived in their own house, their porch chairs had been some kind of plastic. Tonight, after locking his scooter in the garage, he looked around. Dirty Saturns and Geos. Old Buicks and rusting Cutlasses.

A little drive-by, he'd thought. What harm could it do?

The answer was, plenty.

This morning he'd believed that Audrey Reed sat only a few rows away from him, within striking distance, but he'd been wrong. She lived in another country.

He walked to the elevator, and when the door opened, he didn't bother to hold his breath. He just closed his eyes and stepped in.

"Hi," his mother said when Clyde slipped into the apartment. "Were you gone a long time, or did it just seem like it?"

"It wasn't that long," he said, and fell silent.

His mother was studying him. "Did you get what you wanted?"

No, he thought. But he said, "Yeah," and sat down beside her to watch TV. His mother was still watching her cooking shows. At the moment, the chef was twisting the knuckles of cooked lobster claws, the kind of skill, Clyde supposed, you might actually need in another part of town.

Chapter 9
Passersby

The window in front of Audrey's desk overlooked the wide front lawn, and between two white oaks she had a clear line of sight to the street. It was a quiet street—only the occasional car drove by. Tonight she'd looked up when a single headlight slowly passed—a motor scooter, she guessed, from the sound of it—and she'd noticed when, shortly thereafter, it slowly passed again, which seemed odd.

These were the times Audrey wished Oggy were here, or her father.

She switched off her light, opened the window slightly, and positioned herself to the side of it. The headlight didn't come again, but a minute or two later she thought she saw a shadowy form down by the stone wall, a dark outline that looked roughly like a head and perhaps shoulders. And just when she was able to tell herself she was imagining things, it moved, or seemed to move—she wasn't sure.

Audrey slid down to the floor and, with a raised hand, felt for her telephone. She called her father's office—no answer—and then dialed C.C. but got Brian, who turned down what sounded like Gypsy music that he'd been playing loud.

"An intruder?" he said in his stretched-out voice after she'd explained. "Intruders suck hind teat, man."

That seemed helpful. Audrey said, "Let me talk to C.C., Brian."

"She's off power-walking with the mom-creature, but not to worry, I'll be there in five," he said. A few minutes later, to Audrey's utter amazement, Brian and two other boys did appear on the lawn, and began shining flashlights all over the place. Audrey walked out.

"You the damsel in distress?" Brian said when he saw her. Besides a flashlight, he was carrying a baseball bat. So were the other two guys—friends of Brian's, evidently.

"What're the bats for?" she said.

Brian grinned. "If we found the intruder, we were going to apply a little tough love."

"But you didn't find the intruder."

"Yeah, well, that's true, but the other side of the coin is, he didn't find us."

Audrey gave him a long look and said, "There's something seriously wrong with your motherboard," which Brian seemed to view as a compliment.

Across the street, porch lights suddenly came on.

"I think the neighbors are wondering what's going on," Audrey said. "You guys want to come in for a Coke or something?"

Brian shook his head. "We're on duty, lady," he said mock-solemnly, and led his two goofy-looking friends away.

Audrey went back to her window and waited another five or ten minutes, but the rider didn't pass by again.

"Who do you think it was?" C.C. asked when she and Audrey and Lea were having their nightly 9 p.m. conference call.

"No idea," Audrey said.

"Probably a psychopath," Lea said quietly, and both C.C. and Audrey laughed.

When they were all quiet again, C.C. said, "So who do you *hope* it was?"

Wickham Hill, Audrey thought at once, but she said, "Mark Strauss." Mark Strauss had been C.C.'s tennis coach for a while.

"Kind of hard to imagine Mark Strauss out scooter-cruising in Jemison," C.C. said.

Audrey laughed. "Kind of hard, but kind of fun," she said.

Later, while Audrey was lying in bed, it occurred to her that Clyde Mumsford's carrying a helmet around didn't necessarily mean he drove a motorcycle. He could just as easily drive a scooter. And she'd caught him staring at her more than once. She closed her eyes and his image appeared before her. He was halfway handsome, but he was also strange and intense, and always hanging back on the fringes of things, like a . . .

Like a what?

Lea's word came to mind.

Like a psychopath, she thought, and wished for the gazillionth time that her father were in the house, or Oggy.

Chapter 10
Schrödinger's Cat

The next day, Audrey's heart began to race as she approached Mrs. Leacock's classroom. She hoped to see Wickham Hill, but feared what she might feel if she didn't. And she hoped he might talk to her, but worried how much she would blush or stammer if he did.

Inside the classroom, Mrs. Leacock was squeakily writing formulas on the board. Audrey tried not to look too quickly toward her seat, and the seat behind hers, but when she did, she realized it didn't matter.

Wickham Hill wasn't there.

She sat down, and as she looked up at the wall clock, the minute hand moved from 10:41 to 10:42. Three more minutes to tardy.

And then, through the open door, she saw him standing in the hallway, talking to Sands Mandeville, and suddenly Audrey felt small and disheartened and peevish, all at the same time.

Handsome Wickham Hill stood there, loose and comfortable in his own skin, in khaki pants and a black T-shirt, smiling and listening and saying things that made Sands laugh and touch his bare arm. Sands wrote something down on a piece of notebook paper, then tore it off and handed it to him.

Thirty seconds before the tardy bell, Wickham ducked into the room and strolled toward his desk. Audrey averted her eyes.

"Hey," he drawled in a low voice as he slipped into his chair, and when Audrey said nothing, he whispered, "You okay up there?"

"I'm fine," Audrey said in a frosty voice.

Mrs. Leacock walked over to close the classroom door. As she returned, she said, "It would behoove you to take notes. Today we talk about Schrödinger's Cat."

If this had been Patrice's class, someone would have suggested they talk instead about, say, Zondra's dog, or Sands's three asses, but this wasn't Patrice's class, it was Mrs. Leacock's, and everybody was quiet.

Schrödinger's Cat, Mrs. Leacock explained, was Erwin Schrödinger's famous example of the conceptual problems presented by Heisenberg's uncertainty principle. A cat is penned in a steel chamber along with a Geiger counter containing a minuscule amount of radioactive material. If a single atom decays in the course of an hour, the Geiger counter tube releases a hammer that shatters a small flask of hydrocyanic acid, "leaving you," Mrs. Leacock said, "with a—"

"Dead cat," said several students in unison.

"Perhaps. But it is just as likely that no atom has decayed, the acid remains in the flask, and the cat remains alive. Until we open the box, both possibilities co-exist. According to the uncertainty principle, the cat is alive *and* the cat is dead. Two opposing realities are equally true, which Herr Schrödinger found nonsensical."

"Him and me both," Wickham Hill said in a soft drawl, and Mrs. Leacock abruptly stopped talking and looked his way.

"A question, Mr. Hill? Or perhaps some illuminating comment?"

A bare moment passed, and then Wickham said, "A question. If the point of Heisenberg's theory is to make everything doubtful that was previously clear, isn't it going to be pretty hard to test us on it?"

A few muffled snickers, and Mrs. Leacock's stiff expression stiffened further. She twisted the ring on her left hand. "Oh, trust me, Mr. Hill. I'll find a way."

The classroom fell completely still, and Mrs. Leacock continued.

A strange thing then occurred. As Audrey sat listening to Mrs. Leacock, she became gradually more aware of Wickham's presence behind her, the way you might be aware of a sunlamp on your back.

She also realized that her icy feelings toward him had completely melted. She wanted in the worst way to turn and whisper something to him, or even pass him a note, but he was now so clearly the focus of Mrs. Leacock's vigilance that she didn't dare. Finally, the clock ticked to 11:35 and the bell rang.

She was gathering her things together when Wickham leaned close to her and said, "There's some missing data there."

The sugary smell of Christmas hung pleasantly in the air, and she was looking into his brown eyes. "What data?" she said.

He nodded at the cover of her green notebook. "Name. Address." He raised his eyes and let them fall on her. "No phone number."

Audrey couldn't help herself. She said, "Haven't you collected enough telephone numbers for one day?"

A look of confusion passed over Wickham Hill's face. Then, glancing toward the open front door, he seemed to realize what she'd seen. He grinned and shrugged. "Tell you what," he said in his slow, lazy-seeming voice, "you give me your number and I'll throw hers away."

"You would?"

His smile shrank into an expression of pleasant solemnity. "I would."

Audrey felt her whole body going soft. "What would you do with my number if you had it?"

His eyes danced, and he leaned a little closer. "Oh, something really pleasant," he drawled, "is what I'd do with your number if I had it."

Audrey felt herself being transported somewhere she'd never before been. It scared her, but it also pulled at her. "Like what?" she said.

With complete ease he said, "Oh, like calling you to set up a little study session on Heidenger and Schoenberg."

"Heisenberg and Schrödinger," Audrey said.

He grinned. "You can see I'm in need."

Audrey was staring into his eyes and telling herself to look away, but she couldn't.

"How about tonight?" he said.

She nodded.

"Your place or mine?"

Oggy was in Germany and Audrey's father probably wouldn't be home, so she should suggest someplace neutral—

the library, say, or even Bing's—but she heard herself say, "My house is fine."

"Sixish?" he said, and there was something about his assurance that made Audrey realize he'd made dozens of dates like this, possibly hundreds, and that dozens of girls had felt the thrilling buoyancy she was feeling now. But it didn't matter, because this was the first time in her life she'd felt this way.

"Sure," she said. "Sixish is fine."

"You supply the brains and I'll supply the supper."

"You will?"

He smiled and nodded and rose from his chair.

"Do you want me to tell you where I live?"

He stopped and tossed a quick look toward her green notebook. "Already know," he said, and she had the feeling, watching him walk away, that he knew she was watching.

She thought suddenly of an experiment you could perform at the science museum downtown. If you pushed a button, the machine would make a low sound like a foghorn, and if you adjusted the pitch just right, the surface of the bowl of water in the center of the machine would begin to vibrate.

Wickham Hill was the sound, and she was the bowl of water.

Chapter 11
The Yellow Paper

"Did you see this?" C.C. said as Audrey approached the knoll during the lunch break. She was holding up a bright yellow sheet of paper.

"What is it?"

"Take a look for yourself. Lea's already circled the good stuff."

The top of the page read THE YELLOW PAPER, and below that, in smaller letters, *All the News Unfit to Print,* and *The underground newspaper no self-respecting citizens would admit to publishing, so we're not admitting it either.* The masthead featured an old-fashioned engraving of whalers harpooning a barely submerged beast.

There were various columns alleging thinly veiled romantic intrigues (*Word on the street is it's MizK2 and Studly Jr until the 12th of Never and that's a long long time unless say on the 11th MizK should hear about Jr's recent acquaintance with paternity testing*) and odd news stories (*You won't find anything in the official organ—no not that organ and that's not what we mean by keeping your hands to yourself and you know who you are don't you?—about raccoon poo in Room 332 but we're here to tell you there was stated poo found in stated room though absent raccoon tracks there are concerns within The Administration about a Poo Broker so to speak who might've transferred* stated poo from stated animal's woody habitat to teacher's desktop in stated room).

Audrey looked up, grinning. "Not much on punctuation, are they?"

"Big on weird capitalization, though," Lea said.

C.C. said, "Turn it over. Good stuff's on the other side."

In *The Tattler*, the official school newspaper, there was a column called "Shouted" that had at its head a cartoon of a little man shouting into a bullhorn. In *The Yellow Paper*, the same cartoon was used, but the column title had been changed to "Outed."

Lea had circled two items. The first one read:

Hold on to your poles, Bargemen (no, not those poles) but it turns out you aren't alone in your youthful indiscretions . . . Joining you is the teacher hip enough to go by one name and it's not Prince, Cher or Jewel but why not call her Winona because once upon a time (or for you Fact Freaks and you know who you are make that Aug 11, 1972) in Filene's Basement our good teacher acquired several garments Winona-style probably the medication she was taking or maybe a role she was studying for can explain it because we can't but then who are we to hurl the first harpoon? . . .

Audrey looked up. "Yikes."

"Which one?" C.C. said.

"Patrice shoplifting."

C.C. nodded. "Keep reading."

The second circled item in the "Outed" column read:

Zounds! . . . Iz they iz or iz they izn't? . . . Z-Gal's zilent when it comes to the zubject but our zource zites a cosmetic zurgeon in Zaratoga as the zite of the Great Augmentation (our reporters in their unyielding impartial search for Truth & Injustice remain open to personal inspection of the great glands) . . . And this just in from our upstate bureau: A Big Congratz, O Sandy One! . . . Thatz right, the Z-Gal's zandy zidekick's been accepted early decision at Mount Holyoke thereby laying to rest all talk about Holyoke's discriminating against the leotarded ("SATs never tell the whole story," the Vice Dean of Admissions told our reporters. "We take other things, including really good jazz dancing, into account in order to get the diversity we seek.") . . .

"Pretty harsh," Audrey said.

"But I notice you're grinning," C.C. said.

"Well, Patrice, Zondra, and Sands. If you asked me to pick worthy targets—"

Lea said, "Somebody told me *The Yellow Paper* came out a couple of times last year, and the administration had a cow."

C.C. laughed. "Then I guess they're calving again."

"And they never caught them?" Audrey asked.

Lea shook her head no.

C.C. had brought cucumber sandwiches, Audrey's personal favorite, and as she passed them to the others, she said, "Maybe it's not a *them*, then. Maybe it's a *him*."

"The Yellow Man," Audrey said, chewing.

Lea said quietly, "Or the Yellow Girl."

Right, Audrey thought. *Why should one gender have a corner on revenge?* An icy breeze came up, and Audrey shivered.

"That's him," C.C. said suddenly, and Audrey turned to follow C.C.'s gaze to a boy walking alone across the quad. It was Wickham Hill. Spring in the middle of wintry thoughts.

"That's he," Lea corrected, looking, too. "But *who* is he?"

Before Audrey could speak, C.C. said, "The new boy. The dreamy one."

A soft-handed pride held Audrey for a moment.

Lea said "dreamy" seemed excessive.

"You should see him up close," C.C. said.

They all watched as Wickham Hill moved easily into a group of boys in the quad.

"His name's Wickham Hill," Audrey said, almost blurting it out.

"Wicked Hill?" C.C. asked, laughing.

"Wicked Hill," Lea repeated. "It sounds like a skateboard park. Or a rapper."

"It's *Wickham* Hill," Audrey said. "He's nice, and he's coming to my house tonight to study physics."

She didn't look at C.C. or Lea, but she could feel their eyes turning to her, as heliotropes to the sun.

A few seconds passed; then C.C. said, "God, Audrey."

It was the first time in her friendship with C.C. that Audrey had ever felt truly envied.

C.C. said, "Well, if he needs help with French, you let him know Lea and I are aces on the subjunctive."

Audrey smiled. "I will," she said.

Chapter 12
Strangeness

What occurred in Patrice's class that afternoon exceeded
even the expected strangeness. When the tardy bell rang,
Patrice wasn't there, and Sands and Zondra weren't there, but
there was the anticipation of an entrance, so the class was
unusually subdued. And a minute or so later, Patrice and
Sands *did* walk in, followed by the principal, Mrs. Pardoo.
The class fell deadly quiet.

Patrice and Sands went to their desks. Mrs. Pardoo stood
formally in front of the class holding *The Yellow Paper*, which
she now raised for presentation.

"First of all, it needs to be said that what is written anony-
mously is written by cowards." Mrs. Pardoo significantly
dropped the paper into the wastebasket. "Secondly, when the
persons responsible for this paper are apprehended—and
please note I use the word *when*, and not *if*—that person or
persons will be removed from school and turned over to
authorities for legal prosecution." Mrs. Pardoo took a deep
breath. "As for Miss Newman, this school district did a thor-
ough background check and found her not just meeting but
exceeding the high ethical, legal, and educational standards
required for employment."

Which, Audrey realized, was not the same as saying Patrice
never filched a sweater or two at Filene's.

Mrs. Pardoo turned to look at Patrice. "Thank you, Miss Newman. I sincerely regret what has happened today and look forward to setting it right."

After she left, Patrice stood up beside her desk. She seemed different, a little shorter and older than the day before. For perhaps half a minute (though it seemed longer to Audrey), Patrice said nothing and simply stared past the students toward the blank wall at the rear of the room. Finally she brought her gaze back to the students and said in a low voice, "When I was nineteen years old, I made a serious mistake."

She fell quiet again and let her gaze move across the room, from one student to another, systematically, so no one was missed. When her eyes touched Audrey, they left behind a feeling of guilt, which, after a second or two, made Audrey resentful—she'd had nothing to do with *The Yellow Paper*.

The teacher said, finally, "I just want to say one thing. By the time each of you is nineteen—the age I was when I made a mistake—you will have made a mistake, too."

Audrey expected more—when teachers made a moral point, they always seemed to lay it on thick—but Patrice was almost done. "In the future," she said, "please address me as Miss Newman." A pause, then: "I have nothing further to say, but I believe Sands would like to make a statement."

Sands stood immediately, even before everyone's gaze could turn her way. Audrey noticed that, across the room, Clyde Mumsford didn't turn. He sat as he'd sat through both Mrs. Pardoo's and Patrice's speeches, leaning over his desk, doodling with one hand, the other hand draped over his shoulder. He might've been bored. Or sneakily amused.

Unlike Patrice, Sands was assertive and indignant. "I just

want to say that yes, I got into Mount Holyoke, but if anyone had bothered to ask, my SATs are over 1800, which would've gotten me in easy, with or without drill team and the other stuff."

On another day, someone might've made a wisecrack about the nature of the other stuff, but this wasn't another day.

"And as for Zondra," Sands said, "it's not her fault her parents named her Zondra, and also, just for the record, it's not even legal to do that kind of surgery until you're eighteen."

Sounds like you've looked into it, someone would've said on another day, but today the silence was so total, the quick tick of the clock almost startled Audrey.

Sands sat down.

"Okay, then," Patrice said. Her voice sounded tired. "Enough distractions. Let's get back to work."

All Audrey would otherwise remember about the class was how it seemed to last a day, not an hour, and the relief she felt when she finally joined the stream of students exiting the classroom.

"Whew!" C.C. said as she and Lea joined Audrey in the flow. Lea said quietly, "Whew cubed."

As the three girls paused on the steps before setting off in different directions, Audrey gave the others a playful grin and said she was going to go home and brush up on her physics.

"Audrey, honey, don't forget to tell Wicked that if he needs help with French, we're there for him," C.C. said.

"And find out his story," Lea said. "We want all the little details."

As she walked away, Audrey felt ready for anything—if she

hadn't been within eyeshot of Jemison High, she would've broken into a run. *Yeah,* she thought as she walked springily along. *What's your story, Wickham Hill? Inquiring minds want to know.*

Chapter 13
Dr. Yates

That afternoon, Wickham Hill sat in his bedroom on the second floor of his father's old house and listened to his mother run the vacuum downstairs.

There was a desk by the window, and as he sat there with his unopened textbooks, he fingered the place on the black desktop where the initials *J.E.Y. 5/30/56* had been scratched. James Edward Yates, of course. His actual but unofficial father, whom he always referred to as "Dr. Yates," not "Dad" or "Father." The next set of scratches read, *First date: Elaine Harcourt. 8/2/62*. That first date had started a process that led to marriage, and Dr. Yates was still married to the former Elaine Harcourt, which was why Wickham's occasional lunches with Dr. Yates had taken place in Myrtle Beach, two hours away. Nowhere on the desk was Wickham's mother's name or her initials. As Wickham traced the scratches with his finger, he felt little prickles of resentment, and he imagined himself with a piece of steel wool and some acetone, expunging Dr. and Mrs. Yates.

Downstairs, the vacuum noise stopped. Wickham guessed that his mother was listening for the phone, making sure she didn't miss its ring. After a moment, the vacuum whirred to life again.

His mother didn't call what had happened between her

and Dr. Yates an affair. She said they "saw" one another. They had been "seeing" one another episodically for eighteen years. She loved him and he loved her, but he had responsibilities. It was, as she put it, "complicated."

It was especially complicated now. Since the big showdown in the courts, Dr. Yates wouldn't even speak to Wickham's mother. He wouldn't return calls made to his office, and he'd changed his cell phone number. Two months ago, Wickham's mother had told Wickham they were moving to a house in New York State that she had, at various times, visited with Dr. Yates. She had a key, she said. She would find a nursing job. He would enroll in school. And then his mother had said, "He'll come to us there when he comes to his senses."

Which, in spite of—or perhaps because of—all the times Dr. Yates had treated them badly or let them down, Wickham wanted to believe as much as his mother did.

Dr. Yates was sentimental about the house—he'd actually been born in one of the upstairs bedrooms—and he'd always told Wickham's mother that this was where they would come and live permanently when finally they could. He'd kept his membership at the country club, and he had open accounts with the florist, the taxi company, In & Out Dry Cleaners, the Little Dragon Restaurant, and Peter's Old Town Market, with the bills going to his office in South Carolina, where they could be discreetly paid by his accountant. For the past few weeks, Wickham and his mother had been charging their purchases to those accounts, and by now the bills should have been sent and received—which, Wickham thought, was about as close as it gets to sending up a flare identifying their exact whereabouts.

Wickham had never been sure whether he ought to like Dr. Yates for the help he provided or despise him for the distance he kept. What Wickham did resentfully understand was that they needed him. If Dr. Yates never spoke to his mother again, they were both in serious trouble. His grades were bad and, without Dr. Yates to help, college was out. What were they going to live on?

The nerves in Wickham's temples felt compressed by the room and the wintry light, and the nausea was getting worse. He took an Excedrin in hopes that he wouldn't need the Imitrex, which cost fifteen dollars apiece, and then he lay down on the blue cotton spread.

All Wickham really knew how to do was get people to like him. He knew how to dress, and how to lean close to girls when he talked to them in a low voice. When he'd been deferential with girls in Cypress—when he'd said "ma'am" to their mothers and "sir" to their fathers—these girls would smile at him; even as they stood planted on their shiny hardwood floors, he could feel them slipping out of their bodies and moving toward him. They opened their doors to him; invited him to the country club and to Sunday dinners overlooking green, glassy ponds; and afterward they kissed him with a longing he sometimes fully returned, and sometimes did not.

Wickham pressed his fingers on his temples, then shifted his body to pull out his wallet and slide from within it a photograph of a dark-haired girl who was laughing so hard she was slightly out of focus. Wickham studied the picture of Jade and thought of Audrey Reed's finger sliding slowly, habitually, through her long hair and then, finally—already it was something Wickham had learned to watch keenly—bunching it with her hand and pulling it to one side of her head, revealing the bare white skin of her neck. He liked the look of Audrey Reed, and he liked the look of her friends. They dressed in that slyly tasteful way of preppy girls, at once prim and revealing. They wore their hair long and fixed it only with bands or ribbons. And they were girls, he could tell, who were accustomed to nice things—especially Audrey, and this drew him to her.

Wickham wondered if eating would make his headache go away. Sometimes meat helped, or sugar, and he was due at Audrey's in less than an hour. He stood up, took the Little Dragon take-out menu from the top drawer, and dialed the number on the cover. When a man answered, Wickham said, "Mr. Wong, hey, I'm placing an order, but first I've got a question. I know you're sending the bills to my dad in South Carolina, but I just wanted to be sure he was getting them and, you know, there were no snafus in getting paid or anything."

Mr. Wong told him only one bill had gone out, but it had been paid, no problem.

Wickham took this in. "Okay," he said, and placed his order. "But don't send it here," he added. "It goes to 1501 Van Buren. Around 6:45, okay?"

"No problem," Mr. Wong said.

Wickham slid Jade's picture back into his wallet and sat back down at the desk. He picked up the telephone and, while arranging for a taxi, heard the click of the downstairs telephone. "I'm on the line, Mom," he said, and she quietly hung up. He knew what she was doing, because he'd seen her do it countless times.

She was making sure the phone worked.

Chapter 14
Messages Written and Not

Audrey knew she shouldn't be secretly relieved that her father was working late that night, but she was. And she knew she should run a space heater in the breakfast room, where they could both eat and study, rather than turn on the forced-air heater, which her father was trying not to use ("Why deplete our natural resources?" he'd joked). But Audrey was afraid that using only the space heater would make the house—and, indirectly, her—seem cold and stingy.

Wickham had said "sixish," but the doorbell rang at 5:55, and though Audrey came to the door dressed, she was still drying her hair. "Hello, you," he said.

As she smiled and said hello, she knew she was beaming and wished she weren't. "You're early," she said, and gave her hair a final toweling. "I just got out of the shower."

Wickham laughed and, after glancing around to be sure no one else was present, drawled, "Then I should've come a few minutes earlier."

Audrey felt her beaming turn to blushing. "Where're your books?" she said, and then, seeing no car under the portico, "Where'd you park?"

"Forgot my book and I got a ride," he said. He smiled at her for a second or two. "I know what you're thinking."

What Audrey was thinking was how she wished her hair

weren't wet, and how amazing it was that a boy this hand-some had knocked on her door, and how strange it was that he hadn't brought his book if he was planning on studying. What she said was, "Okay, what am I thinking?"

"You're thinking I forgot the promised vittles."

Audrey laughed. "Nope. I'd forgotten the vittles com-pletely." Then she said, "It's okay, I can make soup and sand-wiches."

He leaned forward, and she smelled the sugary smell again. For one preposterous, fleeting second, Audrey thought he was going to kiss her. He didn't. He simply said, "The vittles is on their way."

She laughed again. "They is?"

"They is."

"What kind of vittles is they that can be on their way?"

Wickham made a low laugh. "The kind that leave Little Dragon in little cartons."

This is easy, Audrey thought. *I'm here with wet hair talking to Wickham Hill with nobody in the house, and it's easy.*

As they walked down the warm hallway toward the warm dining room, Wickham Hill said, "So what *were* you thinking?"

She pointed him into the dining room. "When?"

"When I thought you were worried I'd forgotten the vittles."

"I don't remember," Audrey said, "other than wishing my hair was dry."

He reached out, touched a strand of her damp hair, and said, "I liked that it was wet." He was looking at her hair, and then he was looking at her eyes. "You have nice hair."

In the next moment, while he held her with his eyes, Audrey inhaled the sweet, sugary smell. Was it cookies? She wished it were Christmas already, and that snowflakes were piling up on the hedges and trees. She made herself break away from his gaze, opened her book to the chapter on Schrödinger's Cat, and said, "Maybe we should get started."

Audrey and Wickham's first hours together slipped easily by. He said he had a little headache, so they put off talking about Schrödinger's Cat until they'd eaten cashew chicken and considered each other's fortunes (his was "Untended friendships bear hard fruit," and hers was "Protect that which is yours and yours only"). Audrey tried to discuss physics then, but he kept slipping amiably to other topics, and they spent most of their time talking.

He asked about her parents, and after she'd talked awhile about them (her father worked all the time, she said, and she only really remembered her mother from photographs), she asked about his family (he was an only child, his mother was a nurse and his father was a doctor, but they were "kind of separated" right now). He was still talking when the phone rang. Audrey looked at her watch and said, "Oh my gosh." It was already nine o'clock.

She picked up the phone and said, "Hi, you guys," and then, "He's still here—can I call you back in a few minutes?"

After she'd hung up, she turned awkwardly to Wickham. "My friends C.C. and Lea. We always conference-call at nine o'clock."

He nodded. "Your good-looking girl chums."

"Have you met them?"

He shook his head. "I've just seen them with you."

That he paid attention to her unobserved was strangely flattering. She said, "Unless the weather's bad, we eat our lunch on a little knoll above the quad. You could come eat with us tomorrow if you wanted."

He took this in. "Tell you what. I'll come eat with you guys tomorrow if you'll have something to eat with me at Little Dragon tomorrow night."

Easy. It all seemed so easy. "You're kind of a big dealmaker, aren't you?"

He laughed, and in his low drawl said, "All I know is, when I eat Chinese food with you, my headaches go away."

He was looking into her eyes again, and she made herself say, "Aren't you the slightest bit worried that you are so not ready for this quiz thing tomorrow?"

He shifted and shrugged. "I've failed better teachers than Mrs. Leacock," he said. Then he let his eyes settle into hers and, in a low, sociable voice of complicity, he said, "Besides, I'll be fine if, while you're taking the test tomorrow, you just lean a little to the right or to the left."

Chapter 15
A Vow

When his alarm clock sounded the next morning, Clyde Mumsford woke up happy.

He'd been dreaming of Audrey Reed. This wasn't the first time he'd dreamed of her, but this one had been the most pleasant. He'd been riding a bicycle along a sunny country road and was weirdly, almost weightlessly happy, but didn't know why until in his dream he turned around and saw Audrey Reed on her own bike, pedaling behind him. She was wearing shorts and a sleeveless T-shirt, and her long sandy hair streamed back from her face. *I'm gaining on you,* she said, grinning.

For a few minutes, while he slept, he'd known what it was like to be Audrey Reed's boyfriend.

"Clyde? You up?" His father, from the front room.

"Getting there," Clyde called back.

There was a freestanding Everlast punching bag in the middle of the room. Clyde got up and gave it a couple of sharp jabs. So what was he going to do about Audrey Reed? Wait around for the next good dream? Nobody said he had to be rich just to talk to her. Who said he couldn't just ask her to study with him the next time he ran into her? *Say, hey, I'm having some trouble with this whole sub-Saharan culture deal and you seem to have it down pat. Would you mind going over it with me?*

He could do that. Maybe he could do that. He could tell Audrey Reed was nice, and once he'd been around her awhile, his words wouldn't come out like croaks anymore. Diminished croakiness would evolve.

After he'd showered and dressed, Clyde went to the living room, where his father was standing at the big window, staring out. His mother was still sleeping. The TV was tuned to a cooking show, but the sound was off. A tray with yogurt and Cream of Wheat sat next to his mother, untouched.

"Going now, Dad," he said on his way out.

His father turned and nodded. In the five years of his mother's sickness, his father's hair had started graying. This morning his skin seemed gray, too.

From behind them, in a dazed, soft voice, his mother said, "Going where, without . . . ?"

Clyde turned. "To school, Mom."

"Without . . . ?"

Without kissing me, Clyde knew, was the whole question.

He walked over, kissed her on the forehead, and patted her nose. She closed her eyes again and seemed to relax.

"Love you," she whispered—it was what she always whispered—and he headed for the door.

Today, he vowed, and took a deep breath before stepping into the elevator. *Today The Mummy talks to Audrey Reed.*

Chapter 16
Another Candidate

"Morbidly shy."

That was the term his doctor had used when talking to Clyde's mother about Clyde's ingrown nature. Clyde was nine or ten at the time. "He's morbidly shy," the doctor had said, "but I wouldn't worry about it too much. Many children go through it, and most outgrow it."

But Clyde hadn't outgrown it. His father had tried to give Clyde's nature a positive spin ("Clyde understands that it's what people do that counts, not what they say"), but his mother worried about the social consequences of Clyde's silence ("It makes you seem so *solemn*," she said), and she'd suggested speech class or Junior Toastmasters or even at-home charades, all without success, and then she'd become sick and more important worries had supplanted this one.

Clyde had read books on the subject (*Start by looking the stranger in the eye and saying, "Hello, I'm Patrick [or, as the case may be, Patricia]"*), but couldn't take them seriously. (In the bathroom mirror, Clyde had looked himself in the eye and said, "Hello, I'm Patrick, or, as the case may be, Patricia.") He'd locked himself in the bathroom and pretended to conduct lighthearted conversations with a stranger, but the slight resulting confidence vanished the moment he stepped out of the bathroom.

Audrey, hi. I don't know if you know me, but I'm Clyde Mumsford, and I was wondering . . .

Clyde practiced these words in his mind again and again this morning as he rode to school, as he locked his Vespa, as he took the steps up into the west wing. *Audrey, hi. I don't know if you know me, but I'm Clyde Mumsford, and I was wondering . . .*

He had a plan. He'd wait until Audrey broke away from her girlfriends after Patrice's class, and then he'd take three deep breaths and walk up to her and start talking. *Audrey, hi. I don't know if you know me, but I'm Clyde Mumsford . . .*

That was his plan.

But then he saw her. As he made his way through the crowded hallway, he saw her up ahead, coming straight toward him.

Alone. She was alone.

Clyde tried to take deep breaths.

He tried to think.

Hi. I don't know if you know . . .

She was closer, and seemed to look at him and then smile the exact same radiant smile he'd seen in his dream and, to his complete and pleasant surprise, something within Clyde relaxed, and he felt his friendly normal self beginning to take over.

He smiled a calm smile and had begun to open his mouth to speak when, just ahead of him, a tall boy he didn't know said, "Well, well, Audrey Reed." Her face brightened further, and the boy in his smooth, slow drawl added, "My long-stemmed study partner," which made her smile even more.

She stopped to talk to the boy, and as Clyde slipped silently past, face burning, she seemed not even to see him.

A kind of blindness came over Clyde. Students and lockers passed in a blur, and when he saw a doorway, he escaped the building and kept walking.

The new kid, that's who it was. The new kid. Who was a face man. And who also looked like money.

Of course that's who Audrey Reed would hang out with. Somebody handsome and smooth-talking and rich.

Clyde turned down a row between temporary classrooms, and was so lost in his thoughts that when he passed the corner of one of the classrooms, he didn't notice the group of boys huddled there. But they saw him.

"Hey, there goes The Mummy."

Clyde turned. It was Theo Driggs's drones, six or seven of them, with Theo himself slouched in their midst. One of the boys said, "How do de mummy do?"

Clyde glanced quickly away and kept walking.

"He can't talk. Mummies can't talk."

Keep walking, Clyde thought. *Just keep walking.* But Theo and his group were moving now, too, following behind.

"The Mummy still scootering to and fro?"

One of Theo's friends made sputtering putt-putt sounds, which at once grew into a chorus of putt-putting, soon mixed with laughter. What felt like a tightening cable ran from Clyde's neck down his arms to his hands, which formed into fists.

He kept walking, but Theo's group followed, continuing their putt-putt sounds. Finally Clyde stopped and turned.

Everything became quiet.

For a muscular boy, Theo Driggs had a surprisingly fleshy

face. His plump lips showed a trace of a smile. "I see the scooter-ist has balled his little hands into little fists. That for a reason?"

Clyde didn't know what to do or say. So he said something he was actually wondering. "What did I ever do to you?"

It came out croakish, and Theo appeared genuinely confused. "Try it again in English," he said.

"What did I ever do to you?" Clyde said, trying to talk slowly.

Recognition spread over Theo's face, and the smile on his plump lips widened. He said, "You entered my field of vision. You uglified the view."

Snickers among Theo's friends.

Theo, still smiling, drew closer. "Why? Does that bother The Mummy?"

Clyde said nothing. He simply glared at Theo.

"Does it?" Theo said, a hardness lining his voice now. "Does that bother The Mummy?" His hand jabbed at Clyde's chest. "Does it? Yes or no?"

There was a long moment of absolute silence. Then Clyde unfolded his fists and, in a low, croaky voice, said, "No."

Theo's whole body relaxed, and his smile returned. "Good. Now why don't you just haul your mummified pansy ass out of my field of vision so I can regain my accustomed serenity."

Clyde turned. From behind, as he walked away, he heard their sputtering putt-putt imitation of his Vespa, followed by derisive laughter.

God. Theo Driggs. Theo Brain-Dead Driggs, who just came sliming out from under a rock. Talk about a candidate for "Outed."

Clyde somehow got through his first class, and then the

next, and the next, hour upon hour, but when last period finally came, he just couldn't bring himself to walk into World Cultures and see Audrey Reed smiling at Patrice and passing notes to her friends and just generally floating along in her happiness, so he slipped out to his Vespa and rode out to the river, where he sat freezing until he was sure his father would have left for work. Then he went home.

"Hello, Clydefellow," his mother said. She'd been asleep, and now barely opened her eyes. Her face looked almost skeletal. "Good day?" she said.

He nodded.

"On a one-to-ten?" Her voice was slightly slurred from medication.

"An eight," he said. "Maybe an eight and a half."

His mother nodded and closed her eyes, and was soon asleep. Clyde went over to the desk and turned on the computer.

Chapter 17
Excellent

A few hours earlier, as Audrey was taking her physics quiz in the quiet of Mrs. Leacock's room, she did something she'd never done before and had never imagined she would ever do. She moved her test paper slightly to the right and then shifted her shoulders slightly to the left, so that her answers might be seen from behind.

The night before, when Wickham had suggested that she might move to the right or left when she was taking her test, the words that formed in her mind were, *That's cheating.* But she didn't say them—she was afraid they would sound nerdy or schoolgirlish—and he'd made his suggestion so casually that it was clear he didn't see it as an ethical issue. But Audrey did. She'd been taught not to cheat, and not to respect those who did. She knew what she needed to say: *I can't do that. I'm sorry, I just can't. It wouldn't be right.*

But she hadn't said anything at all, had pretended in fact not to hear, and when she'd seen him in the hall before school, she felt such a sense of buoyant well-being that she knew there was no point in bringing the matter up, because it was simple—it was something he wanted her to do, and she would do it. And she did—casually, subtly, as if she were merely shifting in her seat as anyone in the world might do.

"Time!" Mrs. Leacock said, and gave Audrey a start.

She didn't look at Wickham as he handed his paper forward; she put hers on top of his and handed the tests to the boy in front of her. As the papers reached the first desk of each row, Mrs. Leacock moved across the front of the room, collecting them and assigning the class some pages to read while she corrected the quizzes.

For the next twenty-five minutes, it was quiet in the classroom except for the turning of pages, the click of the wall clock, and an occasional sniffle or cough. Audrey tried to read, but couldn't concentrate. Her stomach hurt. Her pulse seemed lightning fast. She was certain she would be caught; that she and Wickham would miss the same questions; that somebody had noticed their cheating and penciled a note on his or her test. Audrey watched Mrs. Leacock as she quickly ran her red marker down test after test, checking off incorrect answers, counting them up, scribbling a score. Once Mrs. Leacock raised her head and looked directly at Audrey, who quickly lowered her eyes.

On quiz days, Mrs. Leacock always dismissed the class by calling out names and returning the corrected quizzes.

"Audrey Reed," Mrs. Leacock said first. Audrey gathered her books and walked toward the front of the room even as Mrs. Leacock called the next few names, none of which were Wickham Hill's.

"Well done," Mrs. Leacock said in a low voice as she handed Audrey her quiz—which, Audrey noted quickly, was marked "100." Next to the score, in red pencil, was written *Excellent!*

As she crossed the room toward the door, Audrey knew that what she should have felt was humiliation and shame. But she didn't.

What she felt was relief.

Chapter 18
Three Girls in a Car

It was too cold for the knoll that day, so the Tate girls were sitting in Audrey's old Lincoln eating lunch, Audrey and C.C. in the front seat, Lea in the back. The heater was on, and all the windows were cracked open an inch or two to keep them from fogging.

While they ate, C.C. talked about Brian's bearded dragon. "The thing just lies on its rock and basks under its heat bulb," C.C. said. "I don't know when it moves."

"At night," Lea said in her soft voice. "When it goes looking for warm flesh."

C.C. laughed. Audrey laughed, too, but not much. The relief she'd felt when she received her quiz back from Mrs. Leacock had quickly dissolved, and a bad feeling had taken hold of her and not let go. She thought that if she could just see Wickham Hill and talk to him, the feeling would release her. But now they'd moved from the knoll, where she'd told Wickham she'd be, to her car, where he would never find her.

A sudden wind broadsided the Lincoln, and seemed actually to shake it.

"You okay, Audrey?"

Audrey, brought back to the present, nodded.

Lea said, "She's probably thinking about Wickie-poo."

C.C., going for a mock-sleazy tone, added, "Audrey's personal quantum mechanic."

Audrey blushed only slightly. The girls had already gone over all the details of the study date, or at least most of them. Audrey hadn't mentioned Wickham's suggestion that she move a little to the left or right.

There was a silence, and then C.C. said to Audrey, "This reminds me. My mom said her mechanic—her real mechanic—bought your dad's Jaguar. Supposedly your dad made him an offer he couldn't refuse. What's the deal on that?"

Audrey had no idea. The Exorbitance, as her father called it, was the car he "saved for sunny days." He hadn't mentioned selling it, and she hadn't noticed it was gone because he kept it in the garage most of the time, protecting the paint from all forms of life. She said, "I guess we don't have enough sunny days." Then: "I know he said the repair bills were pricey."

C.C. said, "I think my mom was miffed he didn't offer it to her first."

Audrey closed her eyes, not so much because she was tired as because she wanted to close this line of conversation. Lately, whenever Audrey thought of her father and money, a strange tightness clamped over her—it was as if something were wrong but she didn't know what, and didn't really want to know.

Except for the engine and heater fan, it was quiet in the car. In slow succession Audrey's thoughts drifted to Wickham Hill, to their sitting at her kitchen table, to him smiling his easy smile and suggesting . . .

Tap-tap-tap.

Audrey's eyes flicked open and turned to her window, where—it seemed almost like magic—Wickham Hill was grinning down at her.

"Phys whiz one minute," he drawled, "Sleeping Beauty the next."

He had a red scarf wrapped around the collar of his coat, and you could see his breath in the air.

Audrey push-buttoned her window down and realized that she'd been right—all it took was seeing Wickham's face to make everything feel okay again.

"How'd you find us?" she said.

"I've got my wily ways," he said.

After Audrey had introduced Lea and C.C. to Wickham (they both smiled beamingly up at him), she suggested he get into the car, out of the cold.

He shook his head amiably. "Can't. I've got a doctor's appointment."

From behind Audrey, C.C. said, "So did Audrey get you a passing grade in physics?"

Audrey flinched at the question, but Wickham's genial expression didn't change as he moved his eyes calmly from C.C. to Audrey. "She did," he said.

Audrey said in a soft voice, "What did you get?"

"A seventy-two." He blinked and smiled. "Didn't want to overdo it."

There was an awkward silence; then Wickham said, "Anyhow, I just wanted to make sure we're on for tonight."

Audrey nodded.

He smiled down at her. "How 'bout if I meet you at Little Dragon around six-thirty?"

Audrey realized that what she wanted to do more than anything in the world was to take hold of Wickham Hill's scarf, pull him gently forward, and kiss him. Instead, she nodded and said, "Sure."

After he'd left, the girls sat silent for a while. Then Lea said quietly, "I feel like Mark Strauss just dropped by to check on my tennis elbow." C.C. said, "I'm thinking Aud's made some kind of deal with the Devil," and Lea added, "I'm thinking maybe we should sign up, too."

C.C. was grinning at Audrey. "Wednesday-night study date. Thursday-night dinner date. You getting married on the weekend?"

Audrey felt her cheeks pinkening. "It's not a dinner date, C.C. We're just going to Little Dragon."

But the truth was, she was already trying to figure out what she should wear.

Chapter 19
Little Dragon

Little Dragon was low-key—Audrey had been there a dozen times with her father or Oggy—but tonight she almost made herself sick trying to decide what to wear. She tried on what seemed like everything in her closet before she finally decided on a slouchy, proletarian look—cargo pants and a spaghetti-strap tank top with a cardigan.

Wickham Hill was sitting at a corner table when she walked into Little Dragon ten minutes late. He smiled, stood, and waved her over.

"Sorry I'm late," she said, peeling off her coat, mittens, and scarf.

"Just got here myself," he said, which was clearly not true. He had a drink in front of him that was already half gone.

"What is that?" she said, nodding at his glass.

"Chinese beer. Want to try it?"

She did, and gave him a look of surprise. "How'd you manage to order beer?"

Wickham gave her his easy grin. "Mr. Wong somehow has the impression that I'm twenty-one." He nudged the glass toward her. "Second sip is always better."

It was true, it did seem better. Sweet, even. She said, "I didn't think I liked beer."

"You learn something new every day."

"Really?" she said. "What did you learn new today?"

He leaned forward. "Couple of things. How good a girl can look in cargo pants is one."

Audrey blushed slightly. "And the other?"

"That my long-stemmed study partner is carrying a 4.3 GPA." He waited a second and said, "You're not denying it."

When, soon after enrollment, the three Tate girls had recognized themselves as Jemison misfits, they'd taken as their defense solidarity and achievement. "We'll fly under the radar," C.C. had said. "We'll be studying fools, and then, when we graduate, one of us is going to give the commencement speech." She'd turned to Lea and Audrey. "Deal?" she'd said, and both the other girls had solemnly nodded. So that's what they'd done through the first two months of the school year. They'd stuck together, lain low, and studied hard.

To Wickham, Audrey said, "It'll probably sound nerdy, or presumptuous, or *something*, but Lea and C.C. and I are hoping that one of us can wind up with the top GPA and . . ." Her voice trailed off.

"And be valedictorian," he said.

She nodded but couldn't look him in the eye, it sounded so far-fetched.

But he said, "I don't think it's nerdy. I think it's kind of spunky, actually." When she looked up, he smiled and said, "And you won't get any serious grade-point competition from me."

It was while they were eating that Audrey again began to think of the physics test. She fell silent. After a while,

Wickham, who'd been working hard with his chopsticks, said, "Small thoughts, big thoughts, or no thoughts at all?"

"Oh," Audrey said. "Sorry. I was thinking about the physics quiz."

Wickham kept chewing and gave her a quizzical look.

"It's just that my letting you . . . It made me feel . . . funny. Bad funny."

"Ah," Wickham said. "You're a believer. You believe if the rules get written, they ought to get followed." He chewed some more and smiled. "It's one of the things about you I find endearing."

Audrey said, "And you don't think the rules got written for a reason?"

Wickham swallowed, took a deep breath, and laid down his chopsticks. "Look, the other night I was talking to this taxi driver, a middle-aged guy named John Mokumbu or something like that—he was from Nigeria or Rwanda or someplace, a nice guy with this great cackling laugh—and we were just talking and I said, 'What's the worst thing that's ever happened to you?' and he got quiet and said, 'Something that happened to my son.' His son was a paperboy, and one morning a white kid threw a snowball at him from a passing car and hit this guy's kid in the eye. They did three operations, but he's still blind in that eye."

Wickham sipped from his glass, and Audrey said, "That's horrible."

He gave a somber nod. "It gets worse. The bills were astronomical, but the newspaper that employed the kid didn't pay a penny. Why? Because under the law, that twelve-year-old boy was categorized as 'a little merchant'—not an employee."

He stared at Audrey. "That boy had delivered papers for that company for three years—never late, never missed a day— and because of what you might call 'the rules,' he could be labeled an independent contractor and the newspaper company didn't have to pay a penny."

Audrey saw where this was going. "Look," she said, "there are good laws and there are bad laws. That law seems really unfair, but the no-cheating rule is pretty straightforward." She said now what she'd already formulated in her mind. "It's what protects those who do the work from being equaled or exceeded by those who don't."

Wickham picked up a single chopstick, and for a few seconds used it to draw furrows through his rice. "Here are the facts of the matter," he said, with his eyes lowered. "My dad's back in South Carolina, and my mom and I are here wondering whether we'll ever hear from him again." Wickham looked up. "No, I haven't lost my sight in one eye or anything, but, you know, metaphorically, we've all been hit by icy snowballs." He paused and let his gaze settle on Audrey. "You say the rule keeps those who do the work from getting hurt, but you tell me, who exactly does it hurt that you let me sneak by with a C minus on a physics quiz?"

Audrey studied Wickham's hands. His fingers were flat-tipped, and strangely intimate to her at that moment, as if she had been used to seeing them covered by gloves. "Nobody," she said, somewhat startled by the sound of her voice. Then, with more resolve: "Nobody at all."

He reached across the table and lifted her hand—the very thing, she realized, that she'd been willing him to do. "You have the slenderest fingers," he said, and his touch, combined with these words, seemed to awaken every part of Audrey's body. For just an instant, she thought her eyelids might actually have fluttered.

Mrs. Wong came to the table to ask how everything was. Wickham sat back and, releasing Audrey's hand, introduced Audrey and then added, "Audrey's shooting for valedictorianism."

Mrs. Wong nodded and smiled demurely.

Wickham smiled up at the woman and asked, "When did you know Mr. Wong was Mr. Right?"

Calmly Mrs. Wong said, "First time I see him."

"I'm not the first one to ask that question, am I?"

Mrs. Wong smiled and blinked slowly. "No," she replied, and discreetly left them the bill, which Wickham took care of merely by signing his name. (This was just one more of his mysteries, as far as Audrey was concerned, right along with his serious talks with African cabdrivers. Normally these things would have bothered Audrey, but she felt so overcome by Wickham's handsome face, body, and wry, easy manner that every time her instincts flared up and warned her that she didn't know him very well, she casually snuffed them out.)

Wickham had gotten a ride to the restaurant, so after he signed the check, they drove around in Audrey's Lincoln, which Wickham found amusing. ("My dorm room at Leighton Hall was smaller than this," he said.) They stopped by the Old Town Pharmacy to pick up a prescription his doctor had called in for him ("Imitrex," he told Audrey, "for migraines"), and then they drove along River Road, talking and listening to *The Mikado,* which for a month now had been stuck in Audrey's cassette player.

"So let me get this straight," Wickham said. "The girl is named Yum-Yum, and the guy is Nanki-Poo?"

"Right," Audrey said.

"And they live in Titipu?"

"Right," Audrey said, laughing.

"Well," Wickham drawled, "I just hope I don't have dreams about this."

Two hours streamed past. When Audrey finally pulled up in front of Wickham's house, a trim, two-story brick house in one of Jemison's old, upscale sections, she turned to look at him. Without any hesitation or awkwardness whatsoever, he leaned close and kissed her. His lips were soft and moist and smelled sweetly of sugar, and when he pulled away, she wished he hadn't. It was her first kiss, it was a perfect kiss, and she didn't want it to be over.

He got out of the car and came around to her window. "You know what this is, don't you?" he said.

"What?"

He gave her his easy grin. "The beginning."

And then Wickham Hill walked into the house.

Chapter 20
Audrey's Father

Audrey couldn't sleep that night. Every time she closed her eyes, thoughts of Wickham Hill came swimming into her mind and could only be stopped by opening her eyes. She got up, did some homework, wrote *This is the beginning* in her green notebook, stared out the window, went back to bed, and still couldn't sleep.

At 1:15, she heard her father come home, but instead of him tramping slowly upstairs, the way he usually did, Audrey heard the refrigerator door open and close, then the scraping of a chair, then silence. When Audrey put on her robe and went down, no lights were on, and it took her a moment or two to spot her father sitting motionless in the dark dining room.

"You okay, Dad?" Audrey said.

She could make out his dark profile shifting, his face turning toward her. "Oh, hi, Polliwog. Did I wake you? I was trying to be quiet."

"I was already awake," Audrey said.

"Studying?"

"Yeah," Audrey said. It seemed simpler than the truth.

"Worrying?" her father said.

This was a surprising question, not the kind of question her father ever asked. "No," she said, "not really."

"Because you shouldn't worry," her father said, in a voice so low it was almost as if he were speaking to himself. "You'll get plenty of chances for that later on."

A few seconds passed; then Audrey said, "Dad?"

"What, Polliwog?"

She wasn't sure what she wanted to say, but she didn't like this, standing here in the dark hearing her father ask strange questions and say gloomy things in a quiet voice. "Why can't we turn on the lights?" she said.

This brought her father to life. "What do you mean?" he said. "Has the electricity been turned off?"

This was weirder than anything preceding it. "No," Audrey said, "I meant, do we have to talk in the dark?"

"Oh," her father said, sitting back. "Sure. A little light would be fine."

But when Audrey flipped on the lights, her father visored his hand over his eyes, as if shielding himself from harsh sun. The skin under his eyes sagged in heavy, waxy folds. Beside him on the table was a can of Milwaukee's Best. He was wearing the same worn suit he'd been wearing the last time she saw him.

She said, "So you sold your good car. The one you said was for sunny days."

He nodded, and didn't even ask her how she knew.

"Now what will you do on sunny days?"

He'd turned away from her now. "Walk," he said.

Audrey thought he might explain why he'd sold the car, but he said nothing, and the silence had a heaviness to it.

"Is everything okay, Dad?"

"Everything's fine," he said quickly, and made a grimacing kind of smile. "Just a long day at the office." Another second or two passed, and then he slowly stood up. "Let's hit the hay and dream sweet dreams," he said.

Audrey did finally sleep, but she didn't dream at all that she could remember, and when she awoke early and glanced out the window, her father's everyday car was already gone—which would have depressed her more if she hadn't at that moment remembered that the night before, Wickham Hill had leaned across the broad front seat of the Lincoln and closed his eyes and kissed her.

Chapter 21
Knoll Talk

"He did?" Lea said in a voice soft with wonderment, and Audrey nodded.

"Nuptials on Sunday," C.C. said.

The girls were back on the knoll today, eating with their collars turned up. Lea and C.C. peppered Audrey with questions, which she answered discreetly, trying not to indicate how completely she was smitten. Finally C.C. summed it up: "Well. Your first kiss, and it came from wickedly handsome Wickham Hill." She beamed a smile at Audrey. "Not bad."

Lea frowned. "I'll tell you what bad is. Bad is getting your first kiss from Artie Hall on the squash court."

Audrey laughed and separated a cluster of currants in her hand. Artie Hall was a math genius who'd gone to the Tate School for a while. At the time of the squash-court kissing, Audrey had actually been envious. At least someone had a crush on Lea, even if he looked like a baffled giraffe.

"What does Wickham Hill drive?" C.C. asked.

Audrey shrugged. "He got a ride to the restaurant, and I drove him home."

"He got a ride?" C.C. asked. "Like with his mom?"

"I don't know who gave him a ride," Audrey said. "And I'm not sure I care."

"He seems like the sort of guy who would have a car," Lea mused. "Not the sort of guy who gets rides."

"What difference does it make?" Audrey said.

Lea didn't seem to notice the hint of peevishness in Audrey's voice. "Maybe he left his car behind when he and his mom left South Carolina," she said.

Audrey thought about this briefly. It didn't make sense to leave a car behind when you moved to a new state, but the truth was, she didn't care if Wickham rode to dates in a bus. She just wanted to look at him, and sit beside him in her car, and have him lean forward to kiss her. This morning, before school, he'd sent an e-mail saying, *Problem. Now I can't eat dinner without you. Pick you up at seven?* Audrey counted the separated currants in her palm—seven. *Seven,* she thought. *Seven, seven, seven.*

Lea was saying, "I saw that Clyde Mumsford guy in Mrs. Arboneaux's room a little while ago. He was at one of the potter's wheels, making a pot. Or trying to."

"Really?" C.C. said. "At lunch? Was anyone else in there?"

Lea shook her head. "Just Mrs. Arboneaux."

Audrey stared off into the distance and tried to imagine Clyde Mumsford throwing pots, but it wasn't easy. Pot-throwing didn't seem like the kind of thing vaguely creepy Clyde Mumsford types did.

"Check it out," C.C. said, nodding toward the quad, where Theo and his goons swept through like prison guards. Even from here, Audrey could see kids averting their eyes, looking up again only when Theo's group had safely passed.

"Miscreants," C.C. said. Lea added, "Muckers." Audrey thought, *To-do list,* and didn't say anything at all.

They put their lunch gear away and collected their books. From the knoll, they all went their separate ways, and when Audrey found herself cutting through the art wing, she slowed to peer into Mrs. Arboneaux's room.

Mrs. Arboneaux wasn't at her desk, but, toward the back of the room, Clyde Mumsford's tall body could be seen bent over the potter's wheel, both hands on a wet clay vase, which, as it twirled, grew taller and taller and thinner and thinner until, finally, it collapsed.

Clyde Mumsford's eyes closed, his head dropped, and the wheel began to coast to a stop. For perhaps three seconds he sat, head down, shoulders slumped, perfectly still. Then he suddenly and roughly scraped the clay together and slammed it to the floor. He stared at the flattened mass for a moment. Just as he began to lift his head, Audrey stepped back from the doorway.

Chapter 22
Another Point of View

Clyde had no control over the most important things in his life—the growth of the cancerous nodules within his mother's body, for example, or who Audrey Reed spent her time with—but here, working with the clay and the wheel in Mrs. Arboneaux's room, the results were completely his own doing.

Spending his lunch hours in Mrs. Arboneaux's room had been Clyde's idea, but his mother was the reason behind it. One day, just before school started, she'd been thumbing through a thick-papered catalog and had come upon a blue-and-pink vase with a slight hourglass shape. After staring at it for a full minute, she'd shown it to Clyde and said, "There is the perfect vase for the first lilacs of spring." Then, with a wry little smile, she'd added, "And it's only one hundred and seventy-nine dollars."

Clyde regarded the photo. It was nice, he guessed, but a hundred and seventy-nine dollars? "Kinda pricey," he said. His mother had nodded and continued browsing. A few days later, seeing one of Mrs. Arboneaux's students carrying a vase around, Clyde wondered if he couldn't make one himself, and had paid the art teacher a visit.

"So you want to throw pots?" Mrs. Arboneaux had said.

When Clyde had nodded, she'd said, "Any particular kind of pot?"

From his wallet he'd unfolded the page he'd torn from the catalog and had handed it to the teacher.

Mrs. Arboneaux had laughed, but it wasn't a skeptical laugh. It was merely a laugh of pleasant astonishment. "Well," she'd said, "at least there are no spouts or handles." She kept smiling as she looked directly at Clyde. "Who's this for?"

Clyde looked down.

"Is this for your mother?"

He kept his eyes lowered.

"Okay," Mrs. Arboneaux said. "When do you need it?"

"Before the lilacs," Clyde had said, in such a low voice he had to repeat it.

"Ah," Mrs. Arboneaux said. "Well, we might have time, then."

Two months had passed and Clyde was making solid progress—he'd learned how to knead his clay, center it, and throw it into a basic rough cylinder—but he was having a hard time re-creating the curves of the vase ("bellying out," Mrs. Arboneaux called it). He was supposed to try to let his inner and outer hands pinch the clay lightly, but not too lightly, and the way to do that, Mrs. Arboneaux said, was "to relax and practice, practice, practice."

And so today Clyde had been sitting at the potter's wheel in Mrs. Arboneaux's room, wet clay running smoothly through his hands while his right foot steadily pumped the wheel. One hand was slipped into the interior of the pot; two fingers of the other hand ran along the outside base of the clay. To pull up the walls of the pot, he began gradually to exert a pinching pressure between his inside and outside hands.

When he'd sat down at the wheel today, he'd noticed one of Audrey Reed's friends—the pale, pretty one with the arctic blue eyes—glance in at him, and he'd immediately wondered what she called him in her mind. "Mummy"? "Freak"? "The Croakster"? Because whatever term she used, Audrey Reed would use. He thought of the word written on the front of Audrey's green notebook: *Hopeless. Hopeless hopeless hopeless.* When he'd had to quit Pop Warner because of his mother's cancer, he'd told his father he wanted to keep playing because he wanted to play high school football, and his father had said, "Sometimes you have to put your hopes in a safe place and come back to them another day"—which had made no sense at all to Clyde, because how could you play football later if you didn't learn how to play football now? It was more or less same with Audrey Reed. She was rich now and she'd be rich later, so what was the point of stashing hopes in a safe place?

He thought of the way Audrey Reed's face had lit up the day before when she'd seen the new boy in the hallway.

The easy way the new boy talked to her.

Clyde pinched the clay a little tighter, pumped the wheel a little faster.

The way, as Clyde had passed, she hadn't even seen him.

His hands pinched tighter, the clay thinned in his hands and rose and then, suddenly, it collapsed. He dropped his head, took a deep breath, and let the wheel coast to a stop. He sat slumped over with his eyes closed for a few seconds, then—he didn't know why—he pushed the clay together and slammed it to the floor, where it flattened and sat.

The abject mass, Clyde thought, and as he raised his eyes from it, he sensed movement at the classroom door, though when he looked, there was no one there.

Chapter 23
Transported

It was 6:57 that night, and Wickham was due at seven.

Audrey stood before the full-length mirror in her bathroom and wondered where they were going to eat and whether she was too dressed-up. She'd impulsively bought an outfit that afternoon: new shoes, new hose, new earrings, and a thin black spaghetti-strap knit dress. There was something about the cut that made her seem gracefully slender instead of depressingly flat-chested.

6:58.

Audrey turned sideways and studied her reflection. She'd read in a fashion self-help book that thin girls, by dispensing with bras, could get away with "subtle nipple exposure." She turned to the side to see if she was, indeed, getting away with it. She'd bought a matching beaded cardigan to go with the dress—"the modesty cardigan," as she thought of it. She put it on, thinking that Oggy would never have approved of this dress.

6:59, and a set of headlights swept into the driveway.

Audrey stared again at the mirror, and for the first time she could remember, she felt fine about what she saw. Besides, Oggy was in Germany. She took off the cardigan.

When the doorbell rang, Audrey grabbed the cardigan, headed downstairs, and opened the door. Wickham Hill had his back to her; he was staring out at the grounds. As he turned around, his eyes slowly ran down to her shoes, and up again.

"My God," he softly drawled. "I knew you were great-looking, but I didn't know you were ravishing."

A happy laugh slipped from Audrey. "You're not looking too bad yourself," she said, and felt herself immediately begin to color, though Wickham Hill did not.

"Let me grab my bag," she added.

Wickham Hill stepped into the entry and was peering into the library when Audrey reappeared wearing her winter coat. "Great library," he said, then glanced beyond her. "Should we say something to your dad?"

"Not here. He's working late." She began pushing buttons on the alarm keypad; then, after punching the last number, she said, "Okay. We've got eight seconds to vaminose."

Outside, idling under the portico, was a green-and-white taxi.

Wickham held the back door open and slid in after her.

"This is nice," Audrey said as the taxi pulled slowly away, "but you . . ."

"My mother thinks I drive too fast," Wickham said, "so she set up an account for me with the cab company." He didn't look at her when he said this, but turned now and smiled. "I thought I'd hate it, but it's actually not so bad. At least it's all warmed up for you when you get in."

Wickham Hill settled back into the seat, and Audrey gazed out the window and was glad when he reached forward to take her hand. "Well, that's one mystery solved," she said, thinking that now she could tell Lea and C.C. that Wickham wasn't the sort of guy who got rides, but the sort who paid for them.

"Which mystery's that?"

"How you found yourself talking to a Nigerian taxi driver about his little boy."

Wickham leaned forward and whispered, "Didn't know that was a mystery," and gave her a little kiss, received tinglingly at the earlobe. "Any more mysteries you want solved?"

Actually, there were quite a few, but she wasn't going to ask, so she laughed and said, "Just one. Where're we going?"

The restaurant was called Le Bistro. It was a converted cottage with small rooms, soft lights, and wooden floors. It smelled like rosemary. Audrey and Wickham were shown to a secluded table next to a small fireplace. "My mother suggested I reserve this table," Wickham said. "I guess she and my father always asked for it."

Audrey's gaze moved from the fire to Wickham, whose face in the firelight had the same radiant glow she'd seen the first time she'd laid eyes on him as he walked into Mrs. Leacock's classroom.

"*Très romantique,*" she said, and Wickham himself seemed pleased. His gaze slid away, though, when she said, "Did your parents come here before or after they were married?"

"Before, mostly," he said as the waiter arrived with menus.

Audrey had slipped on the modesty cardigan before entering the restaurant, but it was warm next to the fire, so she slipped it off.

In a mock-solemn voice, Wickham Hill said, "I don't know what large sums were paid for that dress, but I just want you to know it was money well spent."

98

Audrey smiled. The fire shifted and popped. "I was window-shopping at Veni, Vidi, Emi," she said. "Or at least I thought I was until I saw this dress."

"Veni, Vidi, Emi?"

Audrey smiled. "I came, I saw, I purchased."

Wickham nodded and let his eyes move over her. "You know what's funny? When I imagined coming here with you, I pictured you wearing that exact color."

"Which either makes you telepathic or me predictable."

He looked up from buttering a roll. "You're not at all predictable."

"I'm not?"

He shook his head no. "For example, I didn't think you'd have dinner with me, and here you are."

This was interesting to Audrey, and completely unbelievable. "Why didn't you think I'd have dinner with you?"

"I don't know. When I first saw you, you just seemed so . . . beautiful and contained." His face, tight with concentration, relaxed. "Now you just seem beautiful."

Audrey lowered her eyes. "I'm not, though."

"Argue all you want," Wickham said, "but my mind's made up."

They talked easily then, their conversation straying this way and that as men in black suits appeared with food and disappeared with empty dishes. She hardly tasted what she ate—it was all she could do not to just put down her knife and fork and sit listening to Wickham Hill, and looking at him.

After dinner, Audrey had bread pudding ("a guilty pleasure," she called it, and he said he hoped there were others).

Wickham had a glass of vintage port (after discreetly showing a doctored ID indicating his age as twenty-one) before he settled the bill by signing on his father's account.

On the way home, in the cozy privacy of another taxi, Wickham Hill slid his arm around Audrey, who instinctively leaned into his hold. A few seconds passed and then Audrey said, "If ever in my life I'm a little sad, I'm going to think back to that table by the fire."

His arm tightened slightly, and his hand, moving to the edge of her breast, thrilled her nerves.

"Me too," he said in a low voice, almost a whisper. As he turned and leaned close to her, Audrey smelled the sugary sweetness and felt her lips tingling even before his touched hers. When his hand lightly slid her dress strap down her shoulder and gently peeled the dress away from one breast, she felt a surge of almost greedy desire move through her—a desire that later would make her feel ashamed but now, as it flooded through her, seemed irresistible, and wonderful.

Chapter 24
Two Brief, Unsettling Conversations

When Audrey returned home, she was surprised to see a light coming from her father's study, and peered in. Her father had his back to her and was standing over one of his cherrywood file cabinets, dropping handfuls of paper into a shopping bag at his feet. He was still wearing his work clothes—gray slacks, a white shirt, burgundy suspenders—but his gray sports coat hung from one of a row of cherrywood pegs on the wall.

"Hi," Audrey said.

Her father wheeled around quickly, and the startled look that crossed his face was of somebody who'd just been caught at something. But then, seeing her, his face visibly relaxed. "Oh, hi, Polliwog. You gave me a start."

He gave her dress a quick look, and she was glad she'd slipped the modesty sweater back on. Her father had set a gooseneck lamp on top of the cabinet and adjusted it to crane down and shine on the open files, but its harsh light shone on him, too. He looked old to her, old and worried. "What're you doing?" she said.

"Nothing much. You weren't home, so I decided to clean out some old files."

Audrey nodded as if this made perfect sense, though it didn't. She glanced down at the shopping bags stuffed with papers. The nearest one read VENI, VIDI, EMI.

"So how was dinner with the new boy?" he asked.

"Good," Audrey said, trying to sound more or less business-like, which was the way her father liked her to talk about her personal life. "If I'd known you were still up, I'd have brought him in to meet you. You'd like him. He's pretty impressive."

"Next time," her father said, and regarded her. "Presuming there will be a next time."

Audrey made a point of not lowering her eyes. She hoped she wasn't blushing. "I don't know," she said. "It seems possible."

"Ah," her father said in a tone Audrey recognized as carefully neutral.

They were both quiet then, and it seemed to Audrey that her father was ready to resume his file-cleaning work. She yawned, said, "'Night, Dad," and was nearly out the door when her father said, "Audrey?"

It was the voice he used when there was something he felt he needed to talk to her about, but didn't want to. It took him a moment to speak, and when he did, he was almost apologetic. "Look, when I got these shopping bags out of the pantry, I couldn't help seeing the receipts."

Audrey was relieved he wasn't talking about her responsibility to herself and her future, all that stuff—but still, his bringing up money was weird enough. He'd never brought up money before. She didn't know what to say, so she said, "Did I spend too much?"

"No, no, it's not that," her father said quickly. "It's nothing you did." His gaze floated away from her. "It's just that, right now, temporarily, for just a little while . . ." He didn't finish the sentence.

"I can cut down," Audrey said quickly. "I don't need new

stuff." She shrugged and smiled. "New stuff is just, you know, new stuff."

Her father was nodding, but he still kept his eyes averted from hers.

"I can take the new dress and stuff back," Audrey offered.

Her father shook his head vaguely. "You don't have to do that," he said, which Audrey understood was different than telling her not to.

"It's no problem," Audrey said, but the truth was, she had no idea whether it was a problem or not. She'd never returned an article of clothing in her life. Oggy always did that if something didn't fit or turned out to be of poor quality. Returning something because you couldn't afford it seemed a different matter altogether.

Half a mile away, Wickham Hill came home to find his mother sitting at the kitchen table with a magazine and a cup of tea—in theory a comforting scene, but he saw at once that the tea had gone cold and that she wasn't reading the magazine. Crumpled tissues lay nearby.

"What?" Wickham said. His mother glanced up at him, then tugged her earlobe and looked away. Whenever his mother felt fragile, she would begin the earlobe-tugging. Wickham sat down at the table and, more softly now, said, "What?"

His mother was not a plain woman, and when she was happy, she seemed beautiful to Wickham, but tonight she'd been crying, and her washed-out face and runny nose and red eyes gave her a hapless aspect. She dabbed at her nose, took a deep breath, and said, "James called."

Dr. Yates. His actual but unofficial father.

Wickham waited.

His mother opened her mouth, breathed in, breathed out. "He said he'd been getting our bills." Another deep breath. "He said he'd keep paying them, up to a thousand dollars a month for the next three months. I told him I didn't care about the money, I just wanted to see him, but it was as if he didn't hear me. He just said that after three months, the amount he'd pay would go down by one hundred dollars a month." Another pause and earlobe tug. "He called it a one-year weaning period."

Wickham stared at the tablecloth. It was red-and-white gingham, the kind you saw in reassuring depictions of cheerful American kitchens. "What about the house?" he said. "Can we stay in the house?"

"He said that after nine months, we'd receive a ninety-day notice to vacate." Pause, earlobe tug. "He was using his business voice. I've heard him use it with other people lots of times. But he'd never used it with me."

Wickham worked his jaw and with low vehemence said, "And people thought *I* was the bastard."

Quietly his mother said, "No. This isn't him. This is someone else. This is what his horrible wife and that horrible town have turned him into."

These words had a softening effect on Wickham, toward his mother if not his father. He never touched his mother, never took her hand or kissed her, and though he wouldn't now, he wanted to. He wanted to lean forward and kiss her on the cheek before he spoke. Instead, he just used his gentlest voice to say, "No, this is him, Mom, and nobody made him him but him."

Upstairs, Wickham took down his father's boyhood dictionary and skimmed through the "W" section until he found the word he wanted:

> **wean** . . . *v.t.* **1** : To accustom (as a child or other young animal) to loss of mother's milk. **2** : Hence, to detach the affections of; to rec-oncile to a severance—as "to wean one from a life of ease."

Wickham opened the nearest window and, with a quick sidearm toss, sent the dictionary sailing out into the darkness. He heard a dull *thump-shush* as it hit the ground and skidded onto the driveway.

Weaning.

It was just like the bastard to find the one word that fit the circumstance more insultingly than any other in the English language.

Chapter 25
A Single Droplet

"You kissed in the backseat of a taxi?"

Audrey was caught between feeling excited and embarrassed. "A little," she said.

It was Saturday morning, and Audrey, C.C., and Lea were sitting in a window booth at Bing's. Outside, the sky was Indian-summer blue, and for November it was strangely warm—people passed in short sleeves, and newspaper headlines talked of global warming.

Lea, in her quiet voice, said, "What does 'a little' mean?"

Audrey just smiled and stirred Sweet'n Low into her tea.

C.C. leaned forward and said, "Does 'a little' mean a little too much?"

A light, surprised laugh escaped Audrey. "I don't think so, no."

The girls all took bites of their bagels.

"Okay," C.C. said carefully. "How did it make you feel?"

Audrey smiled and blinked slowly. She'd awoken this morning thinking of a legend they'd learned at the Tate School, the one in which the young, brave, and handsome Tristan is sent to Ireland to escort the beautiful Iseult to Britain so that she can join her intended husband, the vengeful and ignoble King Mark, who is also Tristan's uncle. Tristan is sent with a magic potion for Iseult to drink so that she might fall eternally in love with the elderly uncle, but on the way Tristan and Iseult mistakenly drink the potion and fall eternally in love with each other instead.

Audrey said, "I felt as if for the first time in my life I could imagine what Tristan and Iseult felt after they'd drunk the love potion." This seemed to go too far, so she added, "Except I didn't feel like I'd drunk the whole potion or anything. It was more like a single droplet."

Lea and C.C. had stopped chewing while she talked. Now, after a long moment, they resumed.

Audrey said, "Almost the weirdest thing happened after I came home." She was about to describe the money talk with her father when she noticed someone entering the restaurant, and stopped short.

"Uh-oh," she said in a small voice.

It was Theo Driggs with about five of his enormous, slouching friends. They sauntered down the next aisle.

Audrey wanted to avert her eyes, but couldn't—a mistake, it turned out. When Theo noticed her, he silently, exaggeratedly mouthed two words, and Audrey could read his plump lips loud and clear.

Do list.

Audrey looked away. *Mucker,* she thought. *Mucker, mucker, mucker.* She glanced at C.C. and Lea. "Vacate, vacate, vacate," she said, and they all got up.

Outside, in the warm sunshine, C.C. suggested tennis.

"In November?" Audrey said.

C.C. spread her arms and gestured at the blue sky. "Audrey, honey, everything I see says June."

So they agreed on tennis at C.C.'s, but not until after lunch, because Audrey said she needed to run an errand for her father.

"What kind of errand?" C.C. said.

"The boring kind," Audrey said, to deflect any interest in their tagging along. "See you guys after lunch."

Chapter 26
The Return of the Spaghetti-Strap Dress

"Reason for return?"

Audrey was returning the spaghetti-strap dress, along with the shoes and sweater. "The fit wasn't—" Audrey began, but stopped. She didn't want to lie; she didn't know what to say; she'd never done this before.

The clerk, a thin, fortyish woman with a clamped-tight face, lowered her chin and peered over her reading glasses. "You didn't try them on before you bought them?" It was more an accusation than a question.

"I did, but—" She glanced away, searching the aisles and hoping nobody she knew was in the store.

"Was there something wrong with the garments?"

Audrey turned. "No. It's just that . . . my father didn't like them."

The clerk brought the dress close to her face and sniffed it. "I think it's been worn," she said, and again peered down at Audrey. "Has it been worn?"

Audrey lowered her eyes and nodded. Outside, it was the most beautiful, sunny November day ever, and here she was, standing inside a shop, doing this. She wanted to say, *It's okay, I'll just go ahead and keep it,* but her father had looked so worried that she said nothing and waited.

The thin clerk, reading from the receipt, typed some words into the computer and stared silently at the screen. It was too excruciating. Audrey turned and found herself looking at a long, slinky beaded dress that C.C., she knew, would have called fabulous. Audrey stepped close to feel the material, then turned over the price tag: $394.

From behind her, in a weary voice, the thin clerk said, "Okay, you're a good customer. I'm going to go ahead and credit your account."

"Thank you," Audrey said. She wondered how she could feel so grateful to so cold a woman, but she did. She quickly signed the return slip.

It was barely noon, which meant Audrey had a full hour before heading over to C.C.'s for tennis. She walked down the block, bought a smoothie, and was sitting at a sunny table when her cell phone chimed. The caller's number appeared with his name, which all by itself made her feel better.

"Wickham," she said.

"Audrey," he said. "I have an idea."

"You do?"

"Mmm. Let's do something we've never done before."

"Okay."

A low laugh came from his end of the line. "Aren't you going to ask what it is we're going to do that we've never done before?"

"Okay. What're we going to do that we've never done before?"

Wickham Hill's tone turned sportive. "Maybe I should know what it is you wouldn't do that you've never done before."

An easy laugh slipped from Audrey, but she also felt a warning flare of danger. "There are one or two things," she said, knowing there were many. "Skydiving is one I'm willing to talk about. Did you want to go skydiving?"

"No. Tea-dancing."

At first she heard this as "T-dancing" and wondered if it was some sexual activity she'd never heard about. She tried to sound casual. "What's T-dancing?"

"According to the paper, it's what they did at teatime during World War One, only now they do it at night."

"Oh," she said, laughing and relieved. "*Tea* as in *teapot*. When?"

"Tonight."

"Okay. What should I wear?"

Wickham Hill said it sounded semiformal. "Something along the lines of last night," he suggested, "only maybe a little more so."

An image of the long beaded dress in Veni, Vidi, Emi popped into Audrey's mind. "Okay," she said. Then: "Am I saying *okay* too much?"

He laughed. "No." He made his low voice even lower. "I like hearing you say *okay*."

After hanging up, Audrey sat at her table, staring into the distance, trying not to think of the $394 dress. *Something along the lines of last night, only more so.* But she didn't have anything like last night, only more so. At home, the only formal things she had were a suit dress, which was dowdy, and a black velvet skirt, which looked like Sunday school.

Her car was parked in front of Veni, Vidi, Emi. As she walked toward it, she decided to base her decision on luck: if the same horrible salesclerk was at the counter, she wouldn't buy the dress; but if the clerk was gone, she would.

At Veni, Vidi, Emi, Audrey stopped as if to look at some open-toe shoes in the window display, but let her eyes rise to the central desk, where the thin, awful salesclerk stood staring silently back at her.

Audrey turned at once and walked to her car, trying not to feel what she truly felt, which was disappointment.

Chapter 27
Sifting

In the living room of his apartment, Clyde stood at an ironing board, nosing the hot point of the iron around the buttons of his white dress shirt, which he never wore anywhere except to work.

It was Saturday afternoon, and he was working that night at the Jemison Country Club. It was where he worked every Saturday night, busing tables, setting silverware, and serving what he thought of as "pre-food"—baskets with three kinds of bread and ice water with lemon wedges. When he'd interviewed for the job, he'd looked at his hands and said, "I can do anything except talk to people," but he'd said it in such a low mumble that the interviewer, a smiling older woman, had to ask him to repeat himself.

Today Clyde's mother was watching a football game, Michigan-Wisconsin, though she had no affiliation with either school. Watching sports, like watching cooking shows, was just another of the weird by-products of her condition, and though she watched the game impassively, her eyes seemed even more than usually sunken.

Clyde's father sat down at the desk, turned on the computer, and pulled a file of job applications from his briefcase. A moment later, he leaned back from the computer with a startled look on his face.

"What's this?" he said, turning to Clyde. "You been using the company's background-check program?"

Clyde wished there were some way he could say no, but he couldn't think of one. "I was just looking up a couple of addresses," he said.

His father was staring at the screen. "That's what the phone book is for. And Google. I see three names at least. Wickham Hill. Theo Driggs. Audrey Reed." He turned. "Who are they?"

"People from school."

His father took this in. "And why did you need their addresses?"

Clyde shrugged. "Just wondered where they lived, is all."

"But you found a lot more than addresses, didn't you?"

Clyde didn't answer. His father took a deep breath. "Look, Clyde, these are the personal lives of real people. People like you and me and your mother. Who shouldn't have to think about strangers peeping through the keyhole."

His father was staring at Clyde, and from the side, Clyde could feel his mother's eyes on him, too. He felt embarrassed, then defensive. He pointed to his father's file of job applications. "What about what you do with all those?"

In a restrained voice, his father said, "Those are people who have, *in writing,* given the company the right to look into their backgrounds. I doubt that"—he turned to the computer screen—"Wickham Hill, Audrey Reed, and Theo Driggs gave you written permission to go sifting through their private lives."

"I didn't go sifting," Clyde said. Then, more softly: "I didn't understand it was such a big deal."

"Okay, then," his father said.

And so, on that warm Saturday afternoon in November, Clyde's father nodded and resumed his work, his mother stared blankly at a televised football game, and Clyde, feeling even smaller than normal, went back to his ironing.

Chapter 28
Audrey, Courtside

Thwock. Thwock. Thwock.

Eyes closed, Audrey lay on the chaise on the sideline of C.C.'s tennis court, listening to the slow, rhythmic sounds of one of C.C. and Lea's long baseline rallies. Audrey was feeling good. She'd told C.C. about the tea dance, and about how she didn't really have anything to wear and didn't want to waste the afternoon buying something new, and C.C., remembering that her mother and Audrey were the same size, had gone to her mother's closet and found five formal dresses, which she'd laid out on her bed. Audrey had loved them all but chose the filmy, high-necked red one, which fit perfectly. So now she had nothing to do but sit in the strange, warm November sun, letting the pleasant afternoon sun warm her long legs and bare arms.

The thwocking sounds stopped, and C.C. muttered, "Oh, that was clever."

Audrey smiled without opening her eyes.

"Deuce," Lea called, barely audible. Then, following the serve, the sounds began again: *Thwock. Thwock. Thwock.*

C.C. and Lea played the same baseline game, doggedly retrieving side to side and, with looping strokes, sending topspin forehands and two-handed backhands to alternating sides of the opposite backcourt. Audrey, taller and more aggressive, preferred a serve-and-volley game. She made more spectacular shots, but, in the end, the baseline retrievers usually won, especially on clay. Which was fine by Audrey. It meant more time lounging in the sun and thinking about Wickham Hill.

She peeled down the straps of her top to let the sun touch a bit more of her skin.

"No bare ta-tas allowed courtside here, honey," C.C. called between thwocks, and Audrey smiled and turned her top down another half inch.

C.C. said, "I guarantee you"—*thwock*—"my creepy little brother's upstairs with his binoculars on you right now."

Audrey didn't care. A breeze moving through the fallen leaves made a soft shushing sound, and Audrey thought her drowsy hothouse thoughts of Wickham Hill even while her friends' genteel world went on without her, *thwock thwock thwock.*

At the court change, C.C. and Lea sat down nearby, toweling sweat and sipping lemonade. Audrey said, "Who's winning?"

"Lea," C.C. said, and added, "We always think of Lea as gentle and sweet, but in fact she be sneaky and cruel."

Audrey, who'd closed her eyes again, heard Lea's soft laugh.

C.C. said, "What did I tell you? The cretin's up there, watching us." Then, yelling: "We see you, you little deviant!" Slumping down in her chair and tilting her face to the sun, she said, "You know, if this is global warming, I'm not sure I'm against it."

"Where's your mom?" Lea asked.

"The gym. She wanted me to go and take a yoga class with her. I declined and respectfully suggested she take Brian instead. She said she didn't think so. She probably knew he'd pass gas and play dumb."

Audrey laughed without opening her eyes. The truth was, Audrey idolized Mrs. Mudd. She was an attorney, but she never really seemed like one. When they were all twelve or thirteen and began having sleepovers at C.C.'s house, Mrs. Mudd would help them fall asleep by dimming the lights and having them all stretch out on their sleeping bags. She would teach them a few yoga poses: the sphinx pose; the cobra pose; the cat, rabbit, and warrior poses. Then she would tell them to relax in the corpse pose, which made them giggle. After they stopped giggling, Audrey really imagined herself as a corpse—as her mother, lying in the sunken garden, dead but not dead, awake but not conscious. Then Mrs. Mudd would go from girl to girl, lifting up their legs, pulling them gently, and setting them down again, as if their hips needed a slight adjustment. She'd do the same with their arms. Then she would briefly rub Audrey's neck and shoulders, and before drawing away, she would touch the center of Audrey's forehead with the tip of her finger, as if she were turning off some kind of light.

"This morning, I went into my mother's room," C.C. said, "and she was on her yoga mat, doing the most bizarre move. She was on all fours, and all of a sudden she lunged forward, popped her eyes out, and stuck her tongue way, way out. She actually made an animal sound. I'm not supposed to talk to her when she's doing yoga, but I said, 'Would that be the madman-in-the-attic pose?' 'Lion pose,' she said calmly, and did it again."

As Lea and C.C. walked back onto the court, Audrey listened to the shushy scuffle of their shoes on the sandy surface of the clay. Somewhere nearby, a squirrel chattered. C.C. said, "Don't fall asleep, Aud, you're playing the winner." Audrey, without opening her eyes, raised a hand in acknowledgment. Beneath her eyelids, orangy arcs rose and receded in a pleasant pattern, and soon she was again listening to the lazy and reassuring sounds of baseline rallies and thinking of Wickham Hill, with whom she'd soon be dancing.

In the late afternoon, it began to cool sharply. C.C. zipped on a sweatshirt and said, "November returns." They hurried into the house, arms folded against the cold, and Audrey went upstairs to get C.C.'s mother's red dress. Brian's door was open, so she glanced in. He had his back to her, leaning close to his computer in intent concentration. The plump bearded dragon was draped over the back of his neck, asleep.

Brian was searching for something, apparently, because he was scanning down a list of what looked like Web sites. He was so lost in concentration that she was able to creep forward, lean to within an inch of his ear, and say, "Gotcha."

Brian jerked up so suddenly that the lizard half slid and half fell to the ground. "C.C., you . . . !" he sputtered, but then, seeing Audrey, he turned calm.

He bent to pick up the bearded dragon, and Audrey helped check the lizard's body for signs of damage. By the time she was sure she hadn't killed the thing, Brian's screen saver was peacefully showing slides of outer space.

"I shouldn't've sneaked up on you. I just thought you were, you know, looking for naked ladies or something."

"Maybe I wasn't," he said. "And maybe I was." He ran his index finger over the little spikes on the dragon's head. "Speaking of ladies," he added, nodding toward the binoculars that were sitting on his windowsill. "Seeing you down by the tennis courts—sunning the rarely seen territories—that was what I would call extremely stellar."

Audrey grimaced and shook her head. "I've got to go now," she said, and Brian, nodding his head, staring at Audrey, and stroking the lizard in his lap, said, "You don't, but you will."

Chapter 29
Clyde's Ride

Clyde stood waiting for his ride in front of the apartment building. It was early Saturday evening. The sun had already set, and the sky was pink through the bare tree limbs by the duck pond. It had been a beautiful, warm day—weathercasters called it the warmest November 8 on record—but now, without cloud cover, the temperature was down to the mid-forties, and dropping.

Clyde shivered a little in his work clothes—black slacks, black Nikes, black socks, and a white button-down shirt, neatly pressed. He wasn't wearing a jacket—the country club provided the black jacket and tie he wore while busing tables—and he'd told his mother it was too warm for a parka, a mistake, as it turned out. He had to stamp his feet and blow on his hands to stay warm.

As a dirty yellow Geo approached, Clyde raised his hand to signal the round-faced girl behind the wheel. She pulled over, and Clyde opened the door to high-volume ska music. The girl's name was Manda Will, and when she grinned up at Clyde he could see the wide space between her two front teeth.

"Hey," Clyde said, but his voice was swallowed by the music.

Manda lived with four other girls in a two-bedroom apartment not far from Clyde's. She was taking a few units at

LeMoyne and had two or three part-time jobs, including the one at the country club. When she'd learned how close to her Clyde lived, and that he didn't have a car, she'd offered to give him rides, a dollar each direction. "Cheap," she'd said, grinning her gap-toothed grin.

The car was warm and the music was okay, once Manda turned it down a little. Clyde was comfortable with Manda, mostly because she never seemed to mind his quietness. She was wearing a white top with a black skirt, shoes, and stockings. It took about ten minutes to reach the country club, during which time they listened to the Jamaican singers and stared out at brick buildings. Everything looked cold and dead at dusk, the traffic lights glowing in the rising clouds of exhaust. When Manda nosed her car into a parking spot near the back entrance, she reached inside the waistband of her skirt and pulled out a cigarette case. "Stay put, okay?" she said when Clyde started to open the door.

"Okay," Clyde said reluctantly. He knew she hated to smoke alone in the car. He watched her flip open the case and extract a hand-rolled joint. She depressed the dashboard lighter.

"Wanna tootle the flute?" she said. Clyde shook his head no.

A few seconds passed while Manda held the smoke in her lungs. Then she exhaled and said, "How do you do it, Clyde? Without a little reeferization?"

He shrugged. "It's not that bad."

She gave him a look. "That's where you're wrong, Clyde. It *is* that bad, and then some."

But it wasn't for Clyde. Bad was thinking about his mother. Bad was having to explain looking up Wickham Hill, Theo

Driggs, and Audrey Reed on Bor-Lan's LexisNexis program. Bad was thinking about Wickham calling Audrey his long-stemmed study partner. Good was putting on the black jacket that the manager handed out, delivering the pre-food to the diners, pouring water from crystal pitchers. Dying wasn't on people's minds here. Untouchable girls weren't on people's minds. All the workers wanted was to do their jobs, and afterward count their tips.

"Tonight you're doing my tables just like always, okay?" Manda said.

Clyde nodded. Manda waited tables. Clyde bused them.

Manda squinched one eye as she again drew smoke into her lungs. When, after a few seconds, she exhaled, she said, "You don't talk a lot, do you, Clyde?"

Clyde gave so slight a shrug it might, to Manda, have seemed like a twitch.

She said, "I was telling my roommates about you, how you're the strong, silent type. I think one of them wants to meet you. Should I work on that?"

"No," Clyde said flatly, and to his surprise, a quick loud laugh flew through Manda's lips.

"You *do* like girls, though, right?" she said.

"Depends on the girl," Clyde said—a response that Manda also found hilarious. Clyde made a mental note that, once they started serving, he'd better help make sure Manda was taking the right dinners to the right tables.

Chapter 30
Enter Audrey and Wickham

The cab turned onto a familiar tree-lined road that led to the Jemison Country Club, and a man leaned from a window of the gateside kiosk.

Wickham slid a card to the cabdriver, who presented it to the man at the gate, who gave it a glance and waved them through.

"I guess you've been here before?" Wickham said, and Audrey murmured yes. "I like it here," she said. "My father's a member."

The cab pulled up in front of a new building that, because of its shake shingle siding, pale yellow window light, and heavy, chiseled beams, made Audrey think of a tinted postcard of an old Adirondack lodge. Her father hadn't had time to take her here for ages, and she wondered if he knew they'd fixed things up so much. She'd have to tell him.

Faint strains of a swing band came from within, and, as her father had always done, Wickham opened the car door, held out his hand, and helped her step out.

Inside, perfectly pruned dwarf citrus trees, fragrant with white blossoms, filled white-enameled tin planters. Black-jacketed waiters and busboys whisked in and out of the dining room, which was much bigger than the old one. When they were seated, Audrey said, "You know what this reminds me of? Old Cary Grant movies. Do you like Cary Grant?"

Wickham said he didn't really know. He'd heard of him, but he'd never actually watched one of his movies. "I know his real name, though."

"His real name's not Cary Grant?"

"No sirree."

"Then what is it?" Audrey said.

In a playful voice, Wickham replied, "It'll cost you to find out."

"Oh yeah? How much?"

"Plenty," he said, laughing.

Chapter 31
Episode at Table 9

Clyde had used a crumber to clean a white tablecloth and was setting out the china service for coffee when he noticed someone at table 9 who looked a little like Audrey Reed, only older.

Then he saw that the woman didn't just look like Audrey Reed.

She *was* Audrey Reed.

And she was with that new guy from Georgia or wherever, who was all flashed out in a suit and tie. Audrey wore a high-necked red dress that made her look older, and beautiful, and . . . rich. She'd been laughing, but when she stopped and glanced his way, Clyde feared he might need to nod or smile or even speak. But he was wrong. Audrey Reed looked right through him.

Table 9 lay between him and the kitchen. He tucked the crumber into his apron, poured the coffee—one caffeinated, one decaf, though, to be truthful, he wasn't sure now which was which—and then arranged his face into the mask of a person who sees no one he knows. But he had to come back to their table. He had to bring water and bread.

In the kitchen, he looked at his distorted reflection on the rounded side of the steel pitcher. *Hi, I'm Patrick*, he thought.

Or, as the case may be, Patricia. He made himself pick up the pitcher and a basket of bread. Then he walked stiffly back to table 9.

". . . is what he said to me, anyhow," Audrey was saying. She and Wickham fell silent as Clyde poured. He felt Audrey looking at his face. Then she said, "Clyde, right? From Patrice's class?"

Clyde was nodding stiffly. He actually said, "Yup," but in a voice so low that, thankfully, it couldn't be heard. Then, as a finishing touch, he said, in a croaky blurt, "I work here."

Clyde felt sweat glazing his neck, and there followed an awkward silence that made him want to disappear. The new boy stared at him for a moment; then, by smiling and leaning back in his chair, he conveyed a sense of gracious superiority. But Audrey looked slightly pained. "Have you two met at school?" the new boy said.

Clyde nodded.

Audrey fingered her glass and seemed to find her footing. "Wickham," she said, "this is Clyde. Clyde, this is Wickham Hill." Clyde noticed that she knew Wickham's last name, but not his. No one spoke, so Audrey said, "Clyde's in World Cultures with me."

Wickham gave Clyde a reserved smile, and another awkward silence developed.

Suddenly Audrey, with false brightness, said, "Clyde's a smart guy. Maybe he knows Cary Grant's real name."

Clyde's mother loved Cary Grant movies because they always came with a happy ending, and she'd recently read a Cary Grant biography. Clyde hadn't listened very carefully when she read various parts to him. He remembered his real name was a funny one, but he couldn't remember what it was. He shook his head no.

"Yeah, neither do I," Audrey said. Then, gesturing to Wickham, she added, "But he does, only he won't say except for too high a price."

Clyde noticed how smoothly handsome Wickham Hill was, and how adoringly Audrey looked at him. Casually Wickham said, "My price is reasonable and"—he smiled at Audrey—"not negotiable."

"Leach," Clyde blurted.

Audrey turned, a little surprised. "What?"

"Leach," Clyde said in his gravelly voice. "Cary Grant's real name. It's something Leach." It seemed strange that while looking into Audrey's eyes he could think at all, but in fact his faculties seemed suddenly decongested. *"Archie,"* he said. "Archie Leach."

Audrey looked at Wickham, who gave a confirming nod, but not very happily. The truth was, both Audrey and Wickham seemed a little sorry he'd come up with the answer, and Clyde realized suddenly that they were both looking forward to Audrey paying the reasonable, non-negotiable price, whatever it was.

"I told you he was a smart guy," Audrey said. Then, after the barest glance toward Clyde: "Maybe I should pay him the price you were asking."

Wickham drawled, "Not on my watch, Miss Audrey."

Clyde understood he'd become a prop for their flirtation. "I should go," he said, glancing toward the kitchen. Audrey, smiling, nodding, and holding Wickham Hill's hand, said it had been good to see him again. As he walked away, Clyde realized it was not just his neck that was moist with sweat. His forehead was damp, too, and his scalp, and even his hair.

Table 9 was one of Manda's tables, so he should have been the one to deliver their beverages (two ginger ales), but he couldn't bear the thought and got someone else to do it.

"How come?" Manda asked.

"No reason," Clyde said.

Manda glanced back at Audrey Reed and Wickham Hill, who were leaning across the table toward each other while they talked, and said, "Oh, there's a reason, all right."

For the rest of the night, Clyde felt divided in two. Clyde One poured water and coffee and bused tables while Clyde Two kept tabs on Audrey Reed and Wickham Hill, who ate (slowly, and with much quiet laughter); danced (with surprising ease, receiving approving smiles from the other, older dancers); went into the lounge (where they sat alone and close together on a huge, pillowy sofa); and then left early (hand in hand, with glowing expressions).

It was customary at the end of the night, when all but a few of the club members had gone and the band was still playing, for employees to go out on the dance floor, and some of them did. The members seemed to like it, and though Clyde never danced, he liked watching the cooks and the waitresses and the waiters become dancers. But tonight he wandered out to the terrace, where he stood for a few minutes, alone in the cold, before he heard footsteps behind him.

"Hey," Manda said.

"Hey."

"What're you doing?"

He shrugged, and she produced a small stub of one of her reefers. "Good to the last inch," she said, lighting it carefully. Its acrid odor bloomed in the cold air. After exhaling a lungful of smoke, she said, "I looked him up for you."

Clyde gave her a look that said *Who?*

"The tall number and her baby-faced boy. I talked nice to the kiosk guard, and he said they came in a taxi and that the member's name is Yates."

"Yates?"

She inhaled, fished her order tickets out, found a neatly printed note, and finally exhaled. "Dr. James Edward Yates, Cypress, South Carolina. Gold Member." She shrugged and handed him the note. "That makes him a lifer. We're talking big loot."

Clyde said, "But the kid's last name is Hill."

Manda shrugged. "Maybe he's a stepson." She stubbed out the last fraction of her joint, flicked off its black ashy edge, then laid it on her tongue and swallowed it. "Fuh-*reezing* out here," she said. Slipping her arm through his, she began to guide him back inside. "Wanna dance?" she said.

"I don't dance."

"Yeah, that's what I thought." Manda gave his arm a reassuring squeeze. "It's not that hard. Want me to teach you?"

Clyde wanted to, but he also didn't want to. "Maybe next time."

Manda grinned her gap-toothed grin. "How 'bout right now," she said, and, taking his hand, led him past the empty tables and out onto the dance floor. Clyde would have enjoyed the dancing more if he had not been aware, as his feet went *step-step-turn, step-step-turn,* that he now knew Wickham's father's full name. And if he did a little more sifting, he'd learn a lot more. He shouldn't do it, but he knew he would.

Chapter 32
What Wickham and Audrey Did

Audrey received her third kiss in the taxi on the way home. Also her fourth, fifth, and sixth. At some point Wickham said, in a whisper, "My mother's working nights now at the hospital." Then he said, in the same whisper, "Should I tell him to take us to my house?" Audrey, eyes closed, saw the warning flare that meant she had only been seeing Wickham Hill for one week. If Oggy had been home waiting for her, she probably would have said no. But Oggy wasn't at home. Audrey indicated, with the subtlest nod, that yes, the answer was yes.

Chapter 33
A Door to the Past

Sunday night. The radio announcer said it was twenty-eight degrees. Clyde's mother was asleep, and his father had gone out for groceries. Clyde was working on an English assignment, but was stumped for a way to compare William Carlos Williams to Robert Frost. He thought about Wickham and Audrey, about how smoothly Wickham had said, "My price is reasonable and not negotiable." Was that what made Clyde suspicious of the guy—that he was just a little too smooth?

Clyde touched the icon that connected him to the Internet; then, after closing his eyes for a few seconds, he took a deep breath and opened the various virtual gates that led him to the legal records of South Carolina. He took Manda's note out of his pocket. *Dr. James Edward Yates.* Clyde stared at the screen and typed in *Wickham James Hill,* hoping that Wickham would have received one of his father's names as a middle name. Nothing. *Wickham J. Hill.* Nothing. Then, glancing at his watch to see how long his father had been gone, he quickly tried *Wickham Edward Hill,* and text began to appear on the screen:

Cypress County Superior Court, State of South Carolina
People vs. Wickham Edward Hill

Vehicular manslaughter. Guilty. Sentenced: 5 years parole. Driver's license revoked.

Clyde read the words twice, with a tingly feeling. He supposed this was why people became cops and FBI agents: the sensation of opening the right door. Clyde printed the page and carefully folded it in two. He slipped the paper into the literature anthology, between William Carlos Williams and Robert Frost. *What next?* he wondered. Maybe there were newspaper stories about the trial. Clyde stood up to look out the window and saw the headlights of the Corolla swing up, then down, as his father steered gently over a dip in the road. Clyde sat down quickly and logged off. Then he went back to poems about ovenbirds and red wheelbarrows glazed with rain.

Chapter 34
Within the Snow Globe

For Audrey, the daylight hours of the next week passed in slow, agonizing expectation of evenings with Wickham, which themselves passed so quickly they seemed sliced out of time. She worried what her father would say about a relationship that had progressed so far in just two weeks, and when she wrote her weekly letter to Oggy, she talked about tea-dancing and studying, and wished she had not told Oggy in a breathless letter about receiving her first kiss.

"A girl's *Keuschheit* is the one investment that never, never fails," Oggy had told her when the subject of virtue and innocence came up, and Audrey had believed her. She could still call herself a virgin even after time spent on the brocaded sofa downstairs at Wickham's house, but meeting Wickham had made her waver. Feeling good about herself had always been hard for her. Wickham made it simple. He brought a lightness and ease to everything they did—he seemed to float above the conventional rules, and in his company she seemed to float above them, too.

One week to the day after Jemison had enjoyed the warmest November 8 on record, it began to snow. The snow fell lightly in the afternoon and thickened toward twilight, with broad, dry white flakes falling densely from a slate-gray sky. Audrey had spent the morning with Lea and C.C.—first at Bing's, then at the mall, where she kept her purchases to some underwear and a pair of earrings—and had spent the afternoon cleaning the house (carefully), doing her homework (quickly), making a beef stew (nervously), and thinking of Wickham Hill (mostly).

By the time the snow was falling hard, the beef stew filled the house with its mouthwatering aroma and Audrey had gotten a steady fire going in the dining room fireplace. It was like playing house, only more so. For Audrey, this wasn't just make-believe; it felt wonderfully like the real thing.

Wickham appeared at her door carrying a book bag and wearing a beautiful camel-colored coat and a black scarf, which Audrey took hold of in order to gently pull him toward her for a kiss.

"Yum," she said. Then: "What's in the bag?"

Wickham had brought five Cary Grant videos from the library. "But we can only watch one," he drawled, smiling.

Audrey stood, drinking him in. "You're my own personal Cary Grant."

He grinned. "I am?"

"You are," she said, then turned the movies to see their titles. "Which shall we watch?"

He'd unwound his scarf and was unbuttoning his coat. "You choose."

Audrey narrowed her choices down to *An Affair to Remember*, because it was so crushingly romantic, and *Suspicion*, because she'd never seen it. "I'm torn between these two," she said.

He closed his eyes, dramatically extended his hand, and picked *Suspicion*.

As she carried his camel-colored coat to the closet, she felt something hard-edged in the pocket. She put her hand into it and pulled out a cardboard sheet of foil-covered pills. His Imitrex. "Migraine?" she asked him.

"Did have." He smiled. "Now don't."

When Audrey put the pills back in Wickham's pocket, she felt a smooth cylinder that turned out to be lip balm. PEPPERMINT, it read. So that's why he smelled like Christmas.

They ate beef stew with baguette slices while the fire crackled and the black-and-white credits for the movie began to roll. But before the movie had really begun, Audrey realized Wickham wasn't looking at the screen; he was looking at her.

"What?" she said.

"You," he said; then, nodding at the food in front of him and gesturing at the room around him, "This." He was quiet for a moment. "It's all so . . ." His voice trailed off. Finally he was looking again into her eyes. "I wonder if anybody anywhere is this happy."

We are, she thought. But she merely stared at Wickham Hill's beautiful face until the actors in *Suspicion* began to speak, and then they turned and watched and ate.

The movie was pretty interesting. Cary Grant played a charmer who might or might not have murdered his friend and business partner, and Joan Fontaine played a wealthy woman who was in love with Cary Grant but didn't know what to do with her suspicions.

"It's kind of creepy," Audrey said, "not knowing whether to trust Cary Grant or not."

Wickham said, "I'd trust him. I mean, he *is* Cary Grant."

"Yeah," Audrey said, "but this particular Cary Grant might be a wife-murdering Cary Grant."

They had by this time moved to the sofa, and Wickham leaned close to say, "Know what you are?"

"What?"

"Funny," he said. "Funny and smart and extremely smoochable."

They fell easily into kissing, and didn't stop until they heard the heavy *kuh-lup* of the front door closing. In a stiff whisper, Audrey said, "My dad."

The clicking footsteps passed on the tiled corridor and grew faint. Audrey tiptoed across the room and eased open the door in time to see her father slipping into his office. Small traces of snow marked his trail along the hallway.

"What's going on?" Wickham said.

Audrey turned. "Nothing," she said. "He went into his office."

"Want to introduce me?"

"I do," Audrey said, "but he looked really tired."

Wickham shrugged. "Later, then," he said, and they went back to their movie until it became clear that this particular Cary Grant was not a wife-murdering Cary Grant. Then Wickham whispered, "Let's go for a ride in the snow."

Driving the Lincoln in the snow wasn't dangerous unless it turned icy, which it wasn't. "Let me tell my dad," she said, though exactly what she would tell him, she wasn't sure. It turned out that it didn't matter.

When she looked in on her father, he didn't see her. He stood slump-shouldered, staring out the window with his hands in his pocket. He'd turned on the yard lights so he could watch the heavy snow falling. Audrey backed quietly away. On the kitchen tablet they used for messages, she wrote:

Dad,
Went by C.C.'s. Home by 9:00.
Love, A.
P.S. I actually managed to cook stew in crockpot!

It was eerily, beautifully quiet, driving through the snow-muffled streets of Jemison. They drove by C.C.'s house ("Hi, C.C.; hi, Brian," Audrey said in passing so that she could say, technically, that she'd driven by and said hello). They kept meandering through the neighborhoods, watching the snow float through the yellow beams of the headlights. It was warm in the car, and when they came to a cul-de-sac with a vacant lot and paved driveway, Wickham said, "There."

Parked, with the engine off, it was even quieter. For a long time they didn't talk. They just sat in the warmth of the car, looking out. Then Wickham turned to her and said, "You know, I had a girlfriend in South Carolina." He made a low, mild laugh. "Actually, a couple of girlfriends." His voice turned serious. "But I can tell you right now, I've never felt this way before." When he looked into her eyes and said this, it wasn't just a series of words, it was a door opening into a sealed world where nothing could be wrong and nothing could go wrong.

Outside, the snow floated close to the windows of the Lincoln, then melted on the glass. Wickham had begun kissing her, and he smelled like Christmas. *This is like being inside the most wonderful snow globe,* Audrey thought before closing her eyes.

Part Two

He'll fly to the barn,
And keep himself warm,
And tuck his head under his wing.

Chapter 35
Alternating Currents

November 23. The Sunday before Thanksgiving. Dirty snow covered the lawns, and icicles reached toward and away from the McNair house like gnarled fingers. It was dusk. Mrs. Leacock had assigned the class to write a three-to-five-page biography of a physicist, and it was due the next day. Audrey still needed to finish her paper, on Nikola Tesla, and she'd offered to help Wickham finish up his.

Wickham, smelling of peppermint and cold air, took off his pea coat and scarf, and rummaged around in his backpack until he found a single piece of paper, folded vertically down the middle. He hadn't shaved, which to Audrey only added to his handsomeness, but he had the subtly stiff face she'd learned to associate with his headaches.

"You okay?" she said.

"I'm good," he said. "Gooder than good." But the smile he gave her was a stiff one.

"Anything a kiss could cure?" she said, and sat on his lap and kissed his earlobe.

"Maybe," he said. "Very possibly, in fact."

He let his hand wander, and she gently pushed him away— not that she wanted to. "Work before pleasure," she said, and unfolded his paper.

She was shocked how little was there. Less than half a page. She turned it over, but the back was blank.

"Quantitatively," she said, "we're a little short here."

Wickham took no offense. "Yeah, well, that's why I came to you. For inspiration."

Audrey read what he had written, which was a joke about Heisenberg's uncertainty principle: *Heisenberg was driving down the Autobahn at high speed when he was pulled over by a policeman. The policeman asked, "Do you know how fast you were going back there, Herr Heisenberg?" "No," Heisenberg replied, "but I do know exactly where I am."*

Audrey chuckled, then frowned. "So you're starting with this?"

He shrugged.

"Then what? Do you have some dates and anecdotes?"

Wickham looked not only stiff and possibly sick but also lost and vulnerable, which only sharpened Audrey's affection for him. "Not to worry," she said. She slipped off his lap and led him by the hand to the chair in front of the computer, which she leaned over and switched on. "Which search engine do you use?" she asked.

He looked at her blankly.

"Google, Teoma, Yahoo?" she said.

Again the blank look. "Those aren't nomadic tribes of the American Southwest?"

Audrey gave this a polite laugh and leaned over to type *Teoma*, then *Heisenberg*. "Okay," she said, seeing with satisfaction a long list of scholarly-looking sites. "Now you just scroll down until you find something that looks promising and take a look. If it contains information you need, go ahead and print it."

"Where are you going to be?"

She nodded toward a nearby armchair. "Right there, finishing my geometry homework."

"Way over there?"

"Way over there," Audrey said, sounding more curt than she intended. Usually, being with Wickham was like being the only two people in a place isolated by gently falling snow. But tonight that sense of snug communion was gone.

Wickham read aloud—and printed—a few more physics jokes; then he became quiet. Finally he said, "Okay, time for the cavalry," and rummaged in his backpack until he found the familiar cardboard sheet. He popped an Imitrex through the foil and washed it down with a gulp of Coke.

So it was a migraine. Again. Audrey rose and came over to him. "Bad?"

"Pretty bad, yeah."

It wasn't just his face that was stiff now. It was his whole body. He walked carefully to the sofa and eased himself down. Audrey put a pillow beneath his head and brought him a damp, hot washcloth.

"Why didn't you take a pill sooner?" she asked.

He made a faint smile and said, "Trying to conserve. I'm almost out. And they're fifteen bucks apiece."

Audrey wasn't sure which was the news here—the fact that the pills cost so much or the fact that Wickham, who wore pricey clothes and took taxis to pricey restaurants, would care.

When he was settled and quiet, she sat down at the computer and found some even better sources about Heisenberg. (That wasn't cheating, was it? It was like when a librarian steered you toward the right Dewey decimal number.) She looked to see if Wickham was still awake, and when he rubbed his eyes, she said, "Um, we need a thesis statement over here."

Without opening his eyes, Wickham said, *"Herr Doktor Werner Heisenberg, born in 1902, dead some time later, certainly knew how to use uncertainty to his advantage."*

Audrey couldn't help laughing. "He was born in 1901, not 1902, and I'm afraid you're mistaking Mrs. Leacock for someone with a sense of humor."

Wickham kept his eyes closed. "It's just a biography, right?" He sounded tired, or bored, or both. "Heisenberg was born here, his mother did this, his father did that, he disowned them and became famous."

"He disowned his parents?"

"Maybe that was somebody else," he said without much interest. He sighed and said, "So how would you write it, Miss Term Paper?"

"I am not Miss Term Paper," she said coolly.

"Look, Audrey," he said. "I just can't do this right now. Let's skip it, okay?"

"If you skip it, you flunk."

This seemed not to faze Wickham. "Yeah. . . . So?"

Audrey's voice softened. "So I thought we were going to college together."

They had planned it one night in this very room, when her father was working late and they had the house to themselves. They would get married after graduation. They would both go to Syracuse University, her father's school—not Audrey's first or even tenth choice, but her father was always giving money to the school and she thought he might be able to help Wickham get in there. Hadn't her father always wanted Audrey to attend his alma mater?

"I just can't write a paper when my head is doing this," Wickham said. "I'm sorry. Give me an hour and I'll feel better." Then he put the pillow over his face and fell asleep.

Her father came home, and Audrey tracked the sounds of his car door, the front door, and his footsteps on the stairs. He said, "Knock, knock," and stuck his head in.

He looked tired. He always looked tired now. He regarded Wickham on the sofa. As far as Audrey could tell, her father liked Wickham. They had met one afternoon in the kitchen, and Wickham had made a good impression, shaking Audrey's father's hand, calling him "sir," and talking knowledgeably about her father's favorite basketball team. Her father had said afterward that he seemed "genteel—not like most kids today," and when he'd asked if Wickham was smart, Audrey had grinned and nodded yes. For her father, a boy wasn't a candidate for anything if he wasn't smart.

Tonight, her father looked at the sleeping Wickham and said, "Dead of a heart attack at age seventeen?"

Audrey laughed, mostly out of relief, and said, "He's got a migraine."

Her father nodded, but somberly. "It's getting late, Audrey. And if he's sick, he needs to be home."

Wickham slowly sat up. "I'm sorry, sir. It's the medicine I take—it knocks me out sometimes." Absently, he began to fold the blanket Audrey had put over him.

"Can't he stay until ten o'clock?" Audrey asked. "He needs to finish his paper."

Her father silently considered this. It pitted propriety, which Audrey knew he believed in, against getting your homework done, which he also believed in. "Ten's okay," he said finally, "but no later."

What Wickham wrote at the computer that night was shocking to Audrey. He had to be able to spell better than that, and how could someone so charming and witty seem so simple-minded on paper? Maybe it was the migraine—probably it was—but Audrey read the paper with a perfectly blank expression at 9:55 and said it was great, but maybe she should just go through and fix a few commas.

"And whatever else you find wrong with it," Wickham said as he shouldered into his heavy coat. The taxi he'd called had just wheeled into Audrey's driveway. After Wickham kissed her at the front door, she watched him walk out into the snow. She hoped he would turn around to wave good-bye so she could see his face one more time, but he didn't. He just slipped stiffly into the cab, which rolled away.

Audrey went back inside and sat down at the computer. Wickham had gotten some dates wrong (like saying that Himmler had exonerated Heisenberg of charges the SS made against him in 1983 instead of 1938). When she checked that fact, she found a great anecdote he hadn't even used and a few other details that would make the paper more interesting, and she put those in, too. Then she set to work on Nikola Tesla's alternating currents, her own topic. It was 2:15 when she finally crawled into bed.

In the morning she called Wickham.

"Hello, schoolmarm," he said, which hit her the wrong way, especially since it was said in the cheerful tone of someone who'd gotten a good night's sleep. "Don't call me that," she said. Then, softer: "Meet me at my locker so I can give you your paper, okay? I don't think I should be pulling it out of my bag in class. It'd look like we're cheating."

"Which we're not," Wickham said. "You're just my editor, is all. My editress."

Editor. Editress. It was true—that's all she was. Audrey again felt the sensation of snow falling softly outside a room where she and Wickham were safe and warm.

"See you at my locker," Audrey said, and Wickham, in his soft drawl, replied, "Yes indeed."

Chapter 36
Top Collar

The problem with the vase was the top collar. Clyde had gotten to the point where he could shape the basic vase without thinking, but then his hands would rise to the collar, where the gentlest type of two-handed throttle had to be undertaken, and he just couldn't get it right. The more he concentrated, the worse the results. Now, however, he was merely building the basic vase—his hands ran smoothly through the spinning wet clay—and he was left to his own thoughts, which led him to Wickham Hill.

Clyde hated Wickham Hill, hated him in a way he didn't even hate Theo Driggs, because Theo Driggs was just a thug. But Wickham passed himself off as older, richer, and more sophisticated than everyone else.

He had to warn Audrey. Tell her what he'd found out. It would be hard for her at first, but then she'd be grateful to him, and look at him differently. . . . And then, without meaning to but unable to help it, Clyde began thinking of Audrey, the dream Audrey, on her bike on a sunny country road, with her long legs bare and her sandy hair streaming back. And then he thought of how, when Clyde had remembered Cary Grant's name, she'd said maybe she should pay the reasonable, non-negotiable price to Clyde, and Clyde began to think of Audrey Reed standing before him and smiling shyly and undoing a long, thin dress with a line of cloth-covered buttons running down the front—a reverie that was easy to take pretty far, and in fact only ended when Clyde became suddenly aware of the clay gently enclosed in his hands.

The collar was there.

Somehow, the collar was there.

On the spinning wheel it looked weirdly triangular, but he knew that was the way it was supposed to look.

He very gently released his hands, and the triangular shape turned into a circle before his very eyes.

Clyde sat staring at the pot, almost in disbelief.

Look, he thought. *Look what just happened.*

He raised his eyes to his teacher's desk. "Mrs. Arboneaux," he said. "The vase."

She rose and came to his wheel. She stared at it a long time. Then she said, "It's perfect. It's absolutely perfect." She turned to him. "How did you do it?"

"I don't know." He honestly didn't. "I was lost in my thoughts"—he colored slightly at the kind of thoughts he'd been lost in—"and it just . . . happened."

Mrs. Arboneaux laughed. "You let your fingers do the thinking."

"Is it too big?" Clyde said.

"It'll shrink a little in drying, and a little in firing." She gazed again at the vase. "It's just the most beautiful shape," she said. Then, after they'd stared at it in wonderment for perhaps a full minute, she helped him move it from the wheel to a drying tile, which he set on a high shelf, out of harm's way.

Chapter 37
Forewarned

For Audrey, Monday, November 24, was not a good day. First of all, it was freezing. The streets were white with salt, the snow was black with dirt, and the sky was an impenetrable beige. The second issue of *The Yellow Paper* was sticking out of people's backpacks and textbooks and lying facedown on wet, dirty entryways, footprints like postmarks on the edges.

Audrey picked up one that wasn't too grimy and stuffed it into her coat pocket to read after meeting Wickham. He was already waiting for her, leaning casually, handsomely, winsomely against the wall. "Well, well," he drawled when she drew close, "look who looks fetching as can be."

"Thanks," she said, feeling it to be true only when he said it.

She unzipped her backpack and pulled out her physics binder. There was the sepia picture of Heisenberg; there were the neat black letters of his name. Handing the essay to Wickham, though, was like driving down the street with a patrol car behind her. She looked up to see Clyde Mumsford moving down the hall toward them. He glanced at her and at what she was handing to Wickham, and walked on past them. Audrey felt her face go bright red.

"What's the matter?" Wickham asked.

"Nothing," Audrey said.

"This looks professional," Wickham said, thumbing through the pages and nodding. He closed it up again and asked softly, "Did you change the typeface?"

"What?" She was still feeling Clyde's gaze. What had that look been?

"I mean, is it the same as you used for your paper?"

It was. Suddenly this seemed like a dead giveaway. And if there was something to give away, it meant there was something to hide.

"It's the same," Audrey said softly.

"Well, that's okay. It's not that distinctive. Don't worry about it, Aud. You look like you're on trial for murder here. All you did was edit me, remember? Half the papers at this school were radically 'edited' "—here he put his fingers up to make quotation marks—"by overachieving parents."

"Right," Audrey said doubtfully. "Okay. Well, I'll see you in third period."

She started to go, but Wickham pulled her back. He kissed her in the subterranean gray-green hall of a high school she had hated three months earlier. "Thank you," he whispered. Other students looked at them, and somebody let fly with a "Hubba-hubba!"

Audrey felt momentarily happy and weightless except for the one rope that tied her to earth—the suspicion that what he was thanking her for was helping him cheat in school.

"Bye," she said, and hoped that Clyde was not somewhere watching.

Chapter 38
Ignominy

As she headed off toward English, Audrey pulled out *The Yellow Paper*, which was full of the usual tasteless stuff:

URINE TROUBLE NOW!

NOT-WATER BALLOONS

ARE URINIFEROUS

FILL-UP STRICTLY A GUY THING

Ugh. With a mixture of dread and curiosity, Audrey turned the page over and found the "Outed!" column:

Lovers of Yellow Journalism let us as they say get right down to bidness. What Social Science Teacher-type going by the initials D.B.I. might think of changing that middle initial to U? That's correct, Bargefolk, one of our esteemed educational professionals made the police blotter two weeks back with a blood alcohol reading of almost triple repeat triple the legal limit and here's thinking the fact that the nice Police Officer pulled our So-Sci pedagogue over at 2:15 a.m. in the company of a female companion other than his wee wedded wife might explain why our D.B.I. has taken up temporary quarters at the YMCA. . . .

Probably Mr. Ingram, Audrey figured. He taught social science and she thought his first name was David, but he seemed so meek and bland—maybe five foot six, nearly bald, and always wearing the same nerdy cardigan—that it was hard to think of him out drinking with some woman. But that was the thing about people you saw from a distance, or even people close to you—you had no idea in the world what they might do when they thought they were alone. Who would have guessed, for example, that she would do what she did with Wickham? Letting him look over her shoulder during quizzes. Writing his paper for him. Letting him undo her blouse on the sofa in his living room.

Audrey shook her head quickly to dispel these thoughts, and kept walking and reading.

Stiff upper liposuction, Mademoiselle Taylor, but when asked whether your name and cosmetic surgery should be uttered in the same breath we must in all candor confess the answer be oui.

Miss Taylor, the spinster French teacher, whose face, Audrey had to admit, did seem to have that stretched-taut look. She continued reading.

Here's yet another poll to hold on to, Bargemen, and no we don't mean that pole you deviate you. Results from the 1st Annual Large-Margin-of-Error Poll are finally in and we now have winners of awards in categories both coveted and un. Speaking of uncoveted and starting with scalp scurf, The Demonest Dandruff Award goes to . . . drumroll and miscellaneous juvenile sounds imitating flatulence . . . Mr. Dan Hans the Science Man! Your top choice for the Lady-Godiva-Ride-Through-the-Food-Court Award is . . . drumroll and heavy breathing . . . Evie Berkowitz!

Audrey scanned a few more ersatz awards until she came to Theo Driggs's name:

And finally, Fellow Inmates, the award you've all been waiting for, the highly pejorative Biggest Horse's Ass Award for which let's face it there were a wide variety of nominees but this was the one award with a landslide runaway and thumbs-down winner . . . our very own punkster and mugster Theo-the-Sniggering-Stallion-Driggs. That's right, Theodora, you may have the brains and breath of a Shetland pony but the consensus is you are indeed The Biggest Horse's Ass on campus and to be truthful our tireless staff (no not that staff you overly hormonal moron) can think of no one more deserving of this ignominy. (Sorry Theo, but we can't tell you what ignominy means—you'll just have to look it up.)

Audrey wasn't sure whether the Yellow Man was foolish, brave, or both. But she knew one thing for sure: the Yellow Man was in for a serious pulping if Theo ever figured out who he—or she—was.

Chapter 39
Discovering the Yellow Man

"Audrey?"

Clyde Mumsford stepped out from a hallway alcove, where he must have been waiting. He was wearing the pink-and-black bowling shirt again, but he had shaved, and his hair looked wavy instead of helmet-mashed.

Audrey gave him a half smile. "Hi."

"I need to talk to you."

The urgency in his voice made Audrey apprehensive. She glanced toward room 456, where her English class met. "I've got class right now," she said.

He said, "Perry's class, right?"

She nodded, and wondered how Clyde knew this.

"He's late," Clyde said. "I just saw him go into the teacher's lounge."

Audrey hesitated, and Clyde said, "It'll just take a second." From inside his coat, he pulled out a manila envelope.

"What's that?" Audrey said, afraid it was connected somehow with Wickham's Heisenberg paper for Mrs. Leacock.

"It's . . . ," Clyde began, then looked down at the envelope. His long fingers were caked with light brown clay.

Audrey glanced down the hallway—it was almost empty now. If she kept standing here, she was going to be late. "It's *what*?" she said impatiently.

Clyde looked both serious and fearful. "It's . . . information I think you should have."

He extended the envelope toward her, but Audrey wasn't ready to take it. "What kind of information?" she asked.

Clyde sounded almost apologetic. "Important information." He made his voice softer. "About someone you know."

Audrey's voice was sharp. "Who?"

Clyde looked at her uncertainly, then lowered his eyes. "Wickham."

A kind of rage took hold of Audrey. What right did Clyde Mumsford have to be giving her information about Wickham? In a tight voice she said, "So you're here to debrief me about Wickham Hill?"

Clyde stood there, stiff and quiet.

"Where did you get this so-called important information?" Audrey asked, and when Clyde just stood there looking uncomfortable, something occurred to her, something that felt like a revealed truth. She said, "You're the Yellow Man, aren't you?"

He had a caught-in-the-headlights look. "What?" he said.

She held up *The Yellow Paper*. "This is your work, isn't it?"

"Oh, that," he said. "I couldn't tell you who's behind that." He took a deep breath and rubbed some of the dried clay off his hands. "Look, Audrey, I'm giving you this envelope because I'm worried about you."

Audrey had to keep herself from shouting. "*You're* worried about *me*? What right do *you* have to be worried about *me*?"

Down the hall, Mr. Perry stepped out of the teacher's lounge and ambled toward them, carrying a coffee cup and his tattered literature anthology. His hard heels clicked on the concrete floor.

Audrey turned back to Clyde. "I'm not taking that envelope," she said in a hard, low voice. "I don't want your sleazy information, because I think what you're doing right now is sleazier than anything that envelope might contain."

When Clyde spoke this time, his voice had more bite to it. "Well," he said, "that's where you'd be wrong."

Again he extended the envelope in his clay-caked hand.

Mr. Perry, drawing near them, said amiably, "Miss Reed, if you were to beat me through that door, I could avoid marking you tardy."

Audrey glanced at Mr. Perry, then back at Clyde. "Keep your important information to yourself," she said in a tight whisper. "In fact, keep everything about yourself to yourself."

As she turned to go, Clyde, in a rising voice, said, "Then ask Wickham about a girl whose name was Jade Marie Creamer."

Audrey felt as if she were fleeing a bad dream. She hurried through the classroom door and, avoiding all eye contact, slid into her seat.

Mr. Perry, entering the room, said, "Today, fellow lovers of literature, I have the pleasure of introducing you to a book and a boy named Huckleberry Finn."

Audrey stopped listening and went back over the weird conversation she'd just had with Clyde Mumsford.

Jade Marie Creamer.

Who in the world was Jade Marie Creamer? And what did Wickham have to do with her? Images piled up, and questions, until Audrey almost couldn't think.

Up front, Mr. Perry was saying, "So if you will turn to page 1045."

I couldn't tell you who's behind that. That's what Clyde said when Audrey showed him *The Yellow Paper* and asked if he was the Yellow Man. *I couldn't tell you who's behind that.*

Which wasn't the same as denying it, was it?

And if Clyde was writing *The Yellow Paper*—and deep in her bones, she was sure now that he was—what would keep him from using his sleazy information about Wickham in the next installment of "Outed"?

Chapter 40
Mrs. Leacock

Audrey had hoped to see Wickham again before Mrs. Leacock's third-period class, but hadn't. He walked through the door just before the bell, looking calm and assured, carrying his Heisenberg paper, his textbook, and, sandwiched in between, a copy of *The Yellow Paper*. He wasn't alone. Up and down the rows, Audrey could see *The Yellow Paper* lying under notebooks or peeking out of book bags.

Mrs. Leacock must have seen them, too. "Before handing in your papers, people, please pass forward for disposal any copies you may have of the yellow sleaze sheet distributed today—and please, it would behoove you not to protest First Amendment rights. In this small fiefdom, the right of privacy and personal dignity trumps one's right to defame. So please, if you will, pass them forward."

A reluctant rustling; then, from silent student to silent student, the *Yellow Papers* moved forward.

"Careful how you handle them," Mrs. Leacock said. "They're germ-bearing, and the disease is communicable among weaker individuals."

Mrs. Leacock stood at the head of the class, twisting her ring and waiting. She wore one of her striped sweater sets, and her nails were the exact same shade of red as the stripes across her perfectly smooth acrylic sweater. Her lipstick was freshly applied and inhumanly dark. When the *Yellow Papers* were collected into a stack, she held open a plastic bag for a girl in the first row to drop them into. Mrs. Leacock tied the bag's handles and ceremoniously dropped the bag into the metal wastebasket.

"And now," she said, visibly relaxing, "your own papers, please."

From behind, Wickham handed his paper to Audrey. Audrey handed both of their essays—the type fonts like identical twins—to Greg Telman, who added his own and passed them forward.

"Well, well!" Mrs. Leacock said as she flipped through the papers handed to her from one row. "Someone had the nerve to do Freeman Dyson's quest to extend human life into the extreme future."

Audrey regarded Mrs. Leacock's smile—dark-lipped and tight—and realized she had never seen her laugh. Actually laugh. And she couldn't imagine Mrs. Leacock crying. She couldn't imagine Mrs. Leacock's personal life at all, or her past, either. She was always twisting the gold ring on her ring finger, and she was *Mrs.* Leacock—so she must be married—but who, really, would have fallen in love with her? And if she'd had kids, what kind of mother would she have been? Audrey tried to imagine Mrs. Leacock smothering a toddler in kisses, but couldn't.

Lots of her teachers would illustrate things they were teaching with examples from their own lives, but not Mrs. Leacock. No, Mrs. Leacock was there to teach you physics or human biology or chemistry, and you either learned it or you didn't—it was all the same to her—and then, when she drove away from Jemison High and entered her private life, she locked and double-locked the door behind her.

Well, Audrey thought, *that's why it's called your private life—because it's private.*

Or at least it used to be.

But now you knew that Patrice Newman wasn't just a World Cultures teacher, but also a former teen shoplifter. And you knew that Miss Taylor, while teaching French, was afraid of getting old. And when married Mr. Ingram stood in front of your class, you could sit there imagining him trying to walk a straight line while his girlfriend and a cop stood and watched.

And it wasn't just open season on teachers. It was open season on everybody. Audrey had the awful feeling that Wickham was Clyde's next victim. What did Clyde know about Wickham, and how did he find it out?

Mrs. Leacock slipped the fat bundle of essays into a canvas tote bag and turned to the chalkboard. She began to write, and Audrey began to copy, trying not to think about somebody out in the world whose name was Jade Marie Creamer. She thought about writing a note to Wickham and passing it back, but made herself stop.

You will not ask Wickham, she thought. *You will not ask Wickham.*

But she didn't have to.

Chapter 41
People vs. Wickham Hill

Just before lunch that day, Audrey went to her locker and found that two sheets of paper had been slipped through the narrow vents of the locker door. Normally, Lea and C.C. were the ones who took advantage of the built-in mail drops—pushing notes, photographs, and the occasional cartoon inside—so Audrey unfolded the papers expecting diversion, but instead found herself looking at some sort of abbreviated legal printout, which read:

> Cypress County Superior Court, State of South Carolina
> People vs. Wickham Edward Hill
> Vehicular manslaughter. Guilty. Sentenced: 5 years parole.
> Driver's license revoked.

So this was from Clyde Mumsford. This was what he'd wanted to hand her between classes, and when she'd refused the papers, he'd stuffed them into her locker. It made her furious, and she knew she ought to crumple them up without reading them, but she couldn't. She turned to the second page.

It contained a downloaded article from a newspaper called *The Cypress Telegram*, which read:

A Cypress County teenager was charged yesterday with vehicular manslaughter in connection with the death of a juvenile female on March 3 of this year.

The 16-year-old male allegedly lost control of the Toyota sedan he was driving, resulting in the immediate death of Jade Marie Creamer, age 15. Two other passengers in the car were injured. The name of the juvenile driver was withheld by the court.

According to court documents, the accused is enrolled at Leighton Hall, a private school located two miles southeast of Cypress. The *Telegram* has also learned that three of the passengers in the car are enrolled at the school. A spokesman for Leighton Hall would neither confirm nor deny involvement of any of its students.

The deceased girl, Jade Marie Creamer, was a cousin of one of the other passengers in the car. She was a sophomore at Cypress West High, a member of the Thespians Club, the Model UN, and the debate team.

The accompanying photograph of Jade Marie Creamer looked like a school picture. She wasn't a beautiful girl, but she had perfect teeth and an expression that seemed both perky and assertive.

Audrey flipped quickly back to the legal page. Wickham's conviction followed the news account by just less than three months. About the right time. And it would explain why Wickham never drove.

An image returned to Audrey's mind, the scene she'd

dreamed up while Mrs. Leacock was talking about Schrödinger's Cat. Men and women in lab coats stood around a steel box. They said the cat was dead. They said the cat was alive. They said he was both. They checked their watches to see how much longer they had to wait for their observations to change reality. The cat, meanwhile, didn't even know what they were waiting for.

Audrey stuffed the papers back into the envelope. Sweat dampened her shirt and she felt almost dizzy. She headed for the bathroom, the only one she and Lea and C.C. would use, the one tucked between the C and D buildings, where almost nobody ever went.

It is just as likely that no atom has decayed, the acid remains in the flask, and the cat remains alive.

That's what Mrs. Leacock had said, and Audrey had written it down.

It was lunchtime, but she didn't care about lunch. All she cared about was calming down. Calming down and figuring out how to keep Clyde Mumsford from crushing the flask and opening the box. It would be so easy for Clyde. All he would have to do is smear poor Wickham all over the next *Yellow Paper*.

KILLER FROM CAROLINA.

WHO CREAMED THE CREAMER GIRL?

In Audrey's mind, the trapped cat crouched and stared, waiting anxiously for something it could not even imagine, and the cat was Wickham, who had to be saved.

Chapter 42
Two Birds

The C&D bathroom was empty. Someone had written "XES YEKNOM NO SEY" on one of the stalls in red ink, which made no sense to Audrey until she saw it reflected in the mirror—"YES ON MONKEY SEX." What was she doing in a school like this, with people like these? She had no idea. Absolutely no idea.

Audrey pulled back her long hair, twisted it, and tucked the loose ends into her collar, then wetted her face. The water felt cold, but good. She rolled up her sleeves and ran water on her forearms. She was feeling better. She closed her eyes and was touching wet fingertips to her eyelids when, from just behind her, she heard a voice, a *male* voice.

"Just freshening up?"

Audrey's eyes shot open, and she spun around.

Theo Driggs stood to her left, blocking the doorway.

Audrey couldn't think what to say. She said, "You can't be here."

Theo smiled, but not enough to show his teeth. "Yeah, those are the rules. But only losers play by the rules. That's why they lose."

He stepped closer and looked in the mirror at their reflections.

Audrey said to his reflection, "You need to leave now."

Theo didn't move. "Know what I've been thinking a lot

about?" He did something with his eyes. Something that made them lift slightly, as if to put them on high beam. "You. And how far you've worked your way up my to-do list." He leaned close to Audrey's neck and took a deep breath. "God. You smell so good."

Audrey felt a clammy fear enfold her.

Theo leaned closer to the mirror and seemed to be checking his teeth for food bits. As he leaned forward, a folded piece of yellow paper was observable in his shirt pocket. Theo closed his mouth but kept studying his image. His eyes were on low beam now. "A girl told me I have sensual lips. What do you think? Do I have sensual lips?"

Audrey didn't answer.

Theo turned from the mirror to stare at her directly. "You don't think we're compatible, do you?" he said.

Audrey still didn't speak.

"Why is that?" he said, and his eyes shifted to high beam again. "Because you're rich, or because you think you're smarter than me, or what?"

They stood staring at each other.

"You know, you might be smarter than me, and then again you might not. The school makes me go to this lady headshrinker, and she tells me I've got the big IQ." Theo made a false smile. "She thinks I just don't know how to channel my abilities *constructively*."

He laughed a hard, derisive laugh and kept his high beams fixed on Audrey.

From outside, a voice called in: "Hey, Theo, what about it? We going to the car or not?"

Theo stood between her and the door, and the moment

Audrey thought she ought to scream was the moment she knew she couldn't. Screaming wouldn't help.

Theo's tone turned falsely conversational. "The thing is, compatibility's not so easy to read. You need to go for a spin with us, spend a little time with the guys and me, get to know us." He leaned forward, and one side of his mouth slid upward. "We're not so bad," he said, close enough so that she smelled a sour mix of tobacco and licorice on his breath.

He leaned farther forward. Suddenly, without thinking, without really meaning to, Audrey said, "I know who wrote that stuff about you in *The Yellow Paper*."

Theo's eyes, already on high beam, brightened further. "And who would that be?"

"You'll let me out of here?"

A full few seconds passed before Theo nodded.

"You promise?"

He nodded.

"Clyde Mumsford."

Audrey thought she saw Theo's pupils actually dilate and then contract as he absorbed this news. And then he seemed to relax, as if he now had something else to look forward to.

"You can go, Miss Caviar," he said. But when she stepped forward, he didn't immediately move. "Just so you know, you're not off my to-do list." He looked off to the side. "All that's happened is, somebody moved ahead of you." He was looking at her again, fastening his salamander eyes on her, smiling at her. "I'll get back to you after I stop the presses."

Theo stood aside then, and just like that she was past him, out the door, onto the pavement. Three of Theo's friends looked up as she passed, but she kept her eyes straight ahead.

Once she was beyond them, she wanted to stop feeling scared, but couldn't. She also felt like a coward, but what she'd done was what she'd had to do, wasn't it? And besides, she'd killed two birds with one stone. She'd saved herself from Theo and she'd saved Wickham from Clyde.

Chapter 43
Transportation Services

All afternoon, Audrey wanted to be with Wickham, be in a warm house with him while snow fell outside, but when she and Lea and C.C. found him after school, he was at the rusty water fountain near his locker, swallowing his migraine medicine.

C.C. asked what he was taking, and he made a faint smile and said, "Imitrex, and"—he glanced at the water fountain—"swamp water."

He just wanted to go home, he said, and so Audrey drove him, with C.C. and Lea in the backseat asking solicitous questions about the migraines. They seemed to come in streaks, Wickham said. They weren't that bad. He just had to ride them out.

Lea leaned forward. "This is what my dad does for my mom when she has migraines," she said, and began slowly rubbing two fingers in tight circles on his temples.

Wickham leaned back, closed his eyes, and said, "Mmmm."

"Be careful," C.C. said. "If that cures your headache, Lea'll start trying to convert you to her whole homeopathic lifestyle."

In her soft voice, Lea said, "A girl takes a few antioxidants and her friends turn on her."

Wickham said weakly that if she cured his headache, he'd

just say "maybe" to drugs—which got a laugh from everyone, including Audrey.

"I'll call you when the Imitrex kicks in," he said to Audrey as he got out, and after C.C. climbed into the front seat, Audrey backed up the Lincoln to drive C.C. and Lea home.

The roads were lined with hard, dirty snow, and Audrey was trying to remember the night this same snow had fallen and she and Wickham had slipped inside the snow globe. It seemed like a long time ago.

"Any progress on the music front?" C.C. asked Audrey, pointing to the cassette player.

"I tried tweezers," Audrey said. "They didn't work, either."

C.C. sighed. "Then let's visit the one-record record shop," she said, punching the power button and releasing sprightly soprano voices from within: *"Ev'rything is a source of fun. Nobody's safe, for we care for none!"*

From the backseat, Lea said, "I think you need to ditch Wickham."

Audrey gave her a quick look of surprise. "You do?"

Lea nodded.

"How come?"

"So I can grab the discard."

They all laughed, and in the warm familiarity of the car Audrey considered telling them everything—about the quiz, the Heisenberg paper, even the car accident that hadn't been Wickham's fault—but C.C. said, "You guys hear what they did to Miss Taylor?" and the opportunity was gone.

What they'd done to Miss Taylor was superimpose a blowup of her yearbook head shot on a *National Geographic* foldout of a three-thousand-year-old mummified woman.

Then, when no one was there, they used a human pyramid to pin it to the ceiling of her classroom so that it required a janitor and a ladder to get it down. Audrey remembered Mrs. Leacock's warning that the weakest individuals were the ones most likely to be infected by the germs *The Yellow Paper* carried.

"I guess that's funny," Lea said doubtfully, and Audrey, thinking of Wickham, said, "Not if you're Miss Taylor."

Audrey pulled up in front of C.C.'s house, where both C.C. and Lea climbed out. "Okay," Audrey said to both of them. "So you're going to change your clothes and then come over?" They were all going to make cookies and study together, but C.C. needed to bring her own car so she could drive to her aunt's birthday party afterward.

"Right," C.C. said. "See you in ten minutes."

Audrey drove the rest of the way home wondering how she might get Wickham to talk about the accident without her directly mentioning it. She was sitting in the driveway, still wondering, when a big white truck pulled up.

It parked at the curb, and three men in sweatshirts and blue jeans hopped out. Small cursive letters on the side of the truck read, ANCHOR BROS. TRANSPORTATION SERVICES. The men walked up Audrey's driveway and, to her surprise, opened her front door and went in.

Audrey gathered her books, scrambled out of her car, and picked her way across the icy patches of the driveway. There was another, smaller truck already parked behind the house, and it read, ANCHOR BROS., too. Maybe her dad was home. If he wasn't, maybe she shouldn't go into the house. She stood on the porch uncertainly, then pushed softly on the door.

173

"Dad?"

A few seconds passed, and then he called, "I'm in here."

His voice came from the study, where two men in dirty blue sweatshirts had picked up her father's desk and were carrying it out the French doors. The room was freezing, as if the doors had been open a long time, and the office supplies her father had taken out of the drawers and off the top of the desk were scattered across the floor and bookshelves.

Audrey was dumbfounded. "Are we moving?" she said.

"Yes," her father said, opening a cupboard and pulling out a box. He started dumping pens and CDs and paper clips into it even though it was a file box half full of papers.

"To where?"

"A place nearby. Don't worry. You won't have to change schools."

"I hate my school," Audrey said. "What I mind is changing houses."

He didn't look at her. In a strange, lifeless voice, he said, "We all have to give up things."

He scooped up the remaining clips and pens and framed photographs and set them on the leather chair. But the men had come back from the truck and were standing by the chair, waiting to take it. "Oh, for God's sake," he muttered, and tried to scrape up everything again. This time he set the bits and pieces in the trash can, and the men picked up the chair.

"Why didn't you at least tell me so we could pack?" Audrey asked. "I mean, did you decide we were moving *this morning?*"

It scared Audrey that her father was scrambling around his office with pens and paperweights. He was usually so organ-

174

ized. She felt as if she were having one of those nightmares where every door you open leads to a stranger world.

Audrey picked up a framed photograph of her mother to keep it from getting broken. "Are they taking all the furniture to the new house and then coming back for the little stuff?"

One of the men, the only one who was middle-aged, looked at her father when she asked that. Her father said, "Something like that," and looked dully at Audrey. The middle-aged mover turned to the guy standing next to him and said, "Let's roll up this rug now."

Audrey watched them begin to roll up the rug, which she knew from overheard conversations to be a hundred years old and authentically Persian, and heard heavy footsteps upstairs.

"Are they doing *my* room now?" Audrey asked suddenly. She hurried from the study, wondering if her father had actually gone crazy and what she would do if he had. She was starting to take the stairs two at a time when C.C. and Lea walked in the wide-open front door. C.C., who'd been unwinding her scarf, stopped. Lea stood absolutely still, a bag of chocolate chips in her hand. Finally, C.C. said slowly, "Why are the repo men here?"

Audrey looked at C.C. "They're not *repo* men," she said.

"Oh," C.C. said, and her cheeks pinkened. "It's just that my cousin Mark works for Anchor Brothers," she stammered. "I thought that's what he said they do. Maybe I've got it mixed up."

"My dad said we're moving, is all," Audrey said. A few minutes ago, moving had seemed like the most outrageous thing her father could do. Now she climbed into the idea as if it were a lifeboat.

"Why?" Lea asked. "I love this house."

Audrey didn't say anything.

"Where are you going?" C.C. asked.

"Somewhere nearby, my father said. It's a surprise, I guess."

Two men carried a velvet sofa to the doorway and waited for C.C. and Lea to move away from it. On the backs of their dark, dirty sweatshirts were dirty white anchors.

"You could ask them," Lea suggested. "They probably know where they're taking it all."

Audrey sensed the danger in this. She might learn her new address, or she might find out in front of C.C. and Lea that their furniture was, in fact, being repossessed, which meant her father had somehow gone broke. "I doubt it," Audrey said. "They probably just carry the furniture to some warehouse."

C.C. and Lea nodded. "It's freezing in here," Lea said.

Audrey glanced up the stairs. "Look, I have to finish packing. I don't think I can make cookies after all."

"Want us to help?" C.C. asked.

"No," Audrey said, trying to sound normal. "I'll just finish up and call you later, okay?" She looked back at them and realized she was about to cry.

"Okay," C.C. said, and she and Lea stepped uncertainly back. In a soft, regretful voice, Lea said, "Bye, Audrey."

After they left, Audrey moved stiffly up the stairs and then, at the door to her room, stopped short.

Chapter 44
Start-up

She couldn't believe it. She simply couldn't believe it.

Her mattress lay on the floor, and her clothes and bedding lay in a heap on top of the mattress. The dresser, nightstand, and mirror were already gone. The headboard and footboard were gone.

Audrey lay down on the pile of clothes and tried to make herself believe that all of these familiar things would be rearranged in another house as soon as tomorrow, and they would be hers again.

From down the hall, she could hear a man saying, "You're supposed to leave that lamp on. It's some kind of shrine or something."

"Why's the room empty?"

"No clue." He paused. "Okay, then. Let's hit the piano."

Audrey pulled some of the clothes and blankets over her and burrowed into the rest. She lay within the clothes for a long time, but couldn't get warm. Beyond her, heavy scraping sounds and bumps and grunts continued for a while, and then, finally, the house was still. She peered out of the blankets. The light was pale blue in her room, the color of twilight. She lay looking at the walls and remembering Oggy. Did Oggy know they were moving? Were the men taking Oggy's things, too?

"Audrey?" Her father, from downstairs.

Audrey didn't answer at first. He called again.

"Up here," Audrey said.

She sat up and straightened her hair. It seemed to take him a long time to climb the stairs. When he reached her doorway, he came in but didn't flip on the light. Instead, he crossed the room and stood looking out the window at the darkening blue roofs and white skiffs of old snow.

"I lost the house," he said.

Audrey didn't know what to say to this.

"I tried to save it, but that's how I lost it."

Audrey twisted the fringe of a scarf Oggy had knitted for her and wished very, very hard that Oggy were here to stop all of this.

"I was having trouble making the payments and doing the upkeep, so when this start-up company came to me with a proposal for spam-screening software, I thought, *This could really go somewhere*. And it could have. It was a brilliant idea."

Audrey twisted the fringe. She didn't want to hear this story. She wanted Oggy. She wanted her house, and her room, and the life that had always been hers.

"I helped the start-up guys pitch the software and business plan to my employers, but they passed. I felt they were wrong, so I invested myself." He sighed and stared off into the distance. "Some problems developed, and the start-up needed more money."

He'd taken a second mortgage on the house, whatever that meant. He'd sold jewelry. He'd sold the Jaguar. He'd tried to cut back on expenses. And then Mr. Maryonovich had found out he'd invested in the company.

Her father's shirt was white, almost glowing, against the blue of the window. Audrey was hungry now, besides being cold. She pulled on one blue mitten and tried to find the other one. "What's wrong with that?" she asked.

"It was in my employment contract. No private investing in projects presented to but declined by Maryonovich, Siegel and Greenbrier."

Her father was quiet.

From the next-door driveway, Audrey heard a car door slam, and then the engine started. "Be right back!" someone called—probably Mr. Key—but right now, to Audrey, it was just somebody completely different from her, somebody whose life was the same tonight as it had been this morning.

Her father said, "I was fired."

Fired? Her father fired? "When was this?"

Her father breathed deeply in, then out. "Almost a year ago."

A year ago? Audrey found the other mitten and pulled it on. "Then why'd you have to work late all the time?"

Another deep sigh. "Working at the start-up, trying to make it go."

Audrey clenched her mittened hands and waited.

"They filed for chapter eleven two weeks ago."

A silence, then Audrey said, "What about Oggy? When she comes back from Germany, she'll just follow us, right?"

Her father stared out the window and said nothing. Then he said, "I don't think we can afford to bring her back."

Audrey stood up with the mittens on and put Oggy's scarf around her neck. "That's not possible," she said. "Of course she'll come back."

Her father turned to look at her, then stared out at the darkening neighborhood.

"I can't promise that," her father said. Then: "It's just that keeping the house was my way of . . . keeping your mother. A poor way, probably, but . . ."

Audrey was glad the room was dark. She didn't want to see her father's face too clearly, or for him to see hers. She wondered what sort of place they were going to now, and if anyone—her mother, Oggy—could follow them there. No one would keep the light on in the window now, that was for sure.

To Audrey, it was as if all the important lights had just been switched off.

Chapter 45
The Visiting Hour

Clyde's Monday afternoon was no better. He had his book bag over his shoulder and was feeling better than he had in weeks when he reached the parking lot. The vase was done. It would have to dry now and then be fired, and then he could glaze it for the second firing. If everything went just right, both firings could be done by Christmas vacation.

When he got to his scooter, he noticed at once that its footpeg was wet. Which was strange, because although snow was banked at the sides of the lot, the asphalt was dry.

Clyde bent closer to look, then touched a finger to the wetness and brought his finger close to his nose.

"Would you call it 'uriniferous'?"

Clyde, turning, found himself face to face with Theo Driggs. Theo wasn't alone. Stepping out from behind a van and moving closer were four or five of his drones.

Theo moved close to him and pretended interest in the wetness. "Looks like some stray dog took a shine to your scooter." Then: "Looks like a lot of *product* there, though." Then: "Maybe it was a horse of some kind." He turned his smile now to Clyde. "Maybe even a horse's ass."

Clyde didn't say a thing, although he remembered it was the Biggest Horse's Ass award that Theo had won in *The Yellow Paper*. The cold was chafing, and Clyde's bare hands smarted.

Theo said, "So what do you know about *The Yellow Paper?*"

"What?" Clyde said. "I don't know anything about it."

Theo actually chuckled. "I think you do. I think you are a scooterist–slash–spineless yellow journalist."

"I don't know what you're talking about," Clyde said. He had an uneasy feeling that his words made him sound more guilty than innocent.

"I'm talking about a reliable source—a little rich girl who turned stoolie and sang your song."

"What?" Clyde said. Then: "Who?"

"A girl with long legs," Theo said. He looked away, and Clyde followed his gaze. On the horizon was a hilly park, gray-brown and subdued in the wintry air, its trees and bushes stripped. At its edge, two-story houses stuck out of the trees and absorbed what remained of the weak sunlight. Some of the windows were yellow with light, and smoke rose from two or three of the chimneys. Clyde wished he were in one of those houses.

Still looking out, Theo said, "Visiting hour is over."

Clyde was wondering what this meant when the first blows fell from behind.

He turned, and in the flurry and blur of flesh and fists and faces, Clyde tried to find Theo's nose and shot out a series of rights.

"Fight!" someone yelled from across the parking lot, and other voices began chiming in, too. "Fight!" "Fight!" "Fight!"

Chapter 46
Bearbaiting

Bare trees forked upward into the white sky.

This was what Clyde, lying on the ground, first became aware of when he opened his eyes—that, and the seepage of blood through his nose and into his mouth.

"Back off, juveniles," a deep male voice said. "The fun is over."

The tight circle of gawkers around Clyde and Theo loosened slightly, and the man with the deep voice stepped inside. He was one of the security guys, a black man. He looked down at Clyde's face and said, "Oh, Christ."

Behind him, kids still stood around—guys mostly, but girls, too, watching with bright eyes, their faces pink from the cold, their breath like fog.

The guard looked at Theo, who still stood with clenched fists, breathing heavily. Then the guard turned to the onlookers. "What happened here?"

"Just a fight," someone said, and then one of Theo's friends added, "That kid on the ground started it."

"Yeah, I believe that," said the guard, who clearly didn't. "Okay, why don't all you losers except Driggs find yourself a change of venue?" When nobody moved, he growled, "I'm talking *immediately.*"

The students began to move away, grudgingly peeling their

eyes away from Clyde on the ground. They all looked so *interested*, as if he were in one of those medieval street acts where someone came to town with a bear on a chain and people stood around watching a pack of dogs set loose to attack it.

He'd been the bear. He'd been the *it*.

He stared again at the long, spindly tree-fingers pointing up to the sky.

"Get up, Mumsford," the security guard said.

Clyde turned onto his side, breathing hard. He knelt, then stood. His legs felt boneless, ready to buckle.

"Well, I can only hope you screwups had fun," the guard said, "because now we go see Murchison to tote up the bill."

As Clyde took a first step forward, he touched a finger to his upper lip and brought it away smeared with blood.

Chapter 47
How Come

Murchison's office was as bright and clean as an operating room. Clyde and Theo had to sit in a kind of foyer listening to the buzz of the fluorescent tubes while they waited for their "guardians" to arrive. Theo's uncle arrived first, a heavyset man whose half-closed eyelids didn't disguise his pride in the obvious difference between Clyde's damage to Theo and Theo's damage to Clyde. Theo and his uncle went into Murchison's office and closed the door. After they left, Clyde was still waiting.

"Why don't you go wash up before your dad sees you?" Murchison said.

Clyde walked to the bathroom, where he got the blood off his face, but his shirt was hopeless. He tried not to look at himself again, or to touch his swollen eye, or to think about Theo Driggs. He returned to the brown vinyl chairs and closed his eyes until he heard the door open. His father was here. Now he would see.

His father didn't say anything, though. He followed Clyde into the office and listened to Mr. Murchison describe the school policy on fighting, and the number of days—three— Clyde would be suspended. "I understand," his father said, and signed the papers put in front of him.

Clyde stood—gingerly, painfully—and shouldered his knapsack.

As they walked down the hall together, his father put an arm around Clyde and said gently, "So what did the other guy look like?"

"Like he won," Clyde said. His nose hurt when he talked, and there was pain in his teeth. "I can ride the Vespa home," he said.

"Not with one eye you can't," his father said. Then: "So what happened?"

Clyde stared ahead. "I don't really know."

His father gave him a mild let's-not-play-games look, and Clyde gazed down the long, empty hallway. "It's just a guy who's always hated me."

His father took this in. "How come he doesn't like you?"

"Yeah, well, I asked him that once. He said I *uglified* his view."

"Uglified it?"

Clyde shrugged. The gesture made him aware of a deep pain in his ribs.

"I can't leave my Vespa here all night," he said. "Someone'll steal it."

His father said, "We'll come back with Mr. Heathrow's truck." Another tenant in their building.

His father pushed open the school door and they walked out into the twilight. There were halos of frozen air around the yellow sodium lights.

They drove a few blocks in silence, then his father said, "So what's this kid's name—the one whose view you uglify?"

"Theo Driggs," Clyde said, and immediately wished he hadn't.

His father gave him a quick look. "Don't I know that name?"

Clyde knew his father might not figure this out, but probably he would, and, besides, he didn't feel like lying right now. He said, "Theo Driggs was one of the people I was doing, you know, research on with your computer."

His father turned to Clyde. "Was that part of the problem here?"

It would have been part of the problem if Clyde had found anything about Theo, or if he'd written *The Yellow Paper*, but he hadn't, no matter what anybody thought.

"No," Clyde said, "my looking him up had nothing to do with it."

Chapter 48
To Help His Mother Out

Clyde woke up at six the next morning, the first day of his suspension. It was dark outside, and it was cold in the room. He touched a finger to a lower tooth, slightly loose, and the source of sharp pain when experimentally tapped. The rest of him didn't feel that great, either.

Clyde pulled the covers to his chin and went through a logical process he'd been through a dozen times since the fight. Someone had told Theo that he, Clyde Mumsford, was the Yellow Man. Theo had said that this someone was a rich girl. A long-legged rich girl. And the fight occurred only hours after his giving Audrey Reed the stuff about Wickham Hill.

So it was Audrey Reed. It *had* to be Audrey Reed.

It didn't matter how many times Clyde went through this reasoning; the conclusion was always the same, and always just as depressing. How could Audrey have thought he wrote that stuff? And how could Audrey, who he'd liked a lot, and who he'd only wanted to help—how could she have turned him over to Theo?

Clyde wanted to get up, but dreaded leaving his room. His mother had been asleep when he'd come home the night before. She hadn't seen his face yet.

Probably his father had prepared her, but then again, maybe not.

Clyde lay back in bed, turned his extended hands outward, and opened his fingers into what he hoped might be a Zen-like pose. After closing his eyes, he willed his mind to go white, which it would not do—until it did. Clyde was asleep.

At 8:15, he awoke to a knock at the apartment door.

"Marian?" his mother said.

Clyde heard the front door creak open and a cheerful female voice called something that sounded like, "Aye, nane ither!"

"Oh, good," his mother said.

Whoever Marian was, she was jabbering away in the front room even though his mother was hardly responding. Clyde eased himself out of bed, picked out a flannel shirt and buttoned it over a sizable purplish bruise, then tried to sneak into the bathroom so he could wash his face. But when he pushed open the bathroom door, the stranger was there, rummaging through a drawer. She was middle-aged, trim, and wore a bright floral smock, the kind nurses wore in hospitals. Her cheeks were ruddy and her smile spanned a face that seemed unusually broad.

"You must be Clyde," she said. "You're looking no weel, son."

Clyde liked the sound of her voice, but he had no idea what she was saying. That he was or wasn't looking real? He decided not to say anything.

"Been playin' shinty?" she asked.

"Shinty?"

"It's like hockey on dirt."

Clyde pictured himself on the ground below the watching crowd. "Dirt was involved, yeah," he said.

She touched his chin—she smelled heavily of lavender—and studied his face with medical interest. He risked a glance sideways and in the mirror saw his own reddened eye looking back at him through swollen, yellowish lids.

"So who *are* you?" he ventured, keeping his voice low.

From her expression, the question surprised her. "I'm Marian from the hospice, dearie," she said, touching his arm in a friendly way. "Did your father no tell ye?"

"I guess." Clyde had heard his father discussing hospice, but he couldn't remember what it meant. Some kind of nursing care, he thought.

"I've been comin' in for aboot a week."

"For what?"

She looked at him a moment, then seemed to make some kind of decision. "Well, right noo I'm awa to wash your mother's hair with een of these"—she held up two shampoo bottles and read a little from each label. "We can either invigorate fine, lazy hair or . . . calm stressed, anxious hair." She smiled at Clyde. "Fit de ye think?"

Clyde took a moment to translate. Hair was involved, clearly, and shampoo promises. He thought of his mother's hair—singed, it seemed to him, by the chemical meant to kill her cancer. "The anxious one," he said finally.

"Clyde?" his mother called back from the living room.

Clyde turned and called, "In here, Mom."

"Let me look at you."

He stood, wooden.

"On ye go," Marian said in an encouraging voice. "I'm just getting some hot water fae the bath."

As he approached his mother's bed, she craned her head

to see, but almost at once her eyes filled with tears and she let her head drop gently back on the mountain of pillows. "Pretty bad," she said, holding out her hand for him to take. "Your father made it sound like just a black eye. Something boyish." She stared at him again. "But this . . ." Her voice trailed off.

"It looks worse than it feels, Mom. It's not that bad, really." Then, smiling painfully, "I was never going to get the Cary Grant roles anyway."

"Yes, you were," she said. Then, in a more decisive voice: "And you still will."

From the bathroom could be heard the staccato sound of water filling a plastic tub.

"Why's that Irishwoman here?" he said in a lowered voice.

"Scottish."

Clyde gave a painful shrug. "So what is she doing here?"

His mother looked away and seemed to choose her words carefully. "She's here to help me out."

"Help you out with what?"

In an odd voice she said, "That's all. Just help me out."

She'd been looking off toward the big window but now she turned to Clyde, and as soon as her eyes were on him, they brimmed again with tears. "I'm sorry," she said, looking away from him again. "I'm sorry, sweetie."

Marian entered with a plastic tub shaped like the sinks in hair salons. "Help me clear this table, will ye, Clyde?"

Clyde picked up cookbooks and cooking magazines, a tissue box, and two half-empty glasses of water. Marian began to remove pillows and arrange towels, a complex arrangement she worked like a familiar puzzle. Finally his mother leaned back on the towels and closed her eyes, and Clyde turned to go.

"I want to hear about this Theo person," his mother said.

Clyde stopped. "Nothing to tell," he said.

"Dis he play for the ither team?" Marian asked.

"That's pretty much it," Clyde said, because it seemed, suddenly, as true as true could be. "He plays for the ither team."

When she heard Clyde's accent, his mother started to laugh—a full, genuine laugh that made her chest heave beneath the sheets. Marian seemed so pleased with his mother's laughter that she laughed along good-naturedly, too.

"Noo then," Marian said when the laughter subsided. "Nae mare kiddin' on."

Clyde turned quickly away and went into the kitchen. He'd remembered suddenly what "hospice" meant. It meant the very last stage. Hospice workers came to help you die. To help you *out*.

He leaned on the sink, trying to occupy himself with the childhood game of alphabetizing the things outside the window: *asphalt, bucket, Corolla, dirt.*

In the other room, Marian began talking about the laziness of his mother's hair and what this alfalfa shampoo intended to do "aboot it."

Ice, junk, kettle, lilac. The lilac bush by the fence held granules of ice in its clustered branches. It wasn't going to bloom for at least five months. He couldn't wait that long. Maybe he couldn't even wait until Christmas.

"Alfalfa sounds nice," his mother said, her voice quiet. "I can't really smell anything now, so you make me smell good, Marian, okay?"

His mother and the deathwoman sounded like old friends. Clyde stared out the kitchen window. It was starting to snow outside, tiny white bits that lay for only a moment on the wet wood of the windowsill before disappearing. He poured a glass of orange juice and pressed the cold carton to his cheek. He picked up the phone book and turned to F for florists. His mother loved any kind of flower, and he had his tip money. When his mother fell asleep, he'd buy the nicest flowers they had in the shop and set them on her table in full view, so they'd be the first thing she saw when she opened her eyes. For the time being, an old vase would just have to do.

Chapter 49
Take-out

That same Tuesday, four hours after school ended, Audrey Reed and her father parked behind a yellow-brick apartment building on Genesee and started carrying boxes of clothes up a concrete ramp. Her father propped open the heavy metal fire door and led her to an ancient elevator, which they packed so full of boxes that they barely had room to stand. The apartment was on the third floor, at the far end of a well-lighted hallway, freshly carpeted. When her father unlocked the door marked 3-E, Audrey walked slowly in.

The floor was wood. The doorknobs were glass. The walls had recently been painted white. Audrey set down a box of sweaters and went to the radiator, which she touched with a flattened palm. It was warm and ticking.

Her father carried his box into the kitchen, and she heard him set it down. He stepped into the living room, looked around, and gave Audrey an apologetic look. "Pretty grim, huh?"

"No," Audrey said, "it's not that bad. And it'll look a lot better when the Anchor Brothers bring the furniture."

Her father didn't comment on this. Audrey leaned on the radiator and felt the warmth spread through her legs. "So, how many bedrooms does it have?" She was hoping there were three, which would leave one for Oggy.

Her father hesitated. Then: "Just two."

"Oh," she said. "Two."

"But it's just for the time being," he said. "Things will get better."

Oggy was seventy-four. Audrey wondered how fast things would get better, and she almost said so, but her father looked so depressed that she decided she had to say something cheerful. "It's like one of those apartments you see in ads. You know, where a hunky guy and a girl are lying on the floor, eating take-out Chinese among a few tasteful boxes and a ladder."

"Well," her father said, "the take-out Chinese we could manage. But I haven't been hunky since 1973."

"Sure, you have," Audrey said, though he didn't look so hunky now. His black hair had turned gray, and he looked haggard. His shirts were loose on him, and the cloth on the collar was pilled where it rubbed against his neck. Audrey moved toward him and threw an arm over his shoulder. "Now let's go bring in the tasteful boxes."

Setting up the apartment that night was a little better. Audrey pretended she was playing house. Nothing was permanent, she reminded herself. She was just making do. A box could be a nightstand, and her mother's china could go into the built-in, glass-knobbed hutch, and they could camp out for a while.

Audrey even began to picture what it would be like to live with Wickham in an apartment just like this one, to walk to her college classes and then lie on the floor with him and eat take-out Chinese. That's what she was thinking about that night when she finally fell asleep.

Chapter 50
Breaking the News

Audrey forced herself to tell C.C. and Lea about the new apartment on Wednesday when they met at the lockers before the first bell. Audrey expected pity, but Lea said "an apartment" sounded chic.

"Do you have a buzzer?" C.C. asked.

Audrey nodded, and C.C. said, "So, Audrey, honey, we can come to the door downstairs, buzz you, and be buzzed up?"

"Uh-huh," Audrey said. "Unless I decide you're unbuzzable."

This led to a free-ranging discussion of who in the world was unbuzzable (Theo Driggs and Sands Mandeville) and buzzable (Mark Strauss). "And Wickham," Lea said to Audrey in her soft voice. "Wickham is definitely buzzable."

"What about a trash incinerator?" C.C. asked. "Can we throw things down a chute?"

"No incinerator. But you should see the elevator. It's one of those metal-cage kinds from the nineteenth century. I feel like Lily Bart when I get in it." (When they'd read *House of Mirth* at the Tate School, they'd all gone through a Lily Bart phase.)

"Über-urban," C.C. concluded, and Lea added, "Très Über."

Telling Wickham about her moving was somehow harder.

She blurted it out between first and second period, trying to make the arrival of the repo men seem like a funny story.

But Wickham didn't laugh. "I'm not sure I'm with you here," he said. "They're going to auction off your house?"

Audrey nodded.

Wickham seemed hardly to believe it. He looked away. "That was a great house," he said, more to himself than to her. Then, in a voice so thin it seemed brittle, he said, "I'm really, really sorry."

Audrey shrugged. "It was always too much, anyway. Too much space, too much carved wood, too much history." She made a smile. "The only thing I'm worried about is Oggy."

"Oggy?" he asked.

"Oggy," Audrey said. "You know. The woman who took care of me after my mother died."

But when she looked at Wickham, it was hard to tell what she was looking at. He was here physically, but he seemed to be somewhere else. She thought suddenly of Jade Marie Creamer and wondered if Wickham was thinking of her, too.

"Can you come over and see the apartment after school?" she said.

Wickham's eyes came back into focus. "Sure," he said. "Maybe not today, but sure." And his face went vague again.

"Is there something wrong?" Audrey said.

He shook his head. "It's just that I'm, you know, worried about you."

Audrey had the strange feeling that this wasn't quite true, and there followed a miserable silence, which Wickham finally ended by changing the subject. "So did you hear what happened to your friend the busboy?"

"Clyde Mumsford? He's not my friend."

Wickham shrugged as if he didn't quite believe this. "He got suspended."

Audrey felt a prickling in her stomach. So that's why Clyde hadn't been in class yesterday. "Why?"

"Fighting Theo Driggs in the parking lot." He chuckled lazily—a laugh-version of a drawl. "I guess Theo pretty much tenderized him."

"Why?" Audrey asked again, her stomach heavy now.

Wickham shrugged and looked around, as if he were anxious to get going. Without looking at Audrey, he said, "Since when does Theo need a reason?"

The tardy bell rang, and Wickham seemed happy to have an excuse to go. Around them, students everywhere moved into hurry mode, and Wickham, backing away from Audrey, said, "Later."

He turned and fell in with the stream of students moving away from her.

"See you in physics," she called, but Wickham didn't seem to hear.

Chapter 51
See Me

Most teachers would have waited until after Thanksgiving to hand back essays, but not Mrs. Leacock. She had them graded two days after receiving them. Wednesday, November 26, was a half day and everyone was jittery, ready to be off. Some kids were already absent—the lucky ones who were flying to relatives' houses or ski resorts or Florida condominiums. Mrs. Leacock was not in a holiday mood. She wore a familiar light blue sweater and a blue stone pendant that swung from a black silk cord. Audrey watched the pendant swing as Mrs. Leacock called out names and walked from aisle to aisle.

Usually you could tell by the student's face if the grade was good or bad: flushed cheeks and a small, victorious smile, or flushed cheeks and a look of disappointment or even resentment, followed by the flipping of pages to read marginal comments. Audrey waited with more than usual nervousness for the sound of her own name as Mrs. Leacock's blue stone pendant swayed. "Greg Telman," she said. "Leslie Poll."

Audrey licked her lips and studied the backs of her hands, which always cracked this time of year. Tiny white lines crisscrossed her knuckles.

"Audrey Reed."

Audrey felt herself flush, and when she took the essay from

Mrs. Leacock, she saw first the frozen expression on Mrs. Leacock's face, and then the sentence written in red marker: *Please see me after class.*

Audrey sat down as Wickham's name was called. She flipped through the pages of her essay and saw no grade, no marginal comments. *Bad,* she thought. *This is bad.*

As Wickham walked back down the aisle with his paper in hand, he looked as he always looked—comfortable with himself, and pleased with his place in the world—but that, she knew by now, was just Wickham: he might have had an A plus on his paper, or he might have had an F.

Everywhere kids were paging through their essays and stuffing books into bags, which might have provided cover for Audrey to turn and ask Wickham what he'd gotten, but when she glanced up at Mrs. Leacock's desk, Mrs. Leacock's frozen eyes were fixed on her.

The bell rang and there was the usual crush of students in the aisles, hauling sweaters and overloaded bags. Mrs. Leacock was still staring her way, so Audrey couldn't even turn around to look at Wickham. She stood up slowly, and as she walked to the front of the room, she became aware that Wickham was doing the same. He followed her all the way to the desk. Audrey's stomach clenched tighter. He'd received the same message, then.

Mrs. Leacock watched them approach. She didn't smile or say hello, or even take a deep breath. She just said, "So who wrote these essays?"

Audrey, panicked and confused, felt like blurting something out, but Wickham said, in a pleasant voice, "What do you mean?"

"I mean that we have two papers signed with two names written in one voice, a voice that I know pretty well at this point in the term. What I'd like to know is what Audrey's voice is doing in your paper."

"Oh, that," Wickham said. "I can see where the misunderstanding—"

Mrs. Leacock held up one hand. "If you don't mind, Mr. Hill, I'd like to hear what Audrey has to say first. Could you step outside the room?"

Wickham looked at Audrey. His eyes were transmitting strength. Strength to lie, or strength to make a good case for the truth? She didn't know. She knew he was good at making muddy water clear, but she wasn't. She'd always told people too much, had always bubbled over with explanations and tangential details, a habit that made her father sigh and say, "You're just too honest."

Wickham strolled out into the hall.

"And close the door behind you," Mrs. Leacock said.

"Yes, ma'am," he said, and after giving Audrey one last encouraging look, he shut the door.

Mrs. Leacock slid the blue stone back and forth along the silken cord. "Why don't you pull up a chair, Audrey?"

There weren't any chairs, only heavy desk-and-chair units. As Audrey pulled one over, it vibrated loudly across the linoleum. Sitting in it made her feel small.

"Okay," Mrs. Leacock said. "Tell me the process by which these two papers were written."

Audrey watched the blue stone go back and forth. She opened her mouth. "How they were written," she said, trying not to panic.

Mrs. Leacock nodded, looking impatient.

"Wickham came over to my house," Audrey said. "He doesn't have a computer, so I let him use mine to do research and write his paper." She touched a finger to her cheek. Was her cheek that warm, or was her hand cold? Probably both.

"All right," Mrs. Leacock said. "And?"

"And he printed it there."

"And you had what kind of input into the way it was written?" Mrs. Leacock asked. She'd let go of the blue stone, but now she absently turned the ring on her hand. Her expression was detached, impassive, cold.

"I read it," Audrey said, fumbling now. "And I . . . I had some ideas about making it smoother." Then: "I shouldn't have helped him, I guess."

If Mrs. Leacock recognized the conciliatory note in Audrey's voice, she didn't show it. She merely said, "And how did you present these 'ideas'?"

Audrey couldn't bring herself to say that she rewrote his paper. It was too terrible. She didn't want to say it, and she didn't want it to be true. "I gave him suggestions for editing it," she said, surprised at the lie but also grateful that she had thought of it. "I helped him fix the grammar and add descriptive details."

"Meaning you wrote, like a teacher, in the margins, and he used your comments to revise the paper on your computer?"

Audrey so intensely wanted this to be true that she almost believed it. "Uh-huh," she said, without looking Mrs. Leacock in the face. She nodded slightly, and blushed. Surely Mrs. Leacock would see she was lying.

Mrs. Leacock was silent for a few seconds. "You realize I'm now going to talk to Wickham alone."

Audrey nodded, and stared at the corduroy knees of her pants.

Mrs. Leacock stood up and went to the door. "Your turn, Wickham," she said, and signaled Audrey to take his place in the hall.

In passing, Wickham smiled at her, looking unworried, and Audrey gave him a solemn look in return.

The hall was cold. She couldn't hear their conversation through the door, and she didn't dare look through the window at them. She leaned against the wall and rubbed her fingernails obsessively across the brown corduroy surface of her thighs. The bell had rung, and students were at lunch. Bits of trash—candy wrappers, an empty plastic cup, a ticket stub—lay at her feet. She checked her watch once, twice, three times. She jumped when suddenly the doorknob turned, and Mrs. Leacock stepped out.

"You may go," she said. Her expression was, if anything, even colder than before. "I need to look at these papers again, and I'll give them back to you on Monday."

Audrey nodded, feeling sick and close to tears. Mrs. Leacock hadn't been fooled, and she, Audrey Reed, was going to fail, or be expelled, or who knew what. Audrey looked shakily at Wickham, who lifted a hand and smiled. Then he strolled away from them both.

Audrey picked up her backpack; murmured, "Thank you" to Mrs. Leacock; and then, walking off in the opposite direction so that she didn't seem to be Wickham's co-conspirator, wondered what there had been to thank Mrs. Leacock for.

Chapter 52
Something Wrong

Wickham sauntered up to Audrey's locker a few minutes later.

"So what did you tell her?" Audrey asked.

"Same thing you did." Wickham grinned. "I listened through a plastic cup."

"What plastic cup?"

"The one right there on the floor."

"That actually works?"

He shrugged. "More or less, yeah."

"So you heard what I said, and said basically the same thing."

"Hey, it's what I would have said anyway."

This might have been enough to convince Audrey, except for the memory of Mrs. Leacock's frozen expression. "But she still doesn't believe us," Audrey said. "I think we're in big trouble here."

Wickham stiffened. "Why?" he asked in a cold voice. "If you'd written in the margin and I'd taken your suggestions and printed the paper myself, how would it be different? You just eliminated the step where I, like some chimpanzee, make the changes." He stared off, his face handsome even in annoyance. "And like I said before, any kid in this school with a college-educated parent is getting more help than that on every paper."

There was something wrong here; Audrey could feel it. She waited a few seconds and said quietly, "What's wrong, Wickham? It's like you not only don't care what Mrs. Leacock thinks about all this, but you don't care what I think, either." She paused. "It's like you're mad at both of us."

This prompted the reappearance of the Wickham she loved. "No," he said, softening his voice and slipping an arm around her waist. "I'm a little torqued with Mrs. Peacock, sure, but how could I be mad at you? None of this was your fault." He nipped her ear and said in a whispery drawl, "You were just trying to help me."

Audrey found herself thinking again of a college apartment where she would live with the very same Wickham who was everything she'd ever wanted, and just like that, everything was clear again. She pushed everything that bothered her to the edges of her mind—or tried to—and wrapped her arms around Wickham, closing her eyes so that the world as he saw it was all she could see.

Chapter 53
A Situation, Colonel

Thanksgiving came and went. Audrey and her father went to a great-aunt's house in Cortland. Audrey had invited Wickham, whose mother was working that day, but he said she should just come over with a piece of pie when she got back. "Nothing like a great-aunt's house to bring on a migraine," he'd said.

He seemed to be avoiding her apartment, always suggesting that she come to his house. Audrey, for her part, avoided the subject of Jade Marie. *Don't ask*, she told herself. And silently, to him, she said, *Don't tell*.

On the Monday after Thanksgiving, the moment Audrey dreaded finally arrived. Mrs. Leacock asked to see them after class. "I do not have good news," she said briskly, holding the two papers out.

Audrey felt her stomach drop. The papers were folded open to pages three and four, and in both, several phrases had been circled in red pencil.

"There are just too many verbal similarities," she said. Audrey read a circled phrase in one paper: *Heretofore the tide had been against him*. She saw that Mrs. Leacock had circled *Heretofore* in the other paper. Both papers also contained *ebullient*, *pilloried*, and several identical phrases.

Mrs. Leacock pressed her lips together, then said, "You will both need to write these papers over, in longhand, after school on Monday, December 15, so that I can watch your personal handwriting flow across the page. It will behoove you to choose different subjects, naturally, and you can bring your research materials with you—books, notes, et cetera, et cetera."

Audrey waited. She could tell there was more to come, and there was.

"What cannot be undone," Mrs. Leacock said, "is the damage to your citizenship grades. You will both receive a U in this class, and while I suspect this will cause little discomfort to you, Mr. Hill, I'm afraid that in Audrey's case, this means I cannot recommend her for the Honor Society"—she paused and let her eyes fall directly on Audrey—"as I had, with pleasure, planned to do."

Audrey blinked and nodded, not risking a word. Her throat tightened, and she was afraid she would cry. Audrey turned, folded the paper, and went blindly through the doorway. In the hall, Wickham caught up with her and said, "Well, that could've been worse."

In a dull voice, Audrey said, "Really? How?"

"Let me count the ways . . . ," Wickham began, but Audrey, numbly, said, "No, Wickham, not now," and turned and headed off.

As she walked, she saw nothing, heard nothing, felt nothing.

"Hello in there?" It was like a voice calling into a cave, and it came again. "Hello in there?"

Audrey stopped and stared at the boy in front of her for a moment before realizing it was Brian.

Into his cupped hand, as if it were a microphone, Brian said, "We've got a situation here, Colonel."

Audrey just stared at him. He was wearing his reggae cap, and pea-sized earphones were wrapped around his neck. Into his cupped hand, he said, "Sleepwalker in lion's den. Repeat, code red, sleepwalker in lion's den."

Audrey stared at him and said, "Leave me alone, Brian."

She walked on, but Brian overtook her. "Whoa," he said softly, as if gentling an animal. "Whoa, now."

She stopped, and the moment she looked into Brian's eyes, her own eyes began to moisten. Brian touched a finger to her face, and it was as if a button had been pushed. Tears flooded down her cheeks.

"What?" Brian said softly. "What?"

Audrey tried to calm herself, sniffing and wiping one cheek with her sleeve. "Sorry," she said.

"Nothing to be sorry for," Brian said. Then: "So what is it?"

"Mrs. Leacock just accused me and Wickham of cheating. I helped him with a paper and . . ." She didn't know how to put it. "We both have to do the papers over now."

Brian stiffened, then took her paper and leafed through it. "Why'd she circle this stuff?"

"Because those words were in Wickham's paper, too."

Audrey knew she should have explained more completely, but she felt too sick and ashamed to go into the details. More tears leaked down her face.

Brian seemed oddly angry. "So, what, like you can't use the same words in two papers? Since when do people get exclusive rights to a word?"

"Well, it was a combination of things," Audrey said, and

began to search for a tissue in her pocket. Maybe she'd get straight U's in citizenship. Maybe she wouldn't even get into Syracuse.

"This isn't right," Brian said. "You should appeal to the ombudsman or something."

Audrey wiped her nose with a ragged tissue and shrugged, but Brian was serious in a way she'd never seen him before. "You don't deserve this, Aud."

"But I do," Audrey said. "That's the bad part. I do. Just forget it, Brian. I got what was coming to me, and now I have to live with it."

Brian stood holding the bent, red-marked paper and shook his head. "No," he said, almost to himself, his face set and hard. "This is wrong."

Audrey took the paper from his hands, balled it up, and threw it in a trash barrel painted with a bargeman and the words GIVE A HOOT!

"Forget it, Bry," she said, touching his arm. "That's what I'm going to try to do."

But Brian didn't change his serious expression—which, Audrey thought later, should have been her first clue.

Chapter 54
The Commodore

Audrey was tired of avoiding things. She was tired of avoiding Clyde, who always looked up, then away, when she came into Patrice's class. She was tired of the excuses Wickham gave for not studying at her apartment. She was tired of pretending she'd never heard about the car accident.

It was the Friday before the makeup essay, two weeks before Christmas. Snow was falling again, and as she drove herself and Wickham home through the whitening neighborhoods, she said suddenly, "Let's go to my apartment."

"Now?" Wickham asked. "We might get snowed in."

"Come on. You've never seen it." She drove slowly straight ahead, passed Wickham's street, followed a bus for blocks without wanting to pass, and then, finally, after making a left onto a street of bland, blockish apartment buildings, she parked in front of her own.

"Home-a-jig," she said cheerfully, trying for her father's tone.

The asphalt sidewalk led between two stunted firs to a blue awning that read COMMODORE. It was only four o'clock, but the front light had come on, and while Audrey was looking for her key to the front door, Wickham stood silently beside her. He had his hands in his pockets and his scarf pulled tight around his neck. His cheeks were attractively pink, as in a J.Crew ad.

"It's not that bad, is it?" Audrey asked, finally locating her key.

"What?"

Audrey pointed up. "The building. The double-hung windows. I love it that there are three together in the living room."

Wickham gave a quick upward glance. "Yeah," he said. "That's nice."

They walked silently into the cavernous lobby, a tiled room without furniture or plants. Someone had set up a fake Christmas tree in the corner, and it was unevenly hung with red satin balls. One wall was lined with locker-style mailboxes, and Audrey went to open hers, saying, "My dad says this tile is called 'hex tile.' And that along the edges is a pattern called Greek key." There was no letter inside the box from Oggy, and no catalogs, either. Just throwaway flyers for things like pizzas and refitted windows.

As she threw the flyers away, Audrey noticed that the hex tile she was bragging about was smeared with muddy boot prints. She led Wickham to the elevator, calling it the Lily Bart Memorial Lift ("Lily who?" he asked without interest), and was just trying to close the heavy brass gate when Beck, the maintenance man, came clomping down the stairs in a pair of work boots and a torn Black Sabbath sweatshirt.

"Hey," Beck said, taking a drag on a stubby cigarette, "I found a table for you. Down in the basement. If you have a sec, I can show you."

Audrey flushed. Her father had finally confessed that the furniture had been repossessed and they weren't getting it back. Beck had come up the night before to fix a toilet problem (and smoke a cigarette), and he'd noticed (as anyone would) that she and her father were eating off a makeshift table—boxes covered with a tablecloth. After accepting a plate of moo goo gai pan, he'd offered to scout around for a kitchen table because he came across a lot of loose furniture in the course of his work. Midnight move-outs, he'd said, tended to leave stuff behind.

"We can do it later, if you want," Audrey said uncomfortably to Beck. She neither opened nor latched the gate. "You're probably busy."

"Well, now would actually be better, because I'm heading up to Oswego after this."

"Okay," Audrey said. She wondered if she should do an introduction, but Beck had snuffed out his cigarette in a pedestal ashtray and was already heading down the stairs.

The Commodore's basement was the most medieval room Audrey had ever seen. There were windows, but they were small, high up, and dirty. A single bulb illuminated the front part of the long, stony room, where a coin-operated washer and dryer stood slightly askew on the uneven floor. They worked fine, but Audrey had done exactly one load before locating a Fluff-n-Fold a few blocks away.

"Creepy little Laundromat you've got here, Beck," she said.

Beck grinned and said she wasn't the first to remark on that. "One tenant, her name was Erica, called it a psycho's dream come true. She thought we should call it Blood-n-Suds." A pause; then, deadpan: "Erica's been missing a couple months now."

Audrey laughed, but when Wickham didn't, she turned the subject back to the table.

"Over there," Beck said, pointing beyond the dryer to a

chrome-legged, Formica-topped table. "Pretty cool, no? It's vintage diner."

"It's nice," Audrey said, though it wasn't, not really. The Formica was scratched, and one leg had been repaired with duct tape. Still, it was a table.

Beck lit another cigarette and offered one to Wickham, who, to Audrey's surprise, seemed to consider taking it before shaking his head no.

"Give me a hand, will ya?" Beck said to Wickham, who seemed reluctant to touch anything down there. As they jockeyed the table out, Beck asked Wickham his name.

"Wickham."

"Anybody call you Wick?"

"Not really," he said in a not-quite-frosty tone, the same tone he'd used with Clyde Mumsford the night she'd introduced them at the country club.

They carried the table up to the elevator and then, on the third floor, maneuvered their way through Audrey's door. The apartment was blissfully warm, as usual, and Audrey relaxed a little. Wickham and Beck put the table down in a little alcove by the kitchen and Beck, tapping ash into his hand, said he was off to Oswego.

After Beck left, Wickham looked around and said, "Is it always this hot in here?" He took off his scarf, coat, hat, and sweater. He sat down on a floor cushion by the windows. "I think the janitor has a thing for you," he said, but without the playfulness he normally used for a remark like this.

"That seems doubtful." She went into the kitchen, mixed cocoa with some water in a saucepan, and lit one of the burners. Wickham sat in the front room, glaring out the window.

"Can you believe that thing with Leacock?" he said finally. "And you know what it comes down to? She thinks I'm too stupid to have written that paper. That's what she's thinking."

"It's my fault," Audrey said, her stomach clenching at the reminder. She wished Wickham would come into the kitchen so they could talk properly.

"It's the whole Southern thing. Yankees believe we're rubes, and then they do whatever they have to do to prove themselves right."

"Could you come in here?" Audrey said. "I'm making hot chocolate and I can't hear you very well."

"Hot chocolate," Wickham said, walking slowly into the kitchen and sitting on the red wooden chair her father had found at St. Vincent de Paul. "What I need is a cold beer. It feels like August in here."

Audrey stirred the cocoa with a sense of dread. It boiled, and she added milk.

"Do you miss South Carolina?" Audrey asked, thinking for the hundredth time of Jade Marie Creamer.

"Sometimes I do, yeah," Wickham said sullenly.

"Now?"

"Yeah, sure. A little."

"What do you miss?" She thought of Schrödinger's Cat again, but she was part of it now, was one of the scientists in lab coats gathered around the steel box.

"I don't know," Wickham said. "The weather, I guess. And some friends."

"Like who?" She knew it was a mistake, but she couldn't stand the uncertainty any longer.

Wickham paused and gave her a measuring look. "You sound like you're hunting for something here."

Audrey poured hot cocoa into two mugs, but when she handed Wickham his, he set it on the counter untouched.

Audrey took a sip and burned her tongue. "I want to know what people you miss," she said, plaintively, and took a deep breath before adding, "and why you don't have a driver's license."

His eyes registered this. "What makes you think I don't?"

Audrey touched the burned surface of her tongue to the roof of her mouth. She couldn't bring herself to say Jade's name. "Well, do you?"

"No." His voice was low. "What difference does it make?"

"None," Audrey said, her anguish growing. The snow was falling outside the kitchen window in thick, heavy flakes. It was like the snowfall at the beginning of things, hushed and pure. "Someone gave me a newspaper story about an accident that happened in Cypress," she went on. She looked into her cocoa and tightened her grip on the cup. "An accident that killed a girl named Jade Marie Creamer."

His expression didn't change, unless it became more set in its stoniness.

"I know it wasn't your fault," she said earnestly. "I just wanted you to know that the story is out there, and people might get it wrong."

Wickham turned to stare out at the falling snow. He still hadn't touched his mug of cocoa, and she realized he hadn't touched her all afternoon. In a sullen voice, without looking at her, he said, "I'll tell you the story, if that's what you want.

But it won't make any difference. Those people who want to get it wrong will make sure they get it wrong."

"I know," Audrey said, "but I'm not one of those people."

He fixed his eyes on her and gave her a significant look. "And this is what you want?"

What did Audrey want besides Wickham? She nodded and managed to say, "Yes." Then she closed her eyes, and the door to the steel chamber swung open.

Chapter 55
Wickham's Version

It was completely dark outside now, and the snow fell past the window in huge, somnolent flakes. Wickham didn't immediately speak. He folded his arms, then unfolded them. The radiators ticked and gave off a peculiar smell, like a curling iron wrapped around hair.

"Okay, then," Wickham said, staring off as if at some distant place. "Jade was in the front seat, seat belt on. Same with me; same with Boze and Herffman, the two guys in the backseat." Pause. "It was a sunny day."

For a moment he just stared silently.

"I hadn't had anything to drink. Nothing. Boze and Herffman had had some beers, but Jade and I hadn't."

Wickham rubbed at a worn spot on his jeans, and Audrey, taking a sip of her cocoa, felt an overwhelming sensation of relief. He hadn't been drinking, and if he hadn't been drinking, how could he have been at fault?

"Jade wasn't my girlfriend or anything," he went on. "She was Boze's cousin, and the other guy, Herffman, had a thing for her, but she wasn't interested in him, probably because he's an idiot. But I was talking to her, and she seemed to be enjoying herself, and that got on Herffman's nerves."

Audrey remembered Wickham in the hallway with Sands Mandeville and the way Sands had touched his arm and laughed. She felt a stab of pointless jealousy, and could sympathize with Herffman.

"Herffman started mouthing off and being a complete ass, and I could tell Jade didn't like it. I was smoking, and he was saying the smoke was just one of the several pollutive emissions I brought into the car. I looked at him in the rearview and said, 'You know, maybe we ought to pull over so we could settle this thing,' but Boze—he was always the peacemaker—Boze calmed us down and I kept driving. But Jade, you know, I think at this point she just wanted to jerk Herffman's chain, so she undid her seat belt and scooched closer to me, and of course Herffman says something really crude, and that was when I made a terrible mistake."

He looked for an instant at Audrey, then beyond her.

"Two mistakes, actually. I sped up, and then I twisted around to say something to Herffman eye to eye."

In the apartment, the relentless ticking of the radiator.

"The car drifted, and when it caught the soft shoulder it was like the steering wheel was jerked out of my hands, and that was it." Wickham took a deep breath. "The car flipped. Jade was thrown like fifty feet." A pause. "They said she died instantly."

Audrey waited.

"I never saw her body." Wickham stared off. "The family wouldn't let me come to the funeral, or even the viewing."

After a few seconds, Audrey said, "How about the other two boys?"

Wickham shrugged. "Boze broke some ribs and so did I." He made an unhappy smile. "Herffman walked away with a few bruises."

"So why was there a trial? It was an accident, right?"

"If someone dies, there's an investigation, and I was the guy who was driving."

The radiator ticked, and Audrey's heart pounded.

"Everybody makes mistakes like that all the time," Wickham said, his voice hardening slightly. "You get mad at someone, you drive too fast, you don't look where you're going, and most of the time, it's a near miss. You could've hurt someone but you didn't, and you're grateful. Well, this time nobody got off the hook. The mistake was fatal. And I paid."

The argument had a strangely organized feel, as if he'd made it before, but it was forceful, and Audrey could feel the truth of it.

"I paid big-time," Wickham said again.

Audrey sat still, trying to picture Wickham with a cigarette. She wondered why he didn't say it was Jade Marie Creamer who paid. She opened her mouth and closed it again. She had a feeling she shouldn't say it, but then she did.

"And Jade," she said.

Wickham lifted his chin and gave her a sharp look. "What? You don't think I know Jade paid? Jade paid huge." He paused. "But she paid fast. I've been paying ever since." Another pause. "And it looks like I'll keep paying as long as I live."

Audrey couldn't help herself. She moved toward Wickham, slid onto his lap, and touched his eyelids closed so that she could kiss them. "I know," she whispered.

But Wickham just opened his eyes and said, "I'd better go. Talking about this stuff makes me feel funny."

This surprised Audrey, and she didn't know what to say. Finally she said, "Want me to drive you?"

He shook his head no.

"You want to call a taxi, then?"

He barely took time to consider this. "I think I'd rather just walk."

It was as if he couldn't stand to be there even long enough to wait for a taxi—that's what it seemed like to Audrey. "Is anything wrong?" she said.

Another shake of the head.

"Will you call me later?"

"Sure."

He shifted so that she would stand up—which she did, though she didn't want to. She followed him to the door, where, instead of a kiss, he gave her a stiff, perfunctory hug. "Bye," he said. He barely looked at her.

"Are you sure nothing's wrong?" she asked as he went down the hall.

He shook his head without looking back, and Audrey could do nothing but watch him go.

Chapter 56
Is That You?

Wickham Hill shoved open the heavy front door of the Commodore Apartments and tightened his scarf against the snow. He knew that if he looked up, he'd see Audrey staring down from the living room windows—as she'd done sometimes from her bedroom in the old house, giving him one last wave—but he didn't want to look up.

Is anything wrong?

How could she ask that? How could somebody so smart be so stupid?

Everything was wrong. Audrey's hot apartment, the forced confession, the way it all sounded, the way it all was. It was like being back in Cypress again, with people looking at him over the produce bins at Piggly Wiggly or the gas pumps at the Shell station. At least once a day, he would run into the mother of a friend from school, a teacher, a neighbor, a nurse from his mother's shift, his dentist. They all said hello, but they never knew what to say after that. Silence, pity, blame. Never just a normal conversation, never again.

Wickham shoved his hands into his pockets and walked with his eyes straight ahead. Snowflakes clung to his sleeves, and he could almost feel Audrey's eyes willing him to look up and reassure her that everything was fine, but he kept walking, and when he turned the corner and knew she couldn't see him anymore, he felt relief.

Wickham crossed the street and, leaning into the snow, climbed a steep hill, past three-story wooden houses, faded and chipped, that leaned out over crooked porches. At the top of the hill, sturdier houses decorated with holiday lights ringed the park.

He walked quickly past the park's forested shadows, and his leather shoes grew damp from the deepening snow. He was closer to the university neighborhood now. Maple trees lined the street, their roots buckling the sidewalk.

His feet were wet and cold, and without knowing why, he blamed Audrey for that.

He should have told her everything. She wanted the truth so badly, he should've given her the story about his father, too, and exactly why he wanted to shut Herffman's mouth. He should have told her about Jade's brown shoulders and back, her delicate vertebrae arching when he rubbed coconut oil between the string tie of her yellow bikini top and the yellow triangle below; about Herffman drinking beers and crunching the cans one-handed and giving them his endless monologue on the mythological significance of the *Star Wars* movies that no one was listening to, least of all Jade.

She was wearing a boys' dress shirt over her yellow bathing suit—the suit was optic yellow, like tennis balls and some BMWs. He tried to remember what her face looked like, but nothing came to him. Well, that was the family's fault, wasn't it, not letting him come to the funeral, which he would have gladly done, even though it would have been hard.

A car passed by, its tires making a shushing noise.

Herffman. He was like those guys that poke alligators to make them bite. On the way back from the lake, Herffman had seen an old newspaper on the floor of the car, a *Cypress Telegram* that had Wickham's father's picture on the front page. It was some story about a fund-raising gala, and Wickham had shoved it under the seat to prevent his mother from seeing the picture of Dr. Yates with his arm around his wife. Herffman held up the newspaper and read part of the article aloud: "*'Dr. James E. Yates and his wife, Elaine, donated $500,000 to build a new children's wing.'* Well, isn't that nice."

Jade gave Herffman a bored look, then undid her seat belt and scooched close to Wickham. That was something he could remember perfectly—the liquid green trees sliding by against a pink twilight and Jade's long brown bare legs inches from the gearshift and his hand.

Then Herffman said, "Does anyone here know Dr. Yates? He seems like such a generous man."

Wickham said nothing, but he speeded up a little. In down-shifting at the next curve, he let the back of his hand graze Jade's bare leg, and a moment later, as he accelerated past the speed limit, she took his hand and laid it there. Looking at Herffman in the rearview, he'd said mockingly, "What are you trying to prove, Herffman? That you can read the news-paper?" Not a great line, he knew, but he was concentrating on the creamy softness of Jade's thigh as a few more hundred feet of forest and pink twilight shot by. Then red ash fell from his cigarette, and when he felt it burning through his cutoffs and into his leg he began madly brushing it off, which is what made Herffman say, "You spanking the monkey up there, Mr. Wickham?"—and that made Boze laugh, and even Jade, so

Wickham had to laugh along with them until things quieted down and he could say, "That's a science you excel in, Hefferman, not me." And that was when Herffman, asshole Herffman, said what he said: "That makes me and your mom, then. She wasn't wasting any opportunities. She seemed to know whose monkey to spank."

Just thinking of it now made him clench up a little, as he had then just before he asked Herffman exactly what he was trying to say.

"Trying to say?" Herffman had said. "Hell, I'm *saying* it. Question: Who did Wicky's mother screw to get him into Leighton Hall? Answer: A doctor with his name first among the 'Y's on the Wall of Patrons."

Who wouldn't have flipped his cigarette out the window and turned back and reached for the guy who'd said that? Who wouldn't have done exactly what he did?

Wickham found himself walking now in a small business district where the windows of shops were painted with big holly leaves and red-capped elves. He was standing on the corner, shivering in his wet socks and cold shoes and wishing he'd called a taxi from Audrey's or at least that he had enough money to buy a pizza, when a voice, a girl's voice, said, "Wickham?"

He turned woodenly, afraid it was Audrey, but it wasn't.

It was a girl in an Audi A6. She'd rolled the window down, but her face was hard to see because she was on the other side of the street. "Wickham?" she said. "Is that you?"

Whoever she was, she seemed pretty and she drove an A6, and so Wickham Hill, who the moment before had been feeling peevish about his wet feet and unfair fate, now fixed his dark eyes on the pretty girl in the A6 and slid into an easy drawl. "That would depend on who's doing the asking"—here his lazy smile widened slightly—"and why."

"It's me," the girl said. "Lea. Lea Woolcott. Audrey's friend." Now she was smiling, too. "You need a ride?"

As Wickham circled the back of the car, he reached into his pocket for his peppermint lip balm and smoothed some across his lips.

Chapter 57
Dark and Stormy

As Wickham opened the car door, Lea was tugging her skirt toward her kneesocks, but not before the overhead light had shone fleetingly on an inch or two of her pale thigh. Her eyes were bright and her cheeks pink, either from the car's warmth or from excitement. She looked out the door and said nervously, "It was a dark and stormy night."

Wickham laughed and climbed in, grateful to close the door against the snow and cold. "You know, that was an actual first line from an actual book."

Lea smiled brightly. "Really?"

"Yeah," Wickham said, rubbing his hands together in front of the nearest heater vent. "Nobody reads the rest of it, though."

Lea looked at the dashboard and clenched the steering wheel a little tighter. She hadn't yet pulled the car from the curb, and seemed uncertain what to do next. She nodded toward his feet. "You want to take off your shoes and socks? You can put them over the heater vent."

Wickham said they'd have to drive around a long time to get them dry.

When Lea glanced at him, he was freshly startled by the paleness of her blue eyes. Her hair looked very soft, and it fell in a kind of white corona over her dark scarf. "Yeah," she said, pulling slowly away from the curb and shops. "So?"

Wickham began to work off his wet shoes. "My pants are wet, too," he said.

Lea glanced over at him again and seemed to regain her wits. "Yeah, well," she said, "I'm afraid you're going to have to keep those on."

Wickham watched her drive. Her white hands on the steering wheel were small and precise. Her eyes, when she turned to him and laughed at one of his jokes, did not see anything wrong with him. The slate was clean, he had no past, and the car was warm and expensive-smelling. "New car?" he asked.

"Yeah. I got it this afternoon. It's an early birthday present from my dad. He came by after school and took me down to the dealership. My mother doesn't even know about it yet." She turned right onto Genesee, away from Audrey's building, and gently accelerated. "She's going to have the grand champion of all cows."

An easy laugh from Wickham; then he said, "How come?"

"Sixteen different reasons, the big ones being that, one, teenagers shouldn't drive ritzy cars and, two, Audis are part of Volkswagen and Hitler helped design the original bug, so Audis are kind of a Nazi car."

This was news to Wickham. "Adolf did that?" he said.

Lea made a grim smile. "Probably. My mom's a demon for facts."

Wickham smoothed a finger over the cherrywood dash; then, closer to Lea's leg, over the soft beige leather. "I don't know," he said, "I wouldn't call this automobile anything but deluxe."

"Yeah?" Lea said, and looked pleased. "I wanted to show it

to C.C., but she's not home, and"—she paused—"it didn't seem right to show it to Audrey right now." She looked at Wickham. "You know what I mean, right?"

Wickham nodded somberly and said he did.

"Losing that house would've killed me," Lea said, "but she's being so brave about it all."

Again Wickham nodded.

"I really admire her for that," Lea said.

Wickham said he did, too. Then he said, "So when's your birthday?"

"Wednesday. December 17. I'll be eighteen, which is actually embarrassing. I'm too old for high school."

Wickham told Lea something he'd never told Audrey. "I'm eighteen already."

Lea seemed pleasantly surprised by this fact. "You are?" she said.

"Yeah. We were moving a lot, so I did third grade over. How about you?"

"My mother didn't believe in an early start, so when everybody else was in kindergarten, I was with my mother in Tunisia helping the locals build a school."

The CD she was playing was some kind of retro thing, and all the lyrics were in French. He was surprised how much he liked it.

"You ever smoke?" Lea said.

The question seemed to come out of the blue. "Yeah, I used to." He gave his next words some thought, then went ahead. "I was smoking when I was in this terrible accident in South Carolina where a girlfriend died, so, I don't know, after that I just told myself I'd quit for a while." He looked out the window and said in a lower tone, "That seems like a long time ago." Another pause; then he turned back to Lea. "But the smoking—you can't believe how much I've missed it."

Lea gave Wickham a sympathetic look, then leaned past him to open the glove compartment and pull out a package of Chesterfield cigarettes.

"You smoke?" Wickham said. This ride with Lea was one surprise after another.

"A little," Lea said.

On the CD, a woman sang, "Non, je ne regrette rien," which Lea translated as "I regret nothing."

Wickham pushed in the cigarette lighter. He tugged the pull strip on the Chesterfields' plastic wrapper. He tapped out two cigarettes.

The car rolled quietly down the snow-covered street.

Part Three

Cold and raw the north wind doth blow
Bleak in the morning early,
All the hills are covered with snow,
And winter's now come fairly.

Chapter 58
What's with the French Music?

Monday, December 15, was bitter cold. On the way to school, Audrey sat in the back of Lea's new car while, up front, Lea drove and C.C. checked everything out ("Lea, honey," C.C. said, "I think I need to own up to a wee bit of envy here"). Audrey stared blankly at the instruments on the cherrywood dash and realized that the "–3F" she was looking at indicated the outside temperature. It was also just about the way she felt. Minus three.

It had been two days since she'd last seen or spoken to Wickham. All weekend long she'd kept expecting him to call, or just drop by, and she'd gotten so worried about it she wouldn't even leave the apartment to go to the market because she was afraid she'd miss him. At first she'd thought something was wrong with his phone—when she called him, all she got was his voice mail—and then, yesterday, when he still didn't call, she thought maybe something had happened to him, or maybe to his mom. Maybe they'd driven back suddenly to South Carolina or something and he hadn't had time yet to let her know.

"Jeez, Louise," C.C. said from up front. "Whose are these?" She was holding up a half-empty pack of cigarettes she'd found in the glove compartment.

Lea actually blushed. "Mine, you big snoop."

C.C. looked incredulous. "Yours? Overnight, you're a nicotine freak?"

Lea said that would be taking it pretty far. "Besides, in forty-eight hours I'm eighteen, and then, legally speaking, these lungs are mine to do what I want with."

For Lea, this was a major policy speech, and C.C. fell quiet for a moment or two. Then she said, "Wow, Lea."

Lea, more softly now, said, "I'm just checking it out." Her pale eyes brightened slightly. "But I kind of like it. It makes me feel different."

"Then why don't you smoke around us?"

Lea smiled. "Haven't got it down yet. I still look like a smoking nerd."

C.C. laughed. "Because that's what you are."

Lea shrugged. "I don't know. I just get sick of being so *virtuous* all the time."

Audrey realized that not only had she not said a word through this exchange, but neither C.C. nor Lea had expected her to. It was as if they'd forgotten about her, or she'd turned invisible. So she said, "Once you get a boyfriend, that won't be a problem anymore."

C.C. turned, and Lea looked into the rearview mirror. "What won't be a problem?" C.C. asked.

"Feeling virtuous."

Lea and C.C. were quiet for a second or two. Then C.C. said, "You okay, Aud?"

Audrey nodded. "It's just this moving thing. It's kind of discombobulating." She looked out the car window. "And the snow. Winter hasn't even officially started yet and I'm already sick of it."

C.C. murmured in agreement. Then, idly, probably trying to dispel Audrey's gloom, she said, "So what did you and Wickham do this weekend?"

Audrey shifted her eyes. "Nothing. He's sick, I think. He said he wasn't feeling well."

"Bummer," C.C. said. "Maybe after school we should brew him some chicken soup."

"Maybe," Audrey said vaguely.

Lea said nothing. The new car moved smoothly down the street, and the girls fell into a silence that C.C. finally broke by saying, "Lea, honey, what's with the French music, anyhow?"

Chapter 59
Interesting

At school, after Lea had walked off in another direction and
C.C. and Audrey were making their way through the
crowded corridor, C.C. said, "So did Lea tell you she didn't
want to celebrate her birthday this year?"

"Uh-uh," Audrey said. Her eyes were scanning the hallway
for Wickham.

"Yeah, she was totally specific. No party, no presents, no
nothing."

This caught Audrey's attention. No presents. Was that
because she'd feel guilty having Audrey spend money? "How
come no presents?" she asked.

C.C. shrugged. "Who knows? Lea's turned into a riddle a
day." They walked a little farther without talking. Then C.C.
said, "Know what I hate?"

"What?" Audrey said.

"When your mother says something she thinks is profound
but you think is silly, and then it turns out she was right."

"What did your mother say?" Audrey asked.

"That what makes people interesting is their secrets."

Audrey stopped short. "Who're you talking about?"

The vehemence of Audrey's question seemed to startle
C.C. "Lea," she said. "And her smoking."

Audrey, relieved, nodded, and when they were walking again, C.C. said, "Who did you think I was talking about?"

Wickham, Audrey thought. But she said, "Nobody in particular."

When they reached the end of the hall, C.C. said, "The thing about Lea's smoking is that, you know, in a weird way it *does* make her more interesting." She paused. "If nothing else, it makes you wonder what other little secrets she's got in the glove compartment."

Audrey didn't answer. She'd hardly heard what C.C. said. She was again busy scanning the hall for Wickham.

Chapter 60
Extra, Extra

Wickham's seat was empty when Audrey walked into Mrs. Leacock's class, and it stayed empty. When Leslie Poll, who took roll, reported his absence, Mrs. Leacock said, loud enough for everyone to hear, "Mr. Hill has effected a transfer out of this class through the good offices of the ombudsman." Mrs. Leacock let her gaze rest for just a moment on Audrey. "It seems Mr. Hill does not believe he was treated with, quote, fairness or respect because of Mr. Hill's, quote, cultural differences."

Audrey could hardly believe her ears. Wickham had filed a grievance with the ombudsman by himself? And he'd transferred out of the only class they had together on the day of the makeup essay?

A kind of panic took hold of Audrey. When was she going to see him? She had to see him, she had to find out what was wrong, but she couldn't see him or talk to him. In her green notebook she wrote, *This is like starvation.*

The period crawled by. She didn't hear anything Mrs. Leacock was saying, and when the class was given time to read and take notes, all Audrey could do was write *Wickham*, over and over, in the same place, until her pen ripped through the paper. She turned back the pages and stared at the words she'd written six weeks before: *Something happening. Something definitely happening.*

The windows in the room were clouded with condensation from the radiators, and occasionally a bead of water would form and suddenly stream down to the sill. Audrey was watching the slow progress of one of these beads when she heard muffled laughter from the hallway outside. Then, turning, she saw sheets of yellow paper slide under the door. Outside, raucous laughter followed, and the echoing sound of running feet.

The room grew unnaturally quiet. Everyone was staring either at the scattered *Yellow Papers* or at Mrs. Leacock, who was herself staring at them.

The *Yellow Papers* told the story of Wickham's accident. Audrey was sure of it, so sure of it that she suddenly stood up and said, "Do you want me to throw them away?"

"No," Mrs. Leacock said, glancing mildly at Audrey, "but thank you."

Mrs. Leacock walked across the front of the room, bent down, and picked up one of the yellow sheets. She walked toward the windows, reading in silence; then, after perhaps ten seconds, she simply let the paper drop from her hands. She didn't look at Audrey. She didn't look at the class. She didn't look at anybody. For a full minute she stood perfectly still; then, finally, she took a step forward and did something Audrey would never in her life forget.

With her finger, Mrs. Leacock wrote three words on the steamy window:

Shame on you

Then Mrs. Leacock picked up her purse and left the room.

After a second or two, students left their seats and began picking up the papers. Audrey picked one up, too.

EXTRA! EXTRA! EXTRA! spanned the top of the page, followed by this:

Feliz Navidad, Kwanzaa, and Hanukkah, dudes and dudettes of all cultures, and no, this isn't another plea for a wholesome charity drive unless you happen to be Sands of Mandeville in which case we could definitely go for some of your unwrapped toys, but, scusi scusi, we digress. What we have here for inquiring minds of the Yellow Nation is a stellar little present, free of charge and straight from the crime files, regarding our very own Mrs. Science, a.k.a. The Behoover, whose hubby while lying in close bedside proximity to the physics whiz in their L.A. digs in the wee hours of a February eve eleven years back died of an overdose the accidentalness of which the L.A.P.D., evidentially speaking, had certain questions about, and so do we, as in, How do a Peacock spell Fowl Play?

There had been a relative quiet while the students in the room read this story, but that quiet now gave way to a hum of excitement. A short boy Audrey didn't know whooped and gave the kind of pelvic thrust she'd seen football players on TV do when they'd made a touchdown. All around her, students were grinning and their eyes were bright. "She killed her husband?" somebody said. Someone else said, "Why does that not surprise me?"

Once the excitement had quieted, students began filing out of the room in twos and threes. Audrey was the last to leave. She picked up the *Yellow Papers* that were still scattered on the floor and threw all but one away. She kept one, folding it in half and slipping it into her green notebook. There was something about it, something just behind the words, that seemed strangely familiar.

Before leaving the room, Audrey looked back one last time. She looked at her own empty desk, and at Wickham's; then she looked at the steamy window. *Shame on you.* A few beads of water had trailed through the words, but Audrey could still read them, and she felt them as if they'd been written only for her.

Chapter 61
A Sighting

She saw him. Suddenly, between fifth and sixth periods, with
a shock of recognition, she saw him, at the other end of the
east hall, and quickly called, "Wickham!" But he was just
turning out of sight and didn't seem to hear.

"Did you say 'Wicked'?"

Behind her, grinning, was Brian. "If it's wicked you want,
I'm your boy."

Audrey felt terrible, but she knew that wasn't Brian's fault.
She made a faint smile and touched her index finger to his
nose. "You're funny."

Brian grinned. "Also, if need be, wicked."

Audrey said she'd bear that in mind, and after they parted,
she drifted to a hallway window and cleared the dampness
with her hand. And there, passing into her field of vision,
waving easily at someone, as comfortable in himself as ever
before, was Wickham again, strolling across the quad, going
who knew where.

He looked the same. That had to be a good sign, didn't it?
Because how could he look the same if everything had
changed?

Audrey was still standing at the window, staring out at the
deserted quad, when the final tardy bell rang.

Chapter 62
Said the Spider to the Fly

Clyde moved warily through the halls. There were two people he didn't want to see—more than two, really, but two in particular: Theo Driggs, who'd pulverized him, and Audrey Reed, who'd set him up for the pulverization.

But who he saw waiting for him at his locker was Sands Mandeville, and she was smiling.

"Hey, Mumsford," she said.

He nodded, and she presented him with a *Yellow Paper.*

"What's that?"

Sands had a pretty face, but her smile was evil. "As if you didn't know."

Clyde stared at *The Yellow Paper.* "I don't want that."

Sands kept her blue eyes on him for a second or two, then took back *The Yellow Paper* and began folding it smaller and smaller. "Guess Theo didn't quite get through to you," she said in a casual voice as she worked, and once the paper was folded into a tiny square, she leaned forward and pulled open his front pocket with one hand before pushing the paper deep into it with the other. As she did this, her breast pressed softly into his arm. Her breath smelled of spearmint, and in a whispery voice she said, "Peruse that at your pleasure."

When she stepped back, she said in a cooing voice, "You

know, for a guy with all the dirt, you're weirdly unaware." She smiled evenly at Clyde. "My boyfriend is Cruz Wolfe."

Cruz Wolfe was a halfback on the football team, a face man with a temper.

"I'm afraid Cruz isn't going to like your yellow reference to my"—her expression was pert—"unwrapped toys."

"What unwrapped toys?" Clyde said.

Sands kept her amused smile. "Here's a little-known fact about Cruz. He and Theo Driggs have been friends since they were just itty-bitty, and while it's true they aren't that tight anymore, they still have, shall we say, a good working relationship." She leaned forward and gently touched a finger to Clyde's swollen eye. "It's a shame, really," she said in a minty whisper. "Things were just beginning to heal."

Chapter 63
A Parley with Theo

After Sands left, Clyde read *The Yellow Paper*, twice, and while he did, his feelings slowly hardened into something fist-like. Crap about Sands, crap about Mrs. Leacock. This was too much. This was too effing much.

Down the hallway, he saw Craig Ashworth, one of Theo's groupies. In seventh grade, Craig and Clyde had traded *Star Wars* cards for a while. Now Craig was wearing a black leather jacket studded with chrome, and his ears were pierced.

Clyde walked over and said, "Hey, Craig. I'm looking for Theo. Do you know where he is?"

Craig nodded and led Clyde out the west exit, past the temps, and out to the auto shop. The shop teacher was bent under a hood, so Theo strolled over. Two of Theo's friends followed him, and Craig stayed.

"So The Mummy wants to parley," Theo said, leading Clyde and the rest of the party out of the auto shop and over to a corner of the adjoining lot made private by hedges. He planted himself there and smiled at Clyde. "So?"

"I just wanted you to know I didn't write that crap about Sands or that crap about Leacock," Clyde said. "I didn't write the other *Yellow Paper*s, and I didn't write this one." He stared directly at Theo, who was still smiling. "So you need to tell me whether you believe me or not, because if you don't, now's the time"—he glanced at Theo's bodyguards—"to discuss it."

Theo kept his eyes fixed keenly on Clyde for a few seconds; then, scanning the schoolground beyond him, Theo unzipped his pants and, still smiling, began to urinate. Clyde stepped quickly back. Steam rose from the wet ground. Craig tugged at a chain on his jacket and one of the bodyguards, a huge guy with bleached hair, stuck out his chin and smiled nastily.

"I believe you," Theo said. "I truly do." A smile. "But if something should come out about my uncircumcised friend here, I'm afraid I'll have to reconsider."

He kept urinating. He was doing it hands free, so that, from the way he was standing, somebody passing at a distance would have no idea what he was doing.

"Anything else?" Theo said.

Clyde—revulsed, almost sickened—shook his head and turned away. As he walked, he could still hear the splashing sounds.

Chapter 64
The Wishing Minutes

When Audrey, Lea, and C.C. had been in grammar school with Edie March, they called 1:11, 2:22, 3:33, 4:44, and 5:55 "the wishing minutes." All day, for the first time in years, Audrey had found herself waiting, first for 1:11, then for 2:22, so she could close her eyes and think, *Please, please, please, in the next hour let me see Wickham and have him tell me everything is okay.*

Between classes, she'd gone to her locker even when she didn't need to, in hopes he'd be there or had left a note, but he hadn't. She went to Mrs. Leacock's room after school to do her makeup essay, but the room was locked and the lights were off. This should have been a relief, but it was a disappointment. She had been ready to clean the slate, and now she couldn't. She stood beside the door for fifteen minutes or so, nervously waiting for Mrs. Leacock to come down the hall, key in hand, but no one came. Lea's car was gone by the time Audrey reached the parking lot, so she walked home alone.

Once inside her apartment, Audrey went straight to the answering machine, where there was no message from Wickham. But there was a brief message from Oggy, who hated answering machines. "Hallo?" she said. "Hallo, Audrey. It's me, Oggy. I get your letter and I write you. Don't worry. My sister have much better—" The machine cut her off. Audrey sat still a moment in frustration, and then flipped on the computer. She checked for e-mail messages from Wickham; there were none. She glanced at the clock: 3:56. She'd missed 3:33. The next wishing minute was 4:44.

She called Wickham's cell phone number and got his voice mail. She'd already left four or five messages and didn't want to leave another, but she couldn't help herself. "Hi, it's me. I haven't heard from you, so maybe my phone's not working or your battery's dead or something. Call me, okay?" Her voice cracked, and she hung up.

Immediately the phone rang, and she picked up on the first ring. "Hello?"

"Hi, Polliwog."

"Oh, hi, Dad," she said, unable to hide her disappointment.

He laughed. "Pretty excited to hear from your dad, are you?"

"It's not that. It's just that I was expecting . . ."

"A call from the beau?"

In a small voice, Audrey said, "I wish you wouldn't call him that. You know I don't like it. Oggy called, though. She got cut off. Did you pick up?"

Her father said no, he hadn't. Lately his tone had grown lighter. He had a new job, and he'd begun to regain his old natural buoyancy. In fact, the reason he was calling was that his new firm was putting him in charge of a big project, "with a nice bump in pay." The boss was taking him to dinner at Le Bistro, and Audrey was invited, too.

Le Bistro, where Wickham had said she was beautiful. "Thanks, Dad, but I've got reading to do. I'll just grab something on my way to the library."

After she put the phone down, Audrey thought of calling Lea or C.C. or maybe, she thought wildly, Oggy, but the truth was, there wasn't one thing in the world she wanted to do except see Wickham, talk to him, touch him, and hear his soft, unbothered voice. Audrey stared at her car keys lying on the ugly Formica table, the one that Wickham had helped carry up from the basement only three days before.

Audrey collected some books as if she were going to study at the library, but once inside the old Lincoln, she didn't drive to the library. She drove straight to Wickham's neighborhood, cruising by his house six or seven times as dusk settled and houses began to sparkle with Christmas lights. At 4:44 she parked in front of Wickham's house, closed her eyes, and said aloud, "Please, let him be home and let everything be like before."

Audrey walked toward the house. The footing was treacherous—no one had shoveled the most recent snow. The columns were cracked and peeling, and a pane of glass on the porch lamp was broken. There were no Christmas lights, but a downstairs room glowed yellow. At Audrey's knock, Wickham's mother came to the door.

"Yes?" she said in a brisk tone; then, seeing who it was, she said, "Oh, hi, Audrey."

Audrey had met her two or three times, but Mrs. Hill had a reserve that kept Audrey at a distance. ("Your mother's quiet," Audrey had told Wickham after first meeting her, and Wickham had said in his casual drawl, "Her quiet is just her outer layer of armor.") Tonight Mrs. Hill was wearing a heavy black-and-white coat and carrying a fashionable red purse, which she held in front of her. "I'm just on my way out," she

said, and Audrey felt something new in Mrs. Hill's reserve—
something slightly chilly.

"I was looking for Wickham," Audrey said, and felt her lip
trembling, but if Mrs. Hill noticed this, she didn't acknowledge it.

"That's the thing with Wickham," she said. "He could be
anywhere, and often is." She made a dry laugh and pulled her
keys from her purse. "I'd like to visit further, but . . ." Mrs.
Hill glanced meaningfully toward the car that would carry
her away from this awkward conversation.

"Oh, sorry," Audrey said, nodding and backing away, "but
will you tell him I came by?" Before closing the door, Mrs.
Hill, in a vague voice, said she would.

From Wickham's house, Audrey drove to Little Dragon and
poked her head inside to see if Wickham might be there, eating
alone and doing his homework; but he wasn't there, and when
Mr. Wong saw her, he didn't seem to recognize her. "Party with
one?" he said, and Audrey shook her head no and departed.

She went to the pharmacy where Wickham got his Imitrex;
she went to a co-op where she'd once seen his brand of lip
balm; she even walked through rows of desks at the library,
hoping to see him.

Nothing.

As she drove from place to place looking for Wickham, the
quiet within the car began to make her edgy, so she turned on
the cassette player, and Yum-Yum, Pitti-Sing, and Peep-Bo
burst out.

> *Three little maids from school are we,*
> *Pert as a schoolgirl well can be,*
> *Fill'd to the brim with girlish glee—*

The tempo was brisk and the soprano voices cheerful. She, C.C., and Lea had done this song at one of the many Tate School talent shows. It had been fun; they had been funny. It seemed like a scene from a life in no way connected to the one she was this minute living.

Ev'rything is a source of fun.

Nobody's safe, for we care for none!

Audrey cruised by Bing's, peering into its bright interior at dozens of bored or happy faces, none of them Wickham's; then she drove slowly back to his neighborhood. The sky was black now, and a mechanical deer made of white lights moved its head up and down. A fat inflatable Santa beamed at the street. Wickham's house was completely dark, and remained dark the three or four times Audrey circled the block. She wrote a note (*Wickham, please, please call me.—A.*), slid it under the knocker of Wickham's front door, and ran back to her car.

At 5:54 Audrey pulled to the side of the street and sat staring at the digital car clock. When it read "5:55," Audrey closed her eyes and said, "Please, please, please . . . ," but she didn't finish the wish. She'd begun to cry. She opened her eyes, and through her smeared vision watched the lighted deer raise its hollow head and stand perfectly still in the snow.

Chapter 65
No Longer in Service

At school the next morning, Audrey saw no sign of Wickham. After sitting numbly through first period, she went to the nurse and said she had a bad headache and needed to go home. This worked, surprisingly, though the nurse called her father and got his permission first. In the car, Audrey dialed Wickham's cell phone number and heard a mechanized voice say, "This mailbox is full. Please call back later."

She drove back and forth in front of Wickham's house until a bald man in a yellow-and-black plaid coat came out and stood on the front walk to stare at Audrey and conspicuously write something down on a notepad. Audrey went home, slept until midafternoon, and then forced herself to go into the kitchen and make English toffee for Lea's birthday. If she made something, at least Lea wouldn't have to feel bad about her spending money.

She was spreading melted chocolate with a spatula when she heard the front door of the apartment open. A few seconds later, her father poked his head into the kitchen. "Hi, Polliwog." He regarded the toffee. "I thought you had a headache, no?"

"I took Excedrin and a nap. Now I'm making a birthday present for Lea. She's eighteen tomorrow."

Her father looked stricken. "Eighteen?"

Every time her father heard how old Lea was, he worried that Audrey was that age, too, and that he'd somehow missed a birthday. "Don't worry, Dad. I'm seventeen next month. Lea started school late."

Her father seemed relieved. "So what're you guys doing for her birthday?"

Audrey shrugged. "Nothing. She just wants to do it by herself so she knows exactly what she's feeling. She calls it a Zen birthday."

Her father, smiling, said, "That's pure Lea, isn't it?"

Audrey said, "I guess so." She was trying to picture a Zen Buddhist smoking a Chesterfield.

Her father made spaghetti that night, but it was pasty, and Audrey had a hard time swallowing it. Her father had turned his little kitchen radio to Christmas music, which annoyed her so much she finally asked if she could turn it off.

"Sure," he said, but he looked abashed, and after she'd switched the radio off, they fell into heavy silence. Her father fork-twirled a bite of spaghetti, but didn't put it into his mouth. He looked at Audrey and said, "Headache come back?"

"No."

"Then what's the matter?"

"Nothing."

"Audrey. It's me. Your dad."

What was she going to tell him? That she'd fallen in crazy-love with Wickham and now he'd vanished and wouldn't even talk to her?

"I'm fine," Audrey said in a leaden voice. She nodded at

the unopened cardboard boxes stacked against the wall. "It's just all the moving, is all."

Her father, staring at her and nodding, said quietly, "Okay."

At midnight, Audrey was still awake and she called Wickham's cell phone number one more time. After two rings a voice said, "This Nextel number is no longer in service, and no new number has been provided."

Chapter 66
"Okay in There?"

On Wednesday, Audrey stayed in school all day even though Wickham was still nowhere to be found. Lea was absent, too, but it was her Zen birthday, so Audrey took the box of toffee by her house after school to leave it with her, and maybe talk to her about what was going on with Wickham. But Lea wasn't there. No one was, so she left the box on the front porch, propped against the door.

Audrey was exhausted. She drove by Wickham's house, but on her third time by, the bald man in the yellow-and-black coat stepped into the street and waved her to a stop. He looked serious.

"Young lady," he said, "my name is Earl—that's all you need to know, just Earl—and I'm captain of the Neighborhood Crime Watch team, and if you drive by here one more time, I'll alert our direct link to the Jemison police department."

Audrey said, "You say your name is Earl?" When the man nodded, Audrey, to her own surprise, said, "Well, Earl, you're just horrid." Then she rolled up her window and drove away.

But, she thought, Horrid Earl had done his job. She was afraid to drive by again. She turned on the cassette—*"Pert as a schoolgirl well can be, / Fill'd to the brim with girlish glee"*—and then drove by Lea's one more time, but there was still no sign of her. Audrey didn't want to go back to the Commodore, so she drove out to the river and parked on the overlook where she and Wickham liked to park. She was sleepy—she'd been sleepy all day. She left the ignition on to run the heater and nodded off, only to awake to a sharp tapping on the car window, which had gotten steamy. She lowered it an inch.

A middle-aged man peered in. "You okay in there?"

"Yeah," Audrey said in a heavy voice. "I just fell asleep."

"You'll want to keep those windows cracked open," the man was saying as Audrey rolled the window back up. After wiping the window with her sleeve, she remembered where she was.

Nowhere, she thought. *That's where you are. Nowhere.*

She wiped the glass one more time and drove slowly away.

At home (no messages from Oggy or Wickham, no e-mail) she noticed that her father had come home for lunch and left a small Christmas tree. He'd placed a box of old decorations next to it, but after sliding off the lid and staring at the miscellaneous colored glass balls covered all over with hairline cracks, Audrey realized she didn't feel like putting them on the tree. She wondered what time it was in Germany. Was it later there, or earlier? She knew Oggy wouldn't mind if she called at the wrong time, but her sister might.

Audrey climbed into bed and made herself pull out her schoolbooks. She read the first page of the assigned selection in her literature anthology and realized she could not remember who the characters were. She could see the edge of the *Yellow Paper* she'd folded inside her notebook, and now she slipped it out and unfolded it.

Audrey stared at the article without reading it and then—she wasn't sure why—she took her blue pen and began circling words the way Mrs. Leacock had done when she was finding evidence of Audrey's influence.

Dudette. Scusi. Evidentially. Stellar.

She looked away from the paper and stared at the green wall of her room.

Brian.

These were Brian's words. Not Clyde Mumsford's, Brian's. Was that possible? She thought back to the other issues of *The Yellow Paper*. To how she and Lea and C.C. had told Brian about Zondra and Sands nailing them in Patrice's class. To how they'd told Brian about Theo putting Audrey on his to-do list. And then to how weird Brian had gotten when she'd told him about Mrs. Leacock catching her cheating.

Still, she'd been wrong once before.

Audrey looked out her window and wished she could call Wickham. He'd know what to do.

But Wickham wasn't here, was he?

Audrey pulled on her jacket.

She was going to Brian's.

Chapter 67
The Yellow Man

Brian and C.C.'s house looked bigger than it used to. It looked massive, in fact. Audrey rang the doorbell and peered through the front window, but no one came to the door. She shook her head, but couldn't get rid of the "Three Little Maids" song that kept running through her head:

> Pert as a schoolgirl well can be,
> Fill'd to the brim with girlish glee,
> Three little maids from school!

Audrey had been to C.C.'s house often enough to know that the Mudds kept a spare key on the back porch, inside a terra-cotta bird feeder. If she went into the house now, she could look in Brian's room and see if there was some real evidence that he was the Yellow Man.

She stepped off the front porch and walked to the back door. The sky was turning pink and the light was coppery. Nothing moved in the nearby yards, where it was too cold for ice to melt or children to play. She reached into the bird feeder and removed the key. When Audrey turned her head slightly, she was startled to see eyes in the neighbor's window: a cat stared fixedly at her, its paws curled under in anticipation.

The lock stuck, but then, almost against her will, it gave.

"C.C.?" she called in. "Brian?"

Breakfast dishes sat unwashed on the counter. "It's Audrey!" she shouted.

The icemaker made a scraping noise.

On the stairs she passed a pair of track shoes, an unopened package of Christmas tree lights, and a pile of folded clothes. The house smelled like fabric softener and slightly sour milk. Brian's bedroom door was closed.

Audrey swallowed and knocked. "Brian?" she said loudly.

A deep stillness.

She nudged the door open. Brian's bed was a swirled mass of sheets and blankets and T-shirts and papers. The room was dim except for a bright edge of light beneath the closed closet door. Brian's computer screen was mostly dark, but a pin-sized light gleamed. Not off, but asleep.

Audrey pushed a key, and tiny icons of games and folders flared up in neat rows, including files called "Doc-u-Mints," "Brian's Bidness," and "Pulitzer-Prize Contendahs." It would take forever to search through all his goofy folders.

Audrey closed her eyes and kept them closed until she heard a scratching sound. Her eyes shot open. The scratching was hard and persistent, and seemed to be coming from the closet door. Audrey felt the acceleration of her heartbeat as she tiptoed toward it. It was coming from the closet, all right. Someone was scratching on the door. "Brian?" she said. When there was no answer, she whispered, "Who's in there?" She half expected Brian to break into his slacker's laugh, but it was quiet except for the scratching, which seemed more urgent now.

Audrey's heart pounded. She forced herself to put her hand on the doorknob. She turned it slowly. The door eased open.

And the bearded dragon waddled out, leaving behind its woody, leafy, closet-sized terrarium. Audrey had never in her life been so happy to see a reptile.

"Hiya, Animal," she said, and watched it waddle across the floor toward a low open drawer. The bearded dragon, in a surprisingly agile move, pulled itself up over the drawer handle, hung on to it, dragged itself up, and flopped inside.

Audrey walked over and looked in. The bearded dragon was wedged between one side of the drawer and several wrapped reams of paper. Audrey reached in and carefully lifted the lizard free, and felt it immediately snuggle its head into her armpit and relax there, which Audrey thought not unpleasant.

She leaned over to close the drawer, but stopped. The outer wrappers of the reams were white, but something made her peel back the end flaps of the top package. The paper inside wasn't white. It was yellow. She peeled open all three reams. They were all yellow.

So it was Brian.

With the bearded dragon still tucked against her body, Audrey took out the top package of paper and shuffled through it. Yellow pages, smooth and blank, like a new fence before some tagger got to it with his spray can.

Depressing. It was all so depressing.

Audrey sat down at Brian's computer and set the ream of paper on her lap. The bearded dragon snuggled between the package and Audrey's stomach. She stroked its head, then scrolled up the computer screen to the sleep option, and a second later the screen was dark. All that glowed now was the pinhole.

Through that pinhole were facts, mistakes, and fantasies: numberless Web sites full of highlighted blue words you could touch with an arrow to find more facts, mistakes, and fantasies. If you knew the right codes, you could find drunk-driving teachers, dead-in-your-bed husbands, and terrible car wrecks. The thought made Audrey tired; staring at the dot of light and stroking the plump lizard, she felt almost hypnotized by it.

Three little maids is the total sum. . . . Nobody's safe, for we care for none!

A downstairs noise: the back door.

Audrey's eyes blinked, but she didn't otherwise move. She just sat with the ream of yellow paper and the bearded dragon, whose head was now raised in awareness of the new presence in the house.

She heard the hard, hollow-sounding footsteps on the limestone entry; then, softer, on the staircase carpet. The footsteps slowed on the hardwood upstairs hallway as they approached the door.

Three little maids who, all unwary, / Come from a ladies' seminary . . .

The door didn't make a sound when it swung open, but there was a slight difference in the light cast in the room.

Audrey didn't turn. She sat with the yellow papers and stared at the screen. Except for the low hum of the computer, it was quiet; then, finally, Brian said, "So, dudette, the question is this: What took you so long?"

Audrey didn't answer.

"I mean, the trail leading here was littered with gigaclues."

She almost imagined Brian would look different to her

when she turned, but he didn't. It was the same old goofy Brian, standing loose-jointed in the doorway.

"So why'd you do it?" she said.

He shrugged. "The first year, it was a little free-speech experiment. But this year, it was mostly for you."

"Me?"

He nodded. "And Lea, too, I guess, and C.C." He let his eyes fall on Audrey. "But mainly for you."

She supposed he hoped this would trigger some response from her, but in fact all she felt was clammy. Not clammy the way she'd felt with Theo, but still clammy. Brian was C.C.'s funny little brother, and she knew she'd never think of him in any other way. "It was nice of you, I guess, but . . ."

Brian, who'd been watching her face, took her meaning and looked away. The lizard wriggled and wanted free. Audrey set it down and watched it waddle toward Brian.

"You have to stop *The Yellow Paper*," Audrey said.

Brian shrugged. "Sure," he said, "that can be done."

"And you have to make this right, at least with Mrs. Leacock."

Brian turned now and, seeing the bearded dragon, picked it up and draped it over his neck, where it settled easily. He looked at Audrey. "Make it up by doing what?"

"I don't know, Brian. That's up to you."

She got up, and he stepped from the doorway to let her pass. But she felt such a strange combination of sadness and fondness that she turned and took both of his dangling hands and set them around her waist, then let him pull her close. The bearded dragon, jostled, adapted by wedging itself between both their shoulders. In a low voice, Brian said, "I think we've been reptilinially bonded," and Audrey laughed and said she didn't think that was a word. She closed her eyes and for a second or two let herself imagine that he wasn't Brian at all, but Wickham Hill. Still, when she felt his male body begin to respond, she eased the bearded dragon back onto Brian's shoulders and said, "I've got to go."

He smiled. "You don't, but you will." Then, as she started to leave, he said, "Where're you going?"

Until that moment, Audrey hadn't given it any thought. "I think I need to find C.C. or Lea. Are they somewhere together?"

Brian's expression went vague. "C.C.'s Christmas-shopping with my mom."

"Then I'll try to find Lea."

She'd gone a few steps when he said, "I wouldn't do that if I was you."

She shot Brian a quizzical look. "Why not?"

The bearded dragon stared unblinkingly at Audrey, but Brian's eyes seemed to slide away. "I just wouldn't," he said.

Chapter 68
In Which the Three Maids
Cease to Sing

Audrey drove first to Wickham's, and even though the house was dark, she went to the door to leave another note. She'd brought a notepad and pen with her, and a penlight she could hold between her teeth while she wrote. But as she was getting ready to write, the fine beam of the flashlight hit a crumpled piece of white paper in a corner of the porch.

She bent, picked it up, and unwadded it. There, before her, were her own words, written two days earlier: *Wickham, please, please call me.—A.*

Someone had found it—Wickham? his mother?—and had been annoyed enough to wad it up and throw it down where . . . Audrey could find it the next time she made another pathetic trip to his front door?

It was horrible. It was all too horrible.

As she backed away from the door, she stepped into an icy drift of snow. Bits of ice fell into her left shoe and had begun to melt before she reached the car.

She put the key into the ignition, but didn't know where to go. She stared straight ahead for perhaps a minute; then, resting her forehead on the steering wheel, she began to cry. She was still crying when a flashlight beamed suddenly into the car.

Audrey wiped her cheeks with her gloved hands and looked up. It was Horrid Earl, looking as if he'd just cornered a serial killer.

"Okay!" she shouted. "I'm leaving!" And she hit the accelerator so hard that the old Lincoln fishtailed before achieving traction and lurching forward.

She headed toward Lea's. C.C. was shopping, but Lea was probably home doing her whole Zen birthday thing and wanting to be alone. Still, this was an emergency, and they were friends. That's what she would say when Lea came to the door: something like, "I'm sorry, Lea, but I'm going through kind of a crisis here," and Lea would smile her soft smile and, in her soothing voice, help her figure out what to do next.

That was what Audrey pretended to believe.

But the truth was, when she got to Lea's brightly lighted house and walked up the curving brick walkway and saw the large living Christmas tree in the front room, wrapped in popcorn garlands; and when she saw, through an archway beyond the tree, a candlelit table with Lea sitting in a black dress with her hair pinned up and looking unfamiliar and beautiful and even older than eighteen; and when she saw a male arm reach past Lea to light the candles on a birthday cake, and saw that this arm was attached to the boy she'd loved and hoped to marry, Audrey was not surprised.

She felt betrayed, but not surprised. The trail to this scene, like the one to Brian's room, was also littered with gigaclues.

Audrey watched Lea lean over the cake and take a deep breath. *From three little maids take one away* . . . Wickham was standing behind Lea with his hands on her waist. *Two little maids remain, and they* . . . Two of the candles stayed lit, and Wickham leaned over to help her.

In the dimmer light, he said something and smiled.

Won't have to wait very long, they say . . .

Lea turned and gave Wickham a long kiss. Audrey stumbled back down the salted steps and the crooked path. She slipped and picked her way to the car over frozen tire tracks in the street. The air smelled of ice and car exhaust. Audrey dropped her car keys and fished for them with slippery gloved fingers. When finally she got the engine started, the cheerful sopranos began to sing—"*Three little* . . . *!*"—but Audrey quickly switched them off.

Chapter 69
Over Cucumber Sandwiches

Audrey fell asleep that night around 4 a.m., and when she awoke she was turned sideways in bed, with the sheets and blankets twisted and bunched. She felt sick, or perhaps more precisely, physically sickened by the thoughts of everything real that she wished were not. Lea and Wickham were at the top of the list, of course, but it didn't stop there. Oggy was never coming back. She hated where she lived. She hated that she'd been caught cheating by Mrs. Leacock, who had trusted her, and she hated that she'd betrayed Clyde Mumsford, who had liked her.

She tried to go back to sleep, but her thoughts wouldn't leave her alone, so she dressed without showering, without even looking at herself in the mirror. It was Thursday, two days before Christmas break. She didn't look for Wickham at school. She didn't look for anybody. She kept the hood of her sweatshirt up and her eyes down, and within her numbness and unkemptness felt oddly protected.

After third period, as Audrey walked toward her locker, C.C. slipped her arm through Audrey's and said, "Guess what?"

Audrey turned and said the first word she'd spoken all day: "What?"

"I brought cucumber sandwiches, your personal fave, and plenty of them."

C.C. seemed so pleased that Audrey couldn't bear to tell her she wasn't hungry. They found a quiet corner of the cafeteria, and Audrey was trying to eat a little and talk a little when C.C., gazing over Audrey's shoulder, said, "Hey, there goes Lea." As the word *don't* formed in Audrey's mind, C.C. called her name.

"Lea! Over here!"

Lea Woolcott hesitated just an instant before turning and coming their way.

"Cuke sandwiches at this kiosk!" C.C. said, pulling another one from her satchel and setting it, neatly wrapped, in front of Lea's place across from them.

Audrey, who didn't think she wanted to see Lea, found she couldn't take her eyes off her. She looked different. Happy.

Lea glanced nervously at Audrey, then directed herself to C.C. "I can't stay—I've got to get on a library computer, if any of them still work."

"The big *if*," C.C. said, and the two of them chatted and ate while Audrey, in silence, regarded Lea. Something had flowered in Lea. It was as if her dormant beauty, hidden until now, had suddenly come to the surface where everyone could see it.

"I thought you were going to be absent today," Lea said to C.C. "Aren't you headed for the hermitage?"

C.C.'s family always spent Christmas at a cabin in the Adirondacks. There was no phone, no TV, no VCR, and you had to approach it on snowshoes in the winter. Audrey thought it sounded like fun, but C.C. said it was like vacationing in Siberia.

"Tomorrow night," C.C. said. "Brian has a test tomorrow he can't miss. So how was the Zen birthday? Was it *beatific*?"

A faint blush rose in Lea's cheeks, and she looked down at her sandwich. "It *was*, kind of."

At one of the other tables there was a sudden disturbance that drew C.C.'s and Lea's attention, but Audrey kept her eyes fixed on Lea. When the distraction was over and Lea had taken another bite of her sandwich, Audrey heard herself say, in a dead voice, "So how far did you go?"

Lea gave Audrey a startled look, and C.C., confused, laughed and said, "How far did Lea go with what?"

Audrey kept her eyes on Lea. "With the Zen birthday."

Lea laid her pale eyes on Audrey for a long second, and then looked down.

"I saw him at your house," Audrey said.

Lea swallowed and looked at her hands.

Audrey said, "How could you do that to me?"

Lea didn't look up. In a soft voice she said, "You might've kept him if you hadn't been so clingy." Then, raising her eyes and looking evenly at Audrey, she said, "That's one thing. The other is, I'm eighteen, a legal adult. I get to make my own decisions."

Lea rose and stepped away, but stopped for one last word. "By the way," she said in her soft voice, "how did you expect someone else to care about you when you don't care about yourself? Have you even looked at yourself in a mirror lately?"

"Hey, c'mon, Lea, play nice," C.C. said, trying to make peace.

Lea glanced at C.C., then Audrey, and walked away.

To Lea's back, Audrey said, "Why don't you ask him about—"

Lea swirled and returned to the table. Her soft voice oozed

contempt. "Ask him about what? About Jade Marie Creamer? I know all about her. I know what a burden her tragedy has been to him and"—Lea's gaze seemed to narrow—"I know how bad you made him feel about it."

Audrey felt something collapse inside her. "Is that what he said?"

Lea nodded, and when she turned and left this time, Audrey was quiet.

C.C. looked bewildered. "So what was that all about?" she asked. When Audrey didn't reply, she said, "Okay, *who* was that all about?"

Audrey looked down at her uneaten sandwich and said, "You know, your mom was only half right. People's secrets can be what makes them interesting. They can also be what makes them awful."

"Audrey," C.C. said in a sympathetic tone, "tell me what's going on."

Audrey said she didn't want to talk about it, but Lea could fill her in. Then she stood and gave C.C. a weak smile. "Guess I'm not looking my best today, huh?"

C.C., because she was Audrey's friend and always would be, said gently, "You look perfect to me," and Audrey, afraid she might cry, mumbled a thank-you and quickly walked away.

Chapter 70
The Place I'm Going

It was Friday, seventh period, World Cultures—the last hour before Christmas vacation—and the minute hand on the wall clock seemed never to move.

Clyde slumped at his desk while images of displaced Indian villagers flashed on the screen at the front of the dim room. Patrice had tried to explain how this documentary "cross-pollinated" with their studies of sub-Saharan tribesmen, but as far as Clyde could see, the connection was pretty sketchy. He stared through the slit of window just below the drawn window shade, watching the ebb and flow of students outside. Most of the teachers seemed to have given up. Even as the video played, the door to Patrice's room kept opening and closing as kids came and went. He glanced at the door as Sands and Zondra slipped quietly out.

Clyde thought of some lines he'd heard once on a CD of his father's: "*I do not like the place I'm coming from. I do not like the place I'm going to. So why do I wait for the bus with such impatience?*"

Clyde hated being here, but he didn't really look forward to going home, where the pleasure of seeing his mother would be immediately swallowed up by the fact that she was dying. But at least today he'd have the vase. It was glazed and fired and dried, and all he had to do was pick it up from Mrs. Arboneaux on the way home.

When the kid at the next table put his head down to sleep, Clyde had a good view of Audrey Reed—and what, he wondered, was up with her? She came into class looking like someone who'd been living in a car, and even though she was with her pal C.C., when the pale pretty one came in, C.C. and Audrey cut her cold. Which was exactly what Clyde had done to Audrey when she glanced back at him as she had entered the room, and of course, after he'd cut her, he felt kind of bad about it.

Through the window he could see Theo sizing up Zondra and Sands. Clyde smirked. *There* was some golden matchmaking.

A whispered "Hey!" Then: "Mumsford!"

He looked up, and a girl with a bored expression handed him a folded piece of paper. He opened it and turned it so it picked up some of the window light. *Clyde,* it read, *I need to talk to you—Audrey Reed.*

He glanced up at Audrey, who seemed to be writing in her notebook in spite of the dark. First she'd avoided him, and then she'd ratted on him and gotten him pulverized in public by Theo Driggs. And now she thought she had the right to lay something else on him. Well, thanks, but no thanks. Under her short note, he wrote:

I didn't write the new Yellow Paper, *if that's what you want to know (just for the record, I didn't write any other* Yellow Paper *either). Please leave me alone.*

He folded the paper, sent it up the tables to Audrey, and then made a point of looking out the window—away from her—as she read it. A few minutes later, the bored girl whispered, "Hey!" again, and handed him another note, but this time Clyde just wrote, *Leave me alone* on the outside and returned it unread.

When, at last, the bell finally rang, Clyde inserted himself in the middle of the outward flow, and once out in the corridor, he headed for Mrs. Arboneaux's room without looking back.

Chapter 71
What're You Doing?
Where're You Going?

As other students drifted off toward lockers and cars, Audrey and C.C. paused in the hallway. "So what was all that note-passing between you and The Mummy?" C.C. said, and when Audrey just shrugged, C.C. gave her a frisky look. "Audrey, honey, are you pulling the Mumsford man off the back burner?"

"No," Audrey said in a tired voice.

"Well, that's a shame, because I think he's got the Heathcliff thing going for him." She grinned. "Your new boyfriend would be *Heathcliffian*."

Audrey was in no mood for this. Clyde was past-tense. He might have been interested, but he wasn't anymore. Everything was past-tense. House. Wickham. Oggy. Everything. "I've got to go," she said.

C.C. nodded. "I'll call when we get back," she said. Her mother had a no–cell phone rule when they went to their cabin.

"Okay," Audrey said. The hall was nearly empty now. Someone had torn down one of the red foil garlands that had been draped overhead and it lay now on the floor. Audrey had never looked forward to Christmas less.

C.C. said, "You know, I'll never forgive Lea for this."

Audrey looked past her, down the hall. A laughing boy she

didn't know was wrapping a laughing girl she didn't know in the red foil garland. Audrey in a dull voice said, "I wouldn't blame Lea too much."

"I do, though," C.C. said stoutly. "We were friends. Sister-women."

Were, Audrey thought. Lea was one more thing in the past tense.

"You okay?" C.C. said.

Audrey nodded without looking at her.

A few seconds passed, then C.C. said, "Look, I've got to buy some stuff for this trip. Want to come with me?" Audrey shook her head, and C.C. said, "So where're you going?"

Audrey shrugged. "Home." The Commodore.

But she wasn't. After C.C. left, she went to Wickham's locker in the east wing. She'd left two notes there in the morning, and before seventh period she'd wedged another between the door and frame of his locker. It was still there.

She sat down on the stairs at the end of the empty hall. She felt too tired to move. She just sat, slowly eating stale currants from an old box in her backpack. She'd been sitting for perhaps twenty minutes when a boy appeared at the other end of the corridor. He kept referring to a slip of paper in his hand as he made his way past the lockers. At Wickham's locker, the boy stopped, looked at the paper in his hand, and began spinning the dial on Wickham's lock.

Audrey, standing, said, "What're you doing?"

The boy had just swung open Wickham's locker. He had dull eyes and a heavily acned face. "Just doing what I was told to do," he said. "Getting stuff for some dude."

"Who?"

"The guy whose locker this is." He pulled out Wickham's leather backpack. "A dude with a drawl."

"Why didn't he come himself?"

The boy gave a who-knows shrug. "Dude just said he'd pay me a couple bucks for a favor and told me what to do, and here I am." The boy looked at Audrey and smoothed a finger feelingly across a swollen whitehead. "He said some girl was, like, stalking him."

Audrey took a step back and fell silent. The pimply boy picked up the note on the floor, and two other notes Audrey had fed through the locker's vents. As the boy walked away, he detoured to a GIVE A HOOT! barrel and dropped them in.

She supposed he'd been told to do that, too.

Chapter 72
Safely Under His Arm

The vase was done, and it was perfect.

True, Mrs. Arboneaux had helped with the glazing, but still, the vase itself was Clyde's work, and nobody else's. So on this Friday afternoon before vacation, after helping Mrs. Arboneaux pack away her papier-mâché Santas and woolly reindeer, Clyde wrapped the vase in newspaper secured with masking tape, and gave Mrs. Arboneaux a nod on the way out. "Thanks," he said.

The teacher smiled. "Hope she likes it."

"She will."

"Clyde?"

He turned, and the teacher smiled. "Merry Christmas."

"Same to you, Mrs. Arboneaux."

Clyde had his book bag over his shoulder and the vase safely under his arm as he headed off toward the parking lot.

Chapter 73
Firebird

"Some girl was, like, stalking him."

That was what the boy had said, and that was what she'd become. Wickham's stalker.

When Audrey pushed open the heavy doors of the west wing, the school's lawn was a deserted expanse of brown grass and frozen mud. The sky was still and gray. Everything seemed empty, as if the field had been turned upside down and everything not tied down had spilled out and rolled away.

She moved along the hedge-lined walkway as if through a cold tunnel. Straight ahead, there were a few bicycles left in the lot, and a couple of motor scooters, but her old Lincoln was one of only four or five remaining cars. One of those, a red Firebird, started up and began to back out after Audrey walked past.

The lock on her car door was nearly frozen, so she tried the passenger-side door, which opened after a few seconds of gentle pressure. The coldness of the car seat went right through her as she slid across to the steering wheel. Three times the engine turned over slowly and stopped, but on the fourth try, it finally caught.

Audrey put the car into reverse, looked into her rearview mirror, and saw the red Firebird pull up behind her and stop. Three boys were getting out of the car and walking toward her. Their movements were casual and unhurried. The chubby one had spiked, bleached hair that seemed more orange than blond. The tall one wore a black leather jacket studded with chrome. The third was Theo Driggs.

Audrey instinctively locked her own door and was reaching for the lock to the passenger door when it swung open.

Theo Driggs peered in with his high, slanting eyes. "Well, well," he said. "Miss Caviar."

He unlocked the door to the backseat for the two other boys. Immediately they slid in behind her and shut the door.

"What're you doing?" Audrey asked, fear already beginning to numb her lips and hands. Theo eased himself into the seat beside her and snapped the last door shut. She was locked in with them now. Three against one.

"What're you doing?" Audrey said. "What do you want?"

Theo pretended real interest in this question. "You know what? That's just what the lady headshrinker asked me the other day. 'What do you want, Theo? And how do you intend to get it?'" Theo's eyes were on low beam. His smile was loose-seeming. "Know what I told her? I said, 'All kinds of things, and however I have to.'" He smiled at Audrey. "That lady headshrinker was taking lots of notes."

Theo's friends shifted in the backseat. They were so big that the car felt weighed down, and the cold air of the car smelled like hair gel and cigarettes. Audrey felt in her coat pocket for her cell phone. If they touched her, she would speed-dial her dad. That's what she would do. It was just one button. Just press "2."

In a voice that sounded too high in her own ears, she said, "I meant, what do you want with *me*?"

Theo peeled off a black glove and with his bare hand unfolded a piece of paper from his pocket. He looked at it for a moment, then turned it for Audrey to see. *To-do List*, it said at the top. There followed a list of names that had all been crossed out—Clyde Mumsford's was the only one she recognized. Just one name had not been crossed out, and that was Audrey's. Maybe she should have told the principal about the list a long time ago.

Theo was grinning and pulling on his tight black glove. "Visiting hour is over," he said.

Audrey felt nauseated now. She worked her thumb into the fold of her phone and tried to flip it open within her pocket.

Behind her, a leathery creaking sound. A hand from the backseat passed a flask to Theo, who unscrewed the lid. "What you need to improve your mood," he said, "is a little *elixir*."

Audrey tightened her lips, and Theo grinned. "It'll put you in the holiday spirit."

"I'm not drinking that," she said, working at the top flap of her cell phone. Her pocket felt suddenly too small, and her hand too large. Then she managed to unfold it.

Theo, smiling, reached forward and pulled her keys from the ignition. He tucked them in his pocket and turned to Audrey. "Last time we met, we made a little deal. You gave me the name of the Yellow Man and I let you proceed with your day." His eyes switched to high beam. "Only you gave me the wrong Yellow Man."

Audrey didn't speak. She felt along the keypad of her cell phone for the "2" button. If she pushed "2," her father's phone would ring. But why were there so many buttons? Was that the top row of numerals she was touching? She didn't know. She couldn't tell.

"So I'm giving you another chance here," Theo said. "Either you give me the right Yellow Man, or you have a cup of holiday cheer with us."

Audrey shivered inside her coat, and she ran her finger over the phone's surface again, trying to feel the pads that were "1," "2," and "3."

"If I drink some of that," she asked, "will you let me go?"

Theo drilled into her with his high-beam eyes. "That wouldn't be much of a deal, would it? No, you have, let's say, three good snorts."

From the boys in the backseat came a rustling.

She pushed hard on the button she hoped was "2." She had feared it would make a beeping sound, but she heard nothing. Nothing. She wanted to bring the phone out of her pocket and see if her father's phone number had appeared on the screen, but she couldn't. She listened. The phone made no sound. It seemed wrong that it made no sound at all.

Theo handed her the flask. She took it with her trembling left hand, but kept her right hand in the pocket. Was that the sound of her phone dialing? Would her father say, "Hello?" She put the flask to her lips, closed her eyes, and swallowed. All at once her throat burned, her eyes clamped more tightly closed, and her body wanted to expel the alcohol even as it trickled down her throat.

"Dad?" she heard herself say.

A keenness came to Theo's eyes. "What do you mean, 'Dad'?" he said, and when she didn't speak, he scanned the parking lot. Audrey could hear the boys in the back scraping against the seats, could see the orange-haired guy craning his neck to see behind the car.

No sound came from the pocket. Where was Wickham, where was her father, where was Oggy? Where were the people who were supposed to save her?

Theo turned back to her, evidently satisfied that no one was coming to her aid. And he was right, she knew that now—no one was. "Daddy's not here," he said. "It's just big grown-up you and big grown-up us." He smiled and nodded at the flask. "That's one snort," he said. "Two more to go."

Audrey took another swallow of the burning alcohol, then a third swallow, and all at once, she began to retch, and it all came back up, along with bile and black currants, onto the seat and floor and Theo's shoes.

Theo drew back and stared down at the mess in revulsion.

Behind her, Audrey felt for the door lock.

Chapter 74
A Choice

Clyde's hard boots made a hollow echo as he walked through the empty halls. He didn't like the halls when they were full of kids and he didn't like them empty, so he guessed that meant he didn't like them no matter what. Not exactly a major newsbreak.

Outside, the street and sidewalks were dirty but dry, a good sign for the ride home. There wasn't a lot of light left, but he didn't feel like hurrying. As he turned the corner to the parking lot, he did what he always did: check to make sure his Vespa was where he left it. It was, but he was immediately distracted by peripheral movement.

A girl half slid and half fell out of a big car and was beginning to stumble away, past a red Firebird, when three boys caught up with her.

Clyde stopped in his tracks.

It was Theo Driggs, Craig Ashworth, and a big thuggish guy from the shop class: Mickey Trammel. The girl was Audrey Reed.

Clyde didn't think anymore. He just ran, his pack bouncing roughly on his back and the wrapped vase cradled in the crook of his arm like a football.

Craig was grabbing Audrey by her upper arms, yanking her upright.

Clyde slowed just enough to set the vase safely on the ground; then, running closer, he yelled, "Hey!"

It was as if he were the director and he'd just yelled, "Cut." Everyone stopped and turned toward Clyde, including Audrey. Theo was the first to digest this development. He grinned and said, "Well, well. Here comes the cavalry."

Audrey was standing on her own, but Craig still held both her arms with gloved hands. Audrey's face looked like white wax. The front of her sweater was wet.

"What's going on here?" Clyde said.

Theo said, "Just visiting."

Clyde looked at Audrey, then at Craig. "Let her go."

Theo was grinning back, working on his next move, when a voice behind Clyde said, "Hey, what's this?"

Clyde turned and saw Mickey Trammel tearing the newspaper off of his vase. "Looks like one of those pottery projects," he said, holding it up.

Theo said to Clyde, "That breakable object yours, Mumsford?"

Clyde didn't answer. He was staring at his vase, which Mickey held casually in one hand.

"Let's see it," Theo said, and Mickey flipped it his way.

Theo caught it. He studied the vase, then Clyde. "Very nice work. Who's it for?"

Clyde didn't answer.

Theo shrugged, then said, "Mickey the T, on a slant pattern." Mimicking a quarterback, he spiraled the vase toward large and flabby Mickey Trammel, who caught it bobblingly against his chest. Mickey trotted it back to Theo, who looked again at Clyde. "I can keep passing, but I can tell you right now, Mickey the T drops more than he catches." He paused. "Now who is it for?"

Clyde stared at the vase in Theo's hand. "My mother," he mumbled.

"What?" Theo said, and cocked his arm as if to pass the vase again.

"*My mother,*" Clyde said louder.

Theo let out a harsh laugh. "Your mama," he said, and began tossing the vase from one hand to the other.

Clyde glanced around. Theo and Mickey were watching him with expectant faces, but Craig, the one who was still holding Audrey's arm, was not. He was staring at the ground. Craig turned to Theo. "Cut him some slack, Theo," Craig said in a low voice. "His mother's sick."

Theo turned to the huge boy named Mickey and looked at him for a long, silent moment. Then he turned back to Clyde. "That true, Mumsford?"

Clyde gave the slightest nod.

Theo stared evenly at Clyde. "Okay, Mumsford, who does the cavalry want to save today? The rich girl who ratted on you, or the breakable object you made for your dying mama?"

Clyde stared at him. It was as if Theo had read his mind.

"I'm serious," Theo said. "You get to save one or the other."

Clyde said, "Let Audrey go, Craig."

Theo laughed. "You either have to say 'the rich girl who ratted on me,' or 'the breakable object I made for my dying mama.'"

Clyde let a second or two pass, then said, "The rich girl who ratted on me."

He looked at Audrey, and Audrey looked at him.

Theo, still holding the vase, shrugged. "Actually, it's ex-rich girl, but still, our Mountie's made his decision." He turned to Audrey. "Adios, Miss Caviar. You've been rescued by a mummy."

Craig released Audrey's arms, and Theo put her car keys into her hand. She moved in wobbly steps to her car. It took her a while to get the key into the ignition, but once she did, the car started and she drove away without looking back.

Clyde stood with the others, watching her go. After she'd turned out of the parking lot, Theo turned to Clyde. "Didn't seem that grateful, did she?"

Clyde didn't speak immediately. Then he said, "Why'd you let her go?"

Theo kept staring at the Lincoln's red taillights receding into the dusk. He shrugged. "I don't know, something hap-pened to that girl when her father went bust. She just . . . kind of lost her shine." He turned to Clyde and broke into a grin. "And then there's the puking. There's something about the libido that doesn't like puke on the shoes."

Clyde realized that under different circumstances, he might have thought that was funny. But these weren't different cir-cumstances. He said, "What do you mean, her father went bust?"

Theo cocked his head slightly. "You really aren't the Yellow Guy, are you? Her father lost the fancy house, the fancy car, the whole fancy shebang." A pause. "The *Yellow Paper* head-line would read, 'Riches to Rags.' "

There was a silence then, and a stirring among Theo's friends. There had been a strange loss of momentum. Mickey

Trammel said, "Okay, Theo, where are we here?" Theo looked at Mickey, then at the vase in his hand, then at Clyde.

"Visiting hour's over," he said, and, still staring at Clyde, he with one quick motion lofted the vase high into the air.

Clyde's eyes lifted to the blue vase spiraling up into the sky, where finally it seemed to stop suspended for a moment, then began plummeting straight down to the asphalt. Clyde shifted, bumped into Craig, but never took his eyes from the vase, even as it settled into his outstretched hands. He'd caught it.

He looked at Theo, who was already turning away. "Merry Christmas, Mumsford," Theo said, and as he made his way to the red Firebird, the others followed.

Clyde stood in the cold, deserted parking lot, holding the vase tight in both hands, watching the low-slung Firebird drive away, and not knowing quite what to think of Theo Driggs, or of Audrey Reed, or of almost anything else in the world.

Chapter 75
The Arrival of a Present

Once out of the parking lot, Audrey pulled her phone from her pocket. The screen looked exactly the same—she'd called no one. She must have hit the "clear" button by mistake. As she held the phone, her hand still trembled. What had Theo and his drones wanted? What were they going to do to her, because that was it, wasn't it?—they meant to do something to her. She should call the police, she should call the school, she should do something.

What she wanted to do was call Wickham.

Pathetic, she thought.

She hit "2" on her phone, then—how had she forgotten this step?—hit "enter" to speed-dial her father, who answered on the fifth or sixth ring. "Hi, Polliwog. Where are you?"

Audrey swallowed. She tried to steady her voice. "On my way home."

"Good. Me too, in about ten minutes—I just have to finish something up here. How about if I stop somewhere and pick up entrees for two?"

Within the car, the air was thick with the smell of vomit. "I'm not that hungry, Dad." She wanted to tell him what had happened, but then he would stop sounding so normal and cheery.

"You'll change your tune when you lay eyes on what I bring home!" he said. "See you in about an hour?"

"Sure." She would tell him later, maybe. She couldn't do it now.

"You okay, Audrey?"

"Yeah." She stopped again. "It's just been kind of a long day." She waited for her voice to even out again. "I'm glad school's out for a while," she said at last. "See you at home."

When Audrey got to her apartment, she took off her foul-smelling clothes and stood in the shower until the hot water ran out. Her father still wasn't home. She put on flannel pajamas and her heavy robe, and climbed into bed. She slept for almost twenty hours.

Shortly before noon on Saturday, Audrey opened her eyes and felt the world she'd escaped again take shape. It was December 20, the first day of vacation. And then Audrey thought, *Vacation from what?*

Wickham was still with Lea.

C.C. was at the cabin.

Her father was still at work.

And somewhere out there Theo Driggs was driving around with his friends.

The apartment was quiet. Outside, the sky was gray. The drone of a heavy truck rose from the street.

Audrey felt dully hungry. In the kitchen, on the chrome table, her father had propped a note against the saltshaker:

Hi, Polliwog—You were sleeping, so I didn't wake you. I figured all that school stuff had taken its toll. I brought

*home chicken potpies last night—yours is in fridge if you
want it. Also, your Christmas present may come today,
so don't be surprised.*

—XXX, Dad

As she took small bites of the cold potpie, she thought of
Clyde Mumsford. How the vase she'd seen him working on
that day at school was for his mother, and how his mother was
sick. And how he'd chosen to keep her, Audrey, safe instead
of the vase. She thought he'd probably made the wrong
choice.

She took her dishes to the sink, but didn't wash them.

She stared for a long time out the window, at the traffic
passing below, seeing many red cars but not Theo's Firebird.

She picked up a book she'd checked out from the library
before Wickham had left. It was overdue. Audrey read a page
and a half before she again fell asleep.

About half an hour later, she was awakened by the buzzing
of the entry intercom.

Wickham. She couldn't help it—she hoped it was
Wickham.

She pushed the intercom button and choked out, "Hello?"

But the voice answering from the lobby wasn't Wickham's.
It was a woman saying, "Is that you, Audrey?"

"Oggy?" Audrey said.

And the woman in the lobby, in a stolid German accent,
said, "Who else?"

Chapter 76
Awakening

There, in the dingy lobby, was Oggy in a blue tweed coat with a fur collar. Oggy in a blue-and-white silk scarf. Oggy with a suitcase and two shopping bags. Oggy with a beaming smile. It was Oggy, Oggy, Oggy. Her hair was silver, her eyes small and black. She looked like a child's illustration of a person you could trust. Audrey threw both arms around Oggy's neck, breathed in her Echt Kölnisch Wasser, and whispered, "It's really you."

Oggy looked Audrey up and down and said, "This is not mine Audrey I left in summer. You look . . ."

Audrey knew she was looking for the right word.

". . . *abgeschlafft.*"

Audrey glanced down at herself. Droopy, she thought it meant. "I've been sleeping," she said. Then she said something that hadn't been true, but now was. "I was just about to get cleaned up."

Audrey took Oggy to the elevator and held open the gate with her foot while they scooted Oggy's heavy luggage inside. The bags filled nearly the whole floor of the elevator, which made Audrey recall the problem that awaited them upstairs. "Did Dad tell you how small this apartment is?"

"I am used to small," Oggy said. "My sister she have one bedroom."

While Oggy unpacked her things in Audrey's bedroom, Audrey washed and brushed her hair. They went together to the market, and within two hours Oggy had cooked warm potato salad, sausages, and red cabbage, and Audrey had told her everything, starting with Theo Driggs and working backward.

Oggy, shaking her head and wiping her hands on her apron, said, "I think Oggy vas vell too long avay."

Audrey nodded. "Yes," she said, and hugged her again.

Telling Oggy everything made her feel better, but it wasn't just that. Having Oggy in the same room with her made her feel like herself again. Everything smelled right again, and looked right, and felt right.

"Now this nice boy, Clyde," Oggy said. "Tell me vat he is like."

Audrey shrugged. "I don't know him. He's quiet and smart and keeps to himself. C.C. thinks he's handsome, but I never thought that because I always thought he was kind of creepy until . . ."

"Until you found out he vasn't," Oggy said.

"Yeah." She thought about it. "I feel so terrible that I got him beaten up when he was really trying to help me, but I was too smitten with Wickham to see it."

Oggy, bleaching the cutting board and the sink, was quiet for a time. Then she said, "You should tell that to this boy, Clyde."

Audrey mentioned how she'd tried to get him to talk to her at school but he wouldn't even answer her notes.

Oggy gave a dismissive shrug. "*Mannesstolz.* The man's pride. You let them parade it, then you try again."

Oggy made it sound so possible. "By calling him?"

The older woman shook her head and gave her a friendly frown. "No, *mein Schatz*. You go to his door."

Chapter 77
Ash

Wickham Hill sat smoking at the black desk in the upstairs bedroom that had once been his father's. Wickham's mother was at work. No one else was in the house. A blunt pencil lay on the desk, but Wickham wasn't writing. He wasn't reading. He wasn't listening to music. He was thinking. The afternoon was nearly gone, the room had grown dim, but he didn't move to turn on a light. When the ash on his cigarette grew long, he tapped it into a small ashtray made of Waterford crystal, a gift from Lea.

A piece of English toffee wrapped in clear plastic also lay on the desk. Audrey had made the toffee for Lea's birthday, but Lea hadn't eaten any. "I can't," she'd said, setting a piece in front of him. "It makes me feel . . . funny." He'd turned down the toffee, too, and then, for some reason he couldn't explain, he put the wrapped square in his pocket when he went home.

He looked at the candy on the desk and thought of Audrey with a strange detachment. It was like poking at skin that had been deadened with anesthesia. He couldn't feel his former affection for her, or hers for him.

He supposed this was how his father was. Yesterday a Christmas card had come in the mail. The preprinted signature said it was *from Dr. James Edward Yates and his entire staff.*

Included were two computer-generated checks for three hundred dollars, one in Wickham's name and the other in his
mom's. There was a handwritten message to Wickham and
his mother: *My family and I are going to the Caribbean for the
holidays. Please don't call my home or office.* Wickham was glad
he hadn't been there when his mother opened the card. She
should have been furious, but probably she was just miserable.
Wickham himself had wanted to rip up the check, which he
supposed was a Christmas present, but then had thought better of it.

He put the cigarette to his lips and pulled smoke deep into
his lungs for a second or two before expelling it.

His mother had decided to go back to South Carolina,
where at least she knew a few people. Wickham hadn't figured out how to tell her he was leaving Jemison with Lea
Woolcott, who, it turned out, was as eager to leave the town
as he was.

Lea was different. Outside, a calm package, but inside,
everything bursting to get out. She was the one who'd said,
"Let's drive the Audi to the Finger Lakes." The one who'd
said, "Let's find a hotel." The one who'd said, "You and I see
each other's secrets, and people who see each other's secrets
should face the fact that they're always going to be together."

It had taken him only the briefest second to see that she'd
meant marriage.

"Not now, maybe," she'd said, looking at him with her arctic blue eyes. "But sooner or later."

Spoken in a tone that he simply could not disbelieve.

"What would be fun," she said softly, "would be a secret
engagement."

But he couldn't support them, he'd said. Not now, and probably not ever.

And in her soft voice, she'd said, "I have a trust. All I have to do to start the checks coming is enroll in college." She'd checked with the school counselor, and it wasn't impossible to go to college early admission. You needed the grades, the credits, the test scores, and a letter from the principal, all of which she had.

"And I don't," he said.

"So you'll get a GED," she said. "Someplace warm, I'm thinking. Someplace far, far away." Her pale eyes turned frisky. "How do you feel about Hawaii?"

Wickham said he'd always wanted to dive in Hawaii.

"There's a honeymoon for you," Lea had said softly. "Not that I'm proposing." A conspiratorial smile. "That would be your assignment, should you choose to accept it."

Now he tapped ash into the crystal saucer.

He would accept it, of course. He would cash his puny three-hundred-dollar check, buy a ring, arrange with a fancy restaurant to hide the ring box in the dessert, listen to her tell all about her secret dreams, do the whole romantic thing.

With Lea, he could get away from everything, including Dr. Yates.

He crushed his cigarette out.

Then he took the blunt pencil and, pressing hard so that the old black paint flaked off, engraved this in the surface of his father's boyhood desk:

W.H.

&

L.W.

Beneath that, he wrote *Engaged,* then added the date and let the pencil drop.

Wickham Hill stood, took the cellophane-wrapped English toffee with him to the window, and looked out. The lawn was yellow, the trees were bare. You could see right through the lilac hedge. He peeled back the plastic wrapper and regarded the chocolate-covered toffee for a moment or two. Then he set the whole piece into his mouth and felt the sweetness of it spread over his tongue. It was delicious.

He stood very still then, staring out, wishing it would snow and cover the yellow lawn and the dirty street and the bare hedge with white and white and more white.

The toffee still lay on his tongue.

As it melted, he moved it to the side of his mouth, between his cheek and his teeth. He'd always been the kind of child who didn't bite his lollipops. He wanted them to last, and so they did last. He sucked on the toffee and waited for the sound of Lea's car.

Chapter 78
An Unexpected Visitor

In the front room of Clyde's apartment, Clyde's mother was hooked up to an intravenous machine that dripped morphine. She slept on one side of the hospital bed. Clyde and his father sat nearby, playing cards on an end table.

It was Sunday afternoon, the woman from the hospice was away, and Clyde and his father were playing casino. His father laid an eight on a two, said, "Tens," and gave Clyde the evil eye. "Better cover that, señor, or I'm going home with the big casino."

Clyde was used to his father's bluffing tactics. "Yeah, you will," he said, and was in the process of matching a jack when the doorbell rang. He got up, peered through the peephole— it was a girl—and then opened the door.

Standing before him was Audrey Reed.

"Hi."

"Hi."

There was an awkward silence, and she said, "Could I talk to you for a second?"

This was different from school, and it was different from a note. Clyde glanced past her down the dimly lit hall. "There're some chairs down there," he said, though when they got to the communal sitting area, they didn't sit. They stood staring through the tall windows toward the park.

Finally Audrey said, "I just wanted to apologize. For what I said to Theo to get you . . ."

"Pulverized?" Clyde said.

She smiled weakly. "Yeah." A pause. "And I also wanted to thank you for what you did on Friday with Theo."

Clyde shrugged. "It's okay."

"It was like a nightmare I wasn't going to wake up from."

Clyde nodded, and after a short silence Audrey said, "I guess Theo broke the vase, huh?"

"No," Clyde said. "He tossed it up in the air, I caught it, and he walked off saying 'Merry Christmas.' . . ." Clyde's voice trailed off.

Audrey looked down, then back up. "For a while I thought you were one of the bad guys. And I thought Wickham Hill was one of the . . ."

"Yeah, well, sometimes the label's kind of hard to read," Clyde said, and suddenly realized he was not uncomfortable. He wasn't blushing or croaking out words or anything else.

"I'm sorry about your mom," Audrey said.

Clyde shrugged. Then, when there didn't seem to be anything else to say, he said, "You want to come in?"

Audrey Reed seemed pleased with the invitation. "Would it be okay? With your mom . . ."

"She's sleeping. Then, when the morphine wears off, she'll wake up and feel okay for a little bit." He didn't mention that the pain would come back soon after and she would need more morphine, which would put her out again.

Chapter 79
"Happy to Meet You"

Clyde pushed open the apartment door, which he'd left ajar, and Audrey followed him down a short corridor that opened into the front room. There was a hospital bed there. It seemed huge, but Audrey wondered if it didn't seem that way because of the smallness of the woman sleeping in it.

She was olive-skinned, with deeply sunken eyes and short gray-black hair. Audrey could see from her features that before the illness she'd been pretty. A card game in progress lay on a little table nearby.

"Clyde?" a voice called.

"In here, Dad."

A moment later, the kitchen door swung open and a middle-aged man who looked like a silver-haired Clyde came walking out with two plates containing sandwiches. Seeing Audrey, he looked surprised. He glanced at Clyde, then smiled at Audrey. "I don't know you," he said, "but how do you feel about chicken salad?"

Audrey laughed, then worried that her laugh would wake Clyde's mother. "I love chicken salad," she whispered, looking at the plates Clyde's father was holding. Two plates, two sandwiches. "But I don't want to take yours," she said.

Clyde's father said there was plenty more where this came

from. Then he said, "I'm Lloyd Mumsford. I'm happy to meet you."

Audrey smiled. "I'm Audrey Reed."

Clyde's father took this in, said, "Ah," and then turned to Clyde.

"See that?" Clyde said, grinning. "That's a knowing look he's giving me. That's because I looked your name up once on one of his programs."

Clyde's father nodded, then said, "Back soon with more grub," and disappeared into the kitchen.

Audrey's eyes moved from the kitchen door to Clyde. "Why did you look me up?" Audrey said.

"Idle curiosity. I wanted to know where you lived."

"So you *could* have been the Yellow Man."

"I just looked at addresses. Except for Wickham. And I didn't tell anybody about him except you."

Audrey remembered the scooter passing by some time ago. "Did you ride by my house on your Vespa?"

He grinned, and didn't seem at all embarrassed. "Maybe."

"More than once?" she said.

"Possibly." He laughed. "Hey, it's a nice house."

"Was," Audrey said. "We lost that house." She was surprised how easy it was to say this to Clyde.

Clyde was quiet, and his father swung through the door carrying a tray and saying, "Okay, here we go. Chicken-salad sandwiches all around."

So Audrey ate a sandwich (it was scrumptious) and finished Clyde's father's hand in casino while he went out to the market. She and Clyde played a few more hands—it was fun when she won, but it was even fun when she lost, too—and then Clyde said he was still hungry. "I make a mean banana split," he said, and Audrey, grinning back at him, said she loved mean banana splits.

It was while Clyde was in the kitchen that Audrey noticed the blue vase standing alone on a simple table in front of the picture window overlooking the park. There were three pink tulips in the vase, and the composition in front of the white window seemed like something from an Asian painting.

Audrey walked over and inspected the vase (it really was beautiful), and then stared out at the park, its bare trees and rock outcroppings and iron benches stark against the brown-and-yellow grounds. Audrey thought of Wickham and felt a deep, almost flu-like pain. She heard the sounds Clyde was making in the kitchen, clinking silverware against glass, squirting whipped cream, and she felt that the pain might go away. Oggy was back, and Clyde had forgiven her. That was something.

She heard a small voice say, "Hello?"

Audrey turned, and Clyde's mother gave her a weak smile. Her eyelids were half closed. Her voice was stretched out, unearthly. "You're real," she said. Her eyelids closed, and after a long second opened again. "I thought you were an angel."

Chapter 80
Resilience

On the first Tuesday afternoon following vacation, Mrs. Leacock was sitting alone at her desk when Audrey walked in to do her makeup essay. Mrs. Leacock had returned to school the day before, looking the same, it seemed to Audrey—the same striped sweater set, the same mahogany lipstick—except thinner. She stood and walked with a wooden erectness, and during classes yesterday and today, Audrey hadn't seen even the beginning of a smile.

When Audrey entered the room, Mrs. Leacock nodded but didn't smile. She glanced at Audrey's note cards, handed her a blank blue essay book, and gestured toward the classroom's empty desks.

"Any of the front ones is fine," she said, and went back to grading papers.

The writing proceeded smoothly, except for the reminders of Mrs. Leacock's strangely leaden presence—a drawer opening and closing, some papers shuffled, a pen uncapped. It made Audrey anxious to finish, that and the fact her car was in the shop, which meant she'd have a long walk home when she was done.

Half an hour passed, and Audrey was nearly done with her essay when the classroom door opened and Brian walked in. He didn't acknowledge Audrey, but he didn't seem surprised that she was there, either. He walked straight toward Mrs. Leacock, who was regarding him with a doubtful expression.

"Do I know you?" she said.

Brian shook his head. His big hands dangled. "Not really."

"Then why are you here?"

Brian breathed deeply in and out. "To apologize."

Mrs. Leacock cocked her head slightly and waited.

"I'm the one who wrote *The Yellow Paper.*"

If Mrs. Leacock was surprised by this announcement, she didn't show it. "Yes, and?"

"And I realized what I did wasn't as funny as I thought."

Mrs. Leacock regarded him for a second or two. "What brought you to this realization?"

It took Brian a second to get started. "Well," he said, "I had it worked out in my mind that it wasn't so bad, that it kind of evened the score or something, but the more I thought about what I'd written about your husband, the worse I felt, and I knew I had to do something, and so . . ."

Mrs. Leacock waited. Her face was white and impassive, and her twirling of the gold ring on her left hand seemed unconscious. When Brian didn't finish the sentence, Mrs. Leacock looked at him coldly. "And so here you are."

Brian nodded.

"And you're willing to suffer the consequences?"

Brian looked down at the floor and nodded again.

"Because otherwise one could argue that this little exercise is more for your good health than mine."

"Understood," Brian said. To Audrey, he seemed at this moment suddenly adult.

In the stillness of the room, Mrs. Leacock looked at Brian for a few seconds before saying, "Anything else?"

Brian shook his head no, and Mrs. Leacock said that he could leave. As he turned to go, Brian let his glance meet Audrey's for just a second, and then she went back to writing. Brian shut the door gently behind him.

For a few minutes there was a heavy silence in the room; then Mrs. Leacock rose. Her shoes clicking on the linoleum floor, she walked to the same window where she'd written the words *Shame on you.*

"Students never think their teachers are human," she said, turning around.

Audrey didn't know how to respond to this.

There was another silence, and then Mrs. Leacock said, "I didn't, either, when I was in high school. My teachers all seemed old. Not like me in any way."

Audrey still didn't know what to say, so she waited.

"Do you know what my husband was? A judge. I'm sure he would have forgiven that boy in an instant. 'They're just kids,' he was always telling me. In his court, he saw everybody as a victim, even the perpetrators. He kept trying to figure out how to punish the right person, but he couldn't." Her gaze drifted to the window. Outside, the sky was a dense gray, growing denser. "He used to say that judges needed an off-and-on switch so they could stop thinking about it. But he didn't have that switch. He thought I did. He told me once that I was the most armored person he'd ever met, and he meant it as a compliment." She paused. "I don't know why I'm telling you this." Another pause. "Maybe so one person will have the story right when I accept the district's offer to transfer to another school."

Audrey didn't move.

Mrs. Leacock took a deep breath. "My husband talked about his suicide ahead of time. He said it was the point to which his life would inevitably lead him." Mrs. Leacock's voice became softer. "He said he didn't have kids to live for. He made it a joke. He said he didn't even have a dog to live for." Pause. "There was a sentence pounding in my head so hard I wanted to scream it. It was *You have me to live for*. But I never said it. I swallowed it back down and never said it."

Mrs. Leacock had been looking off toward the windows, but now she let her eyes settle on Audrey. "I might really have been able to save him, but my pride kept me from it. That's the irony. That boy"—she nodded toward the door that Brian had closed behind him—"got a little information and made a wild accusation, but buried deep inside the hard little heart of it . . ."

She fell silent and returned to her desk. She didn't seem to want Audrey to say anything. In fact, she seemed to want Audrey to leave, as if that would free Mrs. Leacock, somehow, from the embarrassment of this fleeting intimacy. Audrey finished her essay, and as she brought it up, Mrs. Leacock was sizing and squaring the set of papers she'd just graded. Without smiling, she said, "Mr. Hill wasn't worth saving. One day you'll find somebody who is."

Audrey nodded without saying anything. She didn't know which was more surprising: that Mrs. Leacock would talk about her husband's suicide or that she would have something consoling to say about Wickham.

"That boy who was in a while ago," Mrs. Leacock said, "the one who wrote *The Yellow Paper*. By now he will have realized that I didn't ask his name."

Audrey waited for Mrs. Leacock to say something else, or to ask Brian's name, but she merely snapped a clip over her set of graded papers. *She isn't going to ask Brian's name,* Audrey thought. *She is going to forgive him. Like her husband would've done.*

As Audrey handed Mrs. Leacock her blue book, she said, "Thanks."

Mrs. Leacock nodded.

"No, I mean it," Audrey said. "Thanks for everything. And I'm sorry to hear you're leaving. You're a good teacher."

Mrs. Leacock made a small but actual smile. "Thank you," she said.

Audrey turned to go, but Mrs. Leacock suddenly had something else to say. "Do you know what *resilience* means?" she said, and without waiting for an answer went on, in a reciting voice: *"The capability of a strained body to recover its size and shape after deformation caused most especially by compressive stress."* She made a small, unhappy smile. "For years I kept that definition pinned on my refrigerator. The point is, we're all crushed at some time or other. It's true that some of us never recover our size and shape, but"—this time the smile seemed actually hopeful—"most of us do."

She dropped her gaze from Audrey, adjusted herself in her seat, removed a clip from a stack of papers, and went back to being Mrs. Leacock, the physics teacher.

Audrey walked out of the room feeling the strange loneliness of Mrs. Leacock. She moved so much within a cloud of her own thoughts that she didn't notice a lone male figure silently leaning against the far wall of the deserted corridor. She was in fact nearly past him before he said in a low voice, "Hey, Audrey."

At first, she was frightened. She thought Theo had come back. But when she turned and saw Clyde, she grinned.

"Still here?" she asked.

"Still here," he said. "Thought you might want a ride on the Vespa."

"Isn't it kind of cold for scootering?"

"Less cold when two go," he said.

Lesscoldwhentwogo, lesscoldwhentwogo. The words went through Audrey's head like a chant in a foreign language she thought it might be fun to learn. She put her arm through his and headed for the door, sticking her chin down inside her scarf and waiting to go with Clyde out into the cold.

"Hey, look," she said when they pushed open the doors.

In Jemison, it was snowing again.

Acknowledgments

The authors wish to thank Cornelia Zöller-Wolff of Herdecke, Germany, for her tireless assistance in the creation of Oggy, Joan Slattery for her editorial wisdom, Kathy Lambert and all the Knitties for ongoing inspiration, and Jack Duckworth, Mindy McNeal, and Libby Pierce for facts that informed fiction.

About the Authors

Laura Rhoton McNeal is a graduate of Brigham Young University with a master's degree in fiction writing from Syracuse University. She taught middle school and high school English before becoming a novelist and journalist.

Tom McNeal graduated from the University of California at Berkeley and was a Wallace Stegner Fellow and Jones Lecturer at Stanford University. His prize-winning stories have been widely anthologized, and his novel *Goodnight, Nebraska* won the James A. Michener Memorial Prize and the California Book Award for Fiction.

Together, Laura and Tom McNeal are the authors of two award-winning novels set in the same town as *Crushed: Crooked*, winner of the California Book Award for Juvenile Literature and an ALA Top Ten Best Book for Young Adults, and *Zipped*, winner of the PEN Center USA Literary Award for Children's Literature. The McNeals live in Fallbrook, California, with their two sons, Sam and Hank.